MW01253449

# CRAZY IN PARADISE

PARADISE SERIES

BOOK 1

DEBORAH BROWN

CRAZY IN PARADISE
Copyright © 2011 Deborah Brown

ISBN-13: 9781463550622

Cover: Natasha Brown

PRINTED IN THE UNITED STATES OF AMERICA

# CRAZY IN PARADISE

# Chapter One

There should be a law in South Florida that a person can't die during the summer. The death of a loved one was hard enough without the added humiliation of sweat. I felt it rolling down my back like a stream, trapped by the belt of my dress with nowhere to go.

My name is Madison Elizabeth Westin, and I'm seated at the funeral of my favorite aunt, people-watching, of all things. Most of the mourners looked ready for a pool party, some of them in shorts and bathing suit cover-ups. I was the only one dressed in black; even my brother wore khaki shorts.

The minister began, "We are gathered here today to give thanks for the life of Elizabeth Ruth Hart, who shared herself with us. It is in her memory we come together, and for all she meant to us, we are thankful."

My mother had named me after her older sister. Elizabeth had been like a second mother to my brother, Brad, and me. We spent summers with her in Florida, running and playing on the beach, building sandcastles, and she was a regular visitor to our home in South Carolina.

After five years of not seeing her, I had packed for a several-month stay and planned to spend the summer with her. That's when I got a phone call from her lawyer telling me she'd died. I still found it difficult to believe it had happened so suddenly.

When I walked into the funeral home earlier, the heat had smothered me, and the main room was suffocating. The air conditioning wasn't working, and it felt as though it were more than a hundred degrees. The director, Dickie Vanderbilt, had apologized for that, telling me that the central unit had gone out earlier in the day. He informed me that he had all the ceiling fans on high, which, in my opinion, were only circulating hot air.

Dickie Vanderbilt gave me the creeps. He had a slight build, pasty white skin, and long skinny fingers. When he reached out to touch my arm, I tried hard not to squirm.

I'm not a big fan of shaking hands. I find people only want to shake your hand when they can see you're not interested. A friend suggested I perfect the dog paw shake for those who insist. I extend my hand like a paw and let it hang loose. Oftentimes, they jerk their hand away and give me an odd stare, which makes me want to laugh every time.

The minister rambled on. I found him uninteresting, his speech dry. He talked about

Aunt Elizabeth as though she were a stranger to him and everyone there. Apparently, Elizabeth's jerk attorney, Tucker Davis, hadn't given him any information about her. I didn't understand why my aunt had left all the details of her funeral to Tucker. Why would she exclude the people who loved her and knew her best? I wished I had one more day to walk along the beach, laughing, talking, and collecting shells with her.

On Sunday, Tucker had called to inform me that Elizabeth had died in her sleep from a heart attack. "The funeral is Wednesday, 1:00 p.m., at Tropical Slumber Funeral Home on Highway 1 in Tarpon Cove," he told me.

"I want to help plan the funeral."

"All of the arrangements have been made." He sounded impatient, emphasizing his words. "If you want to, you can call anyone else you think should be informed."

"My aunt would've wanted her family to be involved in the decision-making for her funeral. After all, my mother, brother, and I are the only family she had."

"Elizabeth appointed me executor. She left written instructions for everything she wanted done after her death, including her funeral."

I didn't believe him. Aunt Elizabeth loved us. She never would've excluded her family in this way, knowing how important it would be to us.

"I oversaw all the arrangements myself. I'm

sure you'll be satisfied. If you have any other questions, you can call my assistant, Ann." He hung up the phone.

My aunt never once mentioned Tucker Davis to me or anyone else in the family. Yet, here he was, a stranger, handling her estate.

The next day, I called the lawyer back to tell him that Elizabeth's sister, Madeline, her nephew, Brad, and I would attend. He refused to take my phone call, and I was frustrated.

"This is Madison Westin. May I speak with Tucker Davis?"

"I'm Ann, Mr. Davis's assistant. He's not accepting calls at this time. Can I help you with something?"

"I wanted to ask again if there was anything I could do in preparation for Elizabeth Hart's funeral. Surely you can understand how her family would want to be involved in any final decisions."

"Mrs. Hart wanted Mr. Davis to make those arrangements, and he has. She didn't indicate that she wanted anyone else involved in the planning. I can assure you, he's seen to all the details with Mr. Vanderbilt at the funeral home."

"I'll be arriving later today. Would you tell Mr. Davis I'm available to help with anything that needs to be done? He can reach me at Elizabeth's house."

"Does Mr. Davis know you plan to stay in Mrs. Hart's house?"

"I don't need Mr. Davis's permission. I've never stayed anywhere but the Cove Road house, and this trip won't be any different. If Mr. Davis has a problem with my staying there, he can call me," I said.

"Any more messages?" Ann sniffed and, without waiting for a response, hung up on me.

* * *

Tarpon Cove was an unsophisticated beach town situated at the top of the Keys off the Overseas Highway, which began just north of Key Largo and ended in Key West. Tropical Slumber Funeral Home was located on the main street that ran through town. In a previous life, the building had obviously been a drive-thru fast-food restaurant, the kind where you drove through the center of the building to place your order for a hotdog and fries. The new owners hadn't even bothered to take down the concrete picnic tables on one side of the building, but they had replaced the old metal umbrellas with tropical thatched-style ones. A red carpet ran from the parking lot to the front door and continued to the door of the hearse parked behind the building.

After we took our seats on the old rock-hard church pews, I turned to look at my mother. "People are going to hear you laughing," I whispered. "What's wrong with you?"

My mother, Madeline Westin, had aged well; she looked younger than her sixty years, her short blond hair framing her face, and wore a colorful sundress that showed off her long tanned legs.

She put her head on my shoulder. "I think Elizabeth is staring at me," she whispered back.

Mother was right about one thing: it did appear as though Elizabeth was staring at everyone. They'd propped her up in the casket and positioned her to sit straight up. She was dressed in a flowery bright-yellow tent-style dress with a wilted corsage pinned to the front—a dress she never would've chosen for herself. Yellow was her least favorite color, and here she was surrounded by white and yellow daisies and carnations, when she loved bold color and exotic blooms.

I'd tried to speak to Dickie about the arrangements when I first arrived in town, but he told me firmly that he only took instructions from Tucker Davis and wasn't allowed to discuss any of the final details. I wondered why the secrecy, but he was so nervous, I didn't ask any more questions. He told me not to worry; he'd worked hard to make everything memorable.

I'd appealed to him: "Don't family members usually participate in the planning?"

But he was very clear—Tucker Davis's approval was the most important thing to him.

I took a deep breath. Later, our family would

create a lasting tribute to Aunt Elizabeth, showing how much we'd loved and respected her and how deeply we would miss her. But for now, this would have to do, I guess.

I glanced up and saw a man who looked to be in his sixties walking to the podium. He was well-worn and beer-gutted, with dirty-looking grey hair, dressed in jean shorts and a tropical shirt that looked as though he'd worn them for several days.

"Hey, everyone," he said into the microphone. "My name is—" He paused "—well, all my friends call me Quattro." He held up both hands in a friendly two-handed wave.

He was missing the middle finger on his right hand and the thumb on his left. Brad and I glanced at one another and laughed. I mouthed "Quattro" at him and waved four fingers. He turned away, biting his lip.

"I told Dickie I'd speak first because he was worried no one would come up and say anything and it wouldn't look right. I told him don't worry so much." Quattro slowly scanned the crowd. "I reassured him there were a few people here who could think of something nice to say." He ran his fingers through his hair and scratched his scalp. "Elizabeth was a great old broad. Too damn bad she died so young. She seemed young to me. Hell, I'm only a few years younger. You know, she checked out in her sleep and in her own bed. How much better does it get than that?"

I looked around. A few people were nodding in agreement.

"Now that she's kicked the bucket..." He paused. "Well, everyone knows there's no bucket involved." He laughed at his own humor. "Have you ever wondered what the reward is?" He waited as though he expected an answer. "Hmm, I've no idea either. Damn, it's hot in here. You'd think a funeral place would turn on the air conditioning."

"Yeah, I've got sweat in my shorts," I heard someone say. A few others voiced their agreement.

"Keeps the smell down and all," Quattro continued. "I know when it was a drive-thru, the air worked good—sometimes the place was downright freezing."

I saw a few people sniffing. Were they sad? Or were they disappointed they couldn't smell hotdogs and fries?

Dickie Vanderbilt stood off to the side, staring at his shoes and picking at his rather large tie tack in the shape of a flamingo.

"But back to Elizabeth. I called her Betty once, and boy, she got mad."

Mother sobbed loudly, which I knew was actually laughter. People turned to stare. I wrapped my arm around her shoulders and pulled her close. "Mother, please. This funeral is bad enough."

Her body shook with laughter. I gripped her

tightly. "Oww," she whispered.

"Behave yourself or I'll keep squeezing." I shifted again on the bench, having a hard time sitting still when my legs kept sticking to the wood.

"Elizabeth was good to a lot of people," Quattro continued. "Too bad she won't be around to do any of us any more favors." He looked around and rubbed the end of his nose.

I stared wide-eyed at him, wondering if he was about to pick his nose.

"The truth is, I've run out of stuff to say. I know she wouldn't have wanted to die so soon, but the problem is we all think we're going to live forever, and we don't. So, God Bless." He waved and walked away from the podium.

Brad and I looked at one another. *Finally*, he mouthed, even though I could see that he was enjoying the circus more than I was.

I didn't have to wait long to see what would happen next. An elderly woman who seemed very familiar approached the podium. Mr. Vanderbilt walked over and helped her up the stairs. Now what?

Brad motioned to me. "Miss January," he whispered.

"No," I said, shocked at how drastically her appearance had changed.

Miss January was a frail-looking woman who appeared to be in her eighties, of average height and no more than ninety pounds. In truth, she was only in her forties. Twenty years ago, her husband had been shot to death in front of her, and after that, she'd dedicated her life to a daily bottle of vodka and chain-smoking. Two years ago, she was diagnosed with terminal liver cancer, for which she'd refused treatment. Her doctor had told her she could die any day, but she'd just laughed at him. Elizabeth had cared about Miss January because she wasn't capable of caring about herself.

"I liked Elizabeth," she started. She fiddled with the microphone, then blew into it, thoroughly entertaining herself. "I'm drunk!" she yelled. "I drank more than usual this morning, toasting Elizabeth over and over. What the hell! I drink every morning."

I covered my face with my hands.

"Elizabeth wasn't much of a drinker," Miss January continued. "I like vodka." She giggled. "She was always..." She paused. "I mean, Elizabeth would pull me out of the bushes and help me home. At least, I think it was her. Some of the time, anyway. That young hottie who lives next door to me at The Cottages... sometimes, he picks me up and carries me home. I like that a lot."

Someone let out a loud burp. Another person clapped. I sat motionless, afraid to look around.

"You need a chair up here!" she yelled. "When the guy from before said it's hot in this place, he was right. Besides, who wants to stand, anyway?" She swayed from side to side, then tried to grab onto the standing flower arrangement next to her. She missed and fell slowly to the floor, pulling a few long-stemmed gladiolas from the vase in a last-ditch effort to recover.

Mr. Vanderbilt, Quattro, and another man raced up the stairs to the podium, and Quattro picked her up. "Don't worry, folks!" he called. "She'll be all right. She's just drunk." He carried her out.

Mr. Vanderbilt moved to the microphone. What was he doing?

"I'm the owner of this funeral home," he said. "My name is Richard Vanderbilt, but most call me Dickie. I can honestly say I've never had such a tremendous turnout. I want to thank all of you for coming. I'm sorry about the air conditioning, and whichever of you dies next, I promise the unit will be repaired by that time. Think of Tropical Slumber Funeral Home for all your burial needs."

"Enough of this," I whispered to my mother and brother. I flew out of my seat, raced to the podium before another person could walk up, and gave Mr. Vanderbilt a shove in the small of his back, pushing him away from the microphone. "Hello. My name is Madison Westin. I want to thank all of you for showing your love and support by coming out on such a hot day to say good-bye to my aunt, Elizabeth

Hart. She loved life, loved her family, and was a generous friend. This concludes the service today. The graveside service will be family only."

The main entry door flew open. "We're here!" shouted a young boy, who ran in with a blond woman behind him who appeared to be his mother.

Everyone turned around, and I smiled. The boy was laughing and jumping up and down. He was wearing a shark tee shirt and holding a cage with a lizard in it. So far, he looked to be the best part of the day, even though I had no idea who he was.

"Well done, sis," Brad said when I rejoined him and Mother. "They've started to leave."

"This is the most undignified funeral I've ever been to. What would Aunt Elizabeth have thought?" I wrapped my arms around my brother for a reassuring hug.

"Who's the man headed our way?" Mother asked.

"I came over to introduce myself," the man began. "I'm Tucker Davis, Elizabeth's attorney. I was one of her closest personal friends." He smiled, extending his hand. He looked to be in his fifties and then some, tall and greying, with a slick air of self-satisfaction.

My mother and brother shook hands with him.

"I don't shake hands," I said. My mother looked shocked, and Brad laughed. I ignored them. "Funny how you and Aunt Elizabeth were such close personal friends and she never once mentioned your name."

"Madison," Mother scolded. "Today's been a long day for all of us, Mr. Davis, and this wasn't quite the ceremony we expected."

"Really?" he said. "I thought everything went smoothly."

It was clear to me that he didn't give a damn what Elizabeth's family thought. I felt awful for my mother, who'd just lost her only sibling. This wasn't the kind of funeral that brought closure.

"I need to set up an appointment for the three of you to come to my office for the reading of the will," Tucker continued, "possibly in two to three weeks. My assistant, Ann, will give you a call."

"The three of us are here now," Brad told him. "You can do the reading as soon as we're done here."

"Today isn't good for me," Tucker said.

"My mother's returning to South Carolina," Brad told him, "and I run a fishing business. It's the middle of the season, and I have to get back to work. If you can't make time today, then give us the will and we'll read the damn thing ourselves."

"I agree with Brad," I said. "Based on experience, you've been hard to get hold of. We're here now, so let's get this over with."

Anger flashed across Tucker's face and disappeared just as quickly. "Fine. Be at my office in two hours. And don't be late." He turned and walked away.

"He's definitely a man used to telling people what to do," I said. "Dealing with him won't be easy."

"What a tool," Brad said. "Madison, you're going to have to keep an eye on him. When you're around him, I'd keep one eye over your shoulder if I were you."

"Calm down, you two," Mother said. "Everything will be fine. Elizabeth wouldn't leave her affairs in a mess. She was very organized—she would've left her paperwork in order and everything clearly spelled out."

"I certainly hope so," I said. "He acts like he has a personal stake in the estate and doesn't want to share. And I hate the evasive way he answers my questions. Having to work with him and his unfriendly assistant will drive me crazy for sure."

"He'll loosen up when the two of you start working together on settling the estate," Mother said.

"I still can't believe that Aunt Elizabeth is dead." I sighed. "First her death, then this ridiculous funeral, and now the reading of the will, which will make it even more final."

Brad tugged on one of my red curls. "I'll find Dickie Vanderbilt and make sure everything's been taken care of. I wonder if anyone just calls him Dick."

The three of us laughed.

My mother smiled. "Wasn't he an odd little man? He stood at the podium and tried to solicit business!"

"I'm going to walk around, say good-bye to the lingerers, and push them out the door," I said.

"Find out about the blonde who showed up at the end of the service," Brad said.

"You're not going to try to pick someone up at a funeral, are you?" I asked, staring at him. Brad stood six feet tall, with sun-bleached hair and boy-next-door looks.

"Aunt Elizabeth would get a good laugh out of me hooking up with a good-looking blonde at her funeral," he said.

"What about Madison? Maybe we could find someone to introduce her to," Mother suggested.

"Oh no, you don't. You first. How about Brad and I fix you up with the man who had the naked hula girl on his shirt?"

"And did you notice that the shirt gave the illusion you could see inside the grass skirt?" Brad said. "I'll go deal with Dickie. Madison, you get rid of the rest of the people and go find the blond girl."

"What about me? What am I going to do?" Mother asked.

"Behave yourself, and we'll be right back. I know — go outside and smoke." Brad winked at her.

"Nice, Brad, encouraging Mother to smoke. No 'Son of the Year' award for you."

# Chapter Two

"Another charming house that's been converted into commercial property," Mother said as we pulled into the driveway. "I don't care for the idea, but I suppose anything is better than tearing it down and, heaven forbid, putting in a strip mall."

Tucker Davis's office was located in an old one-story cottage-style house painted sea blue, with tropical plants and palm trees in abundance. An old sailboat in the yard held his sign.

"I expected something chrome and glass," I said. "Sterile, like his personality."

"Why couldn't the reading of the will be done at Aunt Elizabeth's?" Brad complained. "I guess I should be happy he agreed to do this today."

The three of us walked into Tucker's office. "Here's your chrome and glass," Mother pointed out. "Nothing in here fits with the charm of the outside."

Tucker appeared in the doorway of his office, his fake smile firmly in place. "Come in. I wasn't sure you'd be on time."

"We could go sit in the car," Brad said.

Tucker laughed as if he thought that was the funniest thing he'd ever heard, then motioned to several chairs placed in front of his desk. Once we were all seated, he opened the folder in front of him. "The will is pretty cut and dried. Elizabeth was explicit in her wishes. The first part is legalese, sound mind and body, etc. And, as you're aware, she appointed me executor."

"What did she say exactly?" I asked. "Since you insisted on a formal reading, we'd like to hear what she wrote instead of a summary."

"This is the way I conduct these types of proceedings," Tucker said. "I'll read the sections that pertain to each of you. Once the will is filed with the court, Ann will send copies out, and you can go over every word in detail. Now let's get started." He put on his glasses, shuffled through the papers, and began reading.

"'Madeline, Madison, and Brad, you are the three people I loved most in the world. I'm sorry this day has come. I wanted you to know I was the lucky one to have had all of you as my family. First, to Madeline, my sister and best friend, thank you for sharing your children with me. They were my greatest joy. Because of your generosity, I never missed having children of my own. I'm leaving you all my jewelry, which you loved so much.'" Tucker stopped to pour himself a glass of water, not offering us anything.

"Mother, are you okay?" I asked.

"I did love her jewelry," she said. "I want to go back to last week, when I could call and ask to borrow a necklace or bracelet and she'd send it to me. Two months ago, when we had lunch in Myrtle Beach, she gave me her emerald bracelet because she knew I loved it."

Tucker looked at us. "Can I continue?"

I nodded, thinking how truly insensitive he was.

"'Brad, you were like a son to me. I was extremely proud of you and enjoyed our business ventures, which were not only fun but profitable. My favorite was the commercial fishing. It was hard work, but being on the water with the wind and sun in my face... there's no better way to spend a day. As you are aware, I have several accounts at Tarpon Cove Bank to be transferred to you and your sister. Go and see Hank at the bank; he has all the necessary paperwork.' Elizabeth left this envelope for you," Tucker said, handing it to Brad. "She also transferred to you her share in all the business interests you own together. All loans have been paid in full."

He looked back at the documents before him. "'Now for you, Madison. You're like a daughter to me and, as you got older, a trusted friend as well. I want you to have the happy life you deserve. Take the letter I left for you, brew a cup of tea, sit by the window, and read it in a private moment. You're to receive the rest of my estate, which includes The Tarpon Cove Cottages. The property is a big responsibility, and I know you're up to the challenge. Tucker can answer any questions that come up.' This concludes the reading," Tucker said. "As I mentioned, each of you will receive a copy in a couple of weeks and can read the will in its entirety." He closed the file. "There's one last issue. I understand you're staying in Elizabeth's house, Madison. Since the Cove Road property wasn't covered in her will, it'll be sold and divided accordingly, and you'll need to vacate as soon as possible."

"I'm not moving anywhere," I told him. "I'm surprised Aunt Elizabeth didn't tell you, but my name was put on the deed years ago with right of survivorship. The house is mine now. Since I plan to stay in Tarpon, I'm making Cove Road my home. You can send any correspondence to me there."

"No, I wasn't aware," Tucker said, looking unhappy at the new information. "I'll be checking with the county recorder to make sure the deed is in order. Elizabeth also wanted me to give you this." He handed me a small skeleton key. "She left no further instructions. I assume you know what it goes to."

I nodded. I knew exactly what the key fit.

"I've received an offer for the house," Tucker told me.

"I'm not interested in selling."

"At our next meeting, we can go over the

contract. It's a package deal that includes The Cottages. It's a very good deal; you should give the idea some thought," he insisted.

I shook my head "Tarpon Cove is my home now."

"This concludes everything we needed to discuss today," Tucker said, sounding a bit irritated, and then turned to me. "In the next couple of weeks, I'll be setting up meetings with you to discuss The Cottages and go over current and future management issues. The property needs hands-on attention, but right now, everything is running smoothly." He stood up, crossed to the door, and held it open. "Thank you for coming."

After leaving Tucker's frigid — in more ways than one — office and returning to the heat of the evening, Brad said, "Let's go to dinner at The Crab Shack and celebrate Aunt Elizabeth."

"Since the three of us are together, it's a good time for a family meeting," Mother said. "So much has happened in a short amount of time."

* * *

The Crab Shack sat off the main highway and looked out over the cool waters of the Atlantic Ocean. The restaurant had a low-key atmosphere, decorated with fake palm trees and fish mounted on walls strung with ropes of lights. Aunt Elizabeth had had a few favorite restaurants, and this one was at the top of her list.

Brad raised his bottle of beer. "To Aunt Elizabeth — sister, aunt, second mother, and the woman we all loved. We celebrate her life." We lifted our glasses in tribute.

"I call to order the meeting of the Westin family," Mother said. "All members are present, including Elizabeth. She'll watch over all of us like a guardian angel."

"Mother, you first," I said.

"One thing we've learned over the past few days is that the people you love shouldn't be taken for granted." Mother smiled at me and Brad. "One never knows what the morning will bring."

"You were a better mother than we sometimes deserved," I said. "You stepped up when Dad died and filled the void, being both mother and father."

Brad put his arm around her. "Don't get all teary-eyed."

"Since I'm going first," Mother began, "my news is that I'm moving to South Miami to be near both of you. Brad's already here, and I was sure you'd stay, Madison. The reason I stayed in Miami for the last few days was to finalize the purchase of a house in Coral Gables."

"Wow." I exhaled, realizing I'd been holding my breath.

"I'm returning to South Carolina in the morning to pack. When I get back, we'll be a family again, close enough to get together for dinners and holidays," she finished.

"That's a great idea," I said. "I love that we'll be living close to one another."

"I agree with Madison," Brad said.

"I'll go last," I said. "You're up next, Brad."

"I can't top Mother. I live the farthest away, but it's only an hour's drive to the Everglades. Come and visit me a few times, and you'll love it as much as I do." Brad finished off his beer, signaling the waiter for another one. "Now that you're going to be living here, I want you both to promise to come to the Glades and hunt alligators." He smiled as we rolled our eyes. "Mother," he continued, "anything you need to make your move go smoothly, just call Madison." He laughed at me. "She can take care of everything."

"You're not funny. Mother knows she can call anytime. I'm not the one joyriding out in the Gulf."

"That's work. From my boat to your dinner plate."

"Stop, you two." Mother turned to me. "Your turn."

"Wait, who's the blonde?" Brad asked.

I ignored him. "Now that Aunt Elizabeth's house is mine, I can't imagine living anywhere else. I promise to care for it and love it as much as she did. I've lots of decisions to make, and I plan to take my time. Mother, could you add my boxes on the back of your moving truck? That will save me a trip back. Jazz is here with me already."

"How'd he like the trip?" Brad asked.

"I had to get him a kitty tranquilizer. Otherwise, he would've howled the entire flight. He likes the house—more room for him to roam around."

"Madison," Mother began, looking at me closely, "I've watched you carefully over the last couple of days; you've changed in many ways. We've a lot of catching up to do."

Where was this conversation going? Brad was smiling at me, a "you're in trouble now" look on his face.

"I think you've been holding out on your dear mother," she continued. "When I get back, we'll have a girl's lunch. I look forward to catching up." She smiled.

"Mother," I said, "of course I've changed. I was married for five years; now I'm divorced and starting over again. Now a lot more changes are on the way, as Aunt Elizabeth left me a lot of responsibility and I want to show her that her faith in me wasn't misguided. What I need from you is to balance being a mother with being a friend." As I spoke, I picked the sand dollars and starfish out of the centerpiece and made piles on the table.

"You're paying for that mess," Mother scolded.

"I'll put them back."

"When did you get so direct?" she asked.

"Less confusion with direct. Lets people know exactly where you stand and how much you're willing to put up with."

"You're going to need to use your new attitude in dealing with that attorney of yours," Brad said. "You need to be on top of your game with Tucker Davis. When you meet with him, be clear about what you expect. He works for you. He came across as manipulative and as if nothing gets done unless it's his idea."

"I can do this," I assured. It'd been a long time since I made all my own decisions. I was going to show my mother, brother, and myself that I could do it.

*Mother*, I mouthed to Brad. I wanted him to understand that if she went into over-protective mode, I was going to reroute her in his direction.

He laughed and shook his head.

"Are we ready to adjourn this family meeting?" Mother asked.

"Not quite yet. What did you find out about the blonde?" Brad asked.

"Her name's Julie," I told him. "Her son, Liam, is ten years old and mature for his age. Talking to him was like talking to an adult. She's single, and no mention of a boyfriend. She lives at The Cottages, does voices for cartoons, and Liam told me she dances at night. She did a couple of cartoon voices for me, and Liam had a few voices of his own to show off."

"Great info, sis."

"I enjoyed the conversation and liked her and her son. If you get involved with her, she's a package deal, complete with a child. Are you grown-up enough for that?"

"Next time I visit, we'll go to The Cottages, and you can introduce me." He winked.

"Do you want to stay with me tonight, Mother?" I asked.

"I'm driving back to Miami. I have an early flight in the morning, and the airport is a lot closer there."

"When you're settled in your new house, we'll throw a family party and invite new friends," I suggested.

"Let's toast," Brad said. "To new beginnings here in South Florida."

We raised our glasses.

# Chapter Three

When I drove up to my aunt's house, I stopped the car for a moment and stared at what was now my new home. My brother and I had spent every summer of our childhood here. I'd always loved this place — it was filled with happy memories.

The house was located down a side road off the main highway in the outskirts of Tarpon Cove. It was a two-story Key West-style home with gingerbread trim and a large porch wrapping around the entire perimeter of the second story. I pulled my Tahoe into the driveway, opened the gate, and pulled into the courtyard, which could easily hold two cars.

I walked around the back and through the pool area, which had always been my favorite part of the house. I used to sit outside under an umbrella and read, diving into the cool water whenever the spirit moved me. I looked forward to doing just that again on a regular basis.

I walked across the patio area and came to an abrupt stop. An exceedingly good-looking man appeared to be asleep in one of the chaise lounges.

"Excuse me!" I called. *Wow, he's good looking.*

He opened his eyes and slowly looked me up and down. They were a deep indigo color, and he had jet-black hair.

"Who are you?" I asked, though honestly, I didn't care. I just wanted to keep him.

"I'm a friend of Elizabeth's."

At this point, anyone could say they'd been her friend, and we couldn't prove otherwise.

"Zach Lazarro. Surely she mentioned me?" He showed some teeth, which he probably thought passed for a smile. "She talked a lot about you, Madison."

*Aunt Elizabeth*, I thought, *you held out on me in a big way. You never mentioned this hunk of hotness.* Suddenly, I noticed blood seeping through his shirt at the shoulder. "Why are you bleeding?" I asked, trying to stay calm.

"A band-aid or two, and I'll be on my way."

"I'm calling 911."

"No, don't. Please don't call. There'll be lots of questions I don't want to answer."

"You're not dying on my patio."

"I promise." He smirked.

"I'm either calling a doctor or 911. Your choice." I was probably overreacting, but I wasn't going to take the chance.

"I'll leave." He tried to stand up, sucked in a breath, pain etched on his face, and quickly sat back down.

"Leaving isn't one of your choices," I told him.

"You're a tough one, just like Elizabeth."

I rummaged around in my purse and found my cell phone. "Well?"

"Call Doc Rivers over on Beach Road. Tell him you're calling for Anthony."

I dialed 411, and while the operator was in the process of connecting me, I swiveled the phone away from my mouth and looked at my patient. "I thought you said your name was Zach?" I questioned.

"Anthony Zach Lazarro, ma'am." He smiled.

*Good God, he's handsome, with big, bad, tough guy written all over him. Just the kind of man you're not supposed to be attracted to.*

"I said hello," said a voice in my ear.

I swiveled the phone back to my mouth. "Is this Doc Rivers?"

"Yes, and I already told you that. Who's this?"

He sounded crotchety and as though he were two hundred years old. "My name's Madison Westin. I'm with Anthony Lazarro, and he's here on my patio bleeding."

"What happened to him?" Doc Rivers asked.

"He wants to know what happened," I asked Zach… or Anthony… or whatever his name was.

"Gunshot wound." It was clear by the way he said it that it wasn't the first time he'd been shot.

I sat down hard in the chair behind me. "Gunshot wound," I repeated. I knew I should have called 911.

"Stupid boy," he growled. "Where're you located, sister?"

"Three Cove Road. Do you need directions?" I noticed Zach grinning at me.

"That's Liz Hart's house. Why didn't you just say so?" He hung up.

I stared at the phone and shook my head. "I don't think he liked me asking if he needed directions."

"Doc Rivers has lived in the Cove his entire life. All the old timers still go to him, even though he says he's retired."

"He called her Liz," I said. "I never heard anyone call my aunt Liz before."

He winked. "I think they're very friendly. He's going to like you. He doesn't show how he feels at first, but he warms up eventually."

"Gunshot wound? Is this the reason you didn't want to go the hospital—because you knew it would be reported to the police?"

"I came here because I knew Elizabeth would help me. Where is she anyway?"

"She died on Sunday. I just came from her funeral," I said matter-of-factly, not in the mood for sympathy.

Zach's face fell. "What the heck happened? I just saw her two weeks ago, and she was fine."

"Heart attack. She passed away in her sleep."

"I'm a private investigator. I've been out of town working on a case and haven't stayed in touch with anyone." He shook his head in disbelief. "Elizabeth and I were good friends. I'll miss her."

"Stay here while I get the first aid kit and some towels to stop the bleeding." *Let's hope this isn't one of those choices that comes back to haunt me,* I thought as I walked into the house.

\* \* \*

"Sit up a little," I instructed when I returned, then sat with half my butt on the edge of the chaise. "Should I cut your shirt off, or do you think you can pull it over your head?"

Zach groaned as he sat up. "Go ahead and cut it off."

I cut his shirt straight up the front and around the sleeve, then pressed a towel against his shoulder to stop the bleeding. You could tell he worked out — broad shoulders and six-pack abs.

He was grinding his teeth, sweat running down his forehead.

"How about some whiskey?"

"Doc will torture me with something when he gets here," he said, his jaw clenched.

Just then, the side gate opened, and through it walked a tall man with a slender build and an amazing head of white hair. He was carrying a doctor's bag and looked every inch the Southern gentleman.

I crossed the patio to introduce myself. "Hi, I'm Madison. Anthony's over here." So, he and Aunt Elizabeth had had something going on — she was certainly a woman with secrets.

"What in the hell have you gotten yourself into this time, boy?" Doc asked.

"Thanks for coming, Doc," Zach mumbled.

"Don't thank me. If it wasn't for your mother, your arm could fall off for all I care." Doc Rivers pulled a patio chair over and sat down, then reached into his bag and pulled out a hypodermic syringe.

"I don't need the shot," Zach said. "Take the bullet out, clean the wound, and I'll leave."

"Who's the doctor here?" Doc asked as he rubbed an alcohol pad on Zach's beautiful, buff upper arm. "You aren't telling me how to do my job, are you?" He stuck the needle in Zach's arm.

Zach yelped. "That fucking hurt!"

"Good." Doc laughed at him.

Zach fell back against the lounger, looking worn out. I realized that I was sitting on the chaise with him, on the side opposite from where Doc Rivers was taking care of things. I didn't remember doing that, but there I was, sitting with half my butt on the seat again, holding Zach's hand tightly.

Doc punched his arm.

"Oww!" Zach yelled.

Doc looked over at me. "He's fine. I gave him a painkiller. Soon, he won't feel a thing." The doctor showed such impressive skill in quickly removing the bullet and bandaging his arm that I wondered if he made these kinds of house calls regularly.

"I'll be right back," Doc said, walking inside to clean up.

"Are you okay?" I asked Zach.

"You can let go." He smiled. "I'm not going to die on your patio." He shook his hand and wiggled his fingers. "Amazing grip."

What a great smile—all those beautiful white teeth. I reached out and brushed his black hair out of his eyes without even knowing I was going to.

"He needs two to three days' rest. Keep the bandages clean and dry," Doc said as he walked back out on the patio. "I'm prescribing some antibiotics," he told me. "And I'll give you a prescription for a painkiller, although he'll resist taking them. Tough guy syndrome. His shoulder will be damn sore, but he'll survive." Doc reached into his bag and pulled out another hypodermic syringe. "You'll never get him to take any medication. He's too hard-headed."

"No," Zach whispered. "I don't want the shot."

"Too bad," Doc said, giving him a shot in the arm. "At least you'll get one dose of antibiotics, and you should sleep through the night relatively pain-free. This one's mostly for the missy here—you'll be easier to manage on drugs. Listen up, Anthony," the old doctor continued. "Promise me you'll stay here for a couple of days to recuperate or I'll call your mother and she can nurse you."

"Elizabeth isn't here," Zach pointed out.

"I know — I just came from her funeral. Never saw such a spectacle." He laughed. "I told that Dickie guy I'd speak. And there were a few others who knew Liz, who would have gotten up and said a few words." Doc shook his head. "Instead, he chooses a couple of drunks. Now, are you staying or do I call your mother?"

Zach turned to me. "Can I stay?"

I nodded, trying hard not to stare at his bare chest and broad shoulders. Call me crazy, but I was looking forward to having him as a houseguest, a diversion from the sadness.

"You did a good job at the funeral, getting rid of everyone," Doc Rivers said to me, giving me a once-over. "Elizabeth was proud of you. She left you a lot — try not to screw anything up." He hugged me. "Liz and I were the best of friends. Call me if you need anything. I better not have to come back here." He glared at Zach, then left through the same gate he'd entered.

*Now what?* I asked myself. "Zach?" I sat down next to him on the chaise again. He opened his eyes, hooked one arm around my neck, wound his fingers in my hair, and pulled me into a kiss. Lightning shot through my body. "Zach, stop," I murmured, though stopping was the last thing I wanted. I was thinking about what it would be like to have sex with him right here on the chaise.

"No. I'll recover faster."

"You can't sleep out here on the patio," I said

between kisses. A small moan escaped my lips, embarrassing me. I pushed away slightly. "The guest room bed will be much more comfortable."

"Can I sleep with you?"

"No, and behave yourself or *I'll* call your mother."

"Good threat." He laughed. "I'm a grown man, and she still scares me sometimes. This is one of those situations she definitely wouldn't like."

"Sit up. We're going to get you upstairs while you're high on drugs. Lean against me, and I'll help you up the stairs."

He got up slowly. I put my arm around his waist and guided him into the house and upstairs. "The first door on the right." I pointed.

"Where's your bedroom?"

"I'll be across the hall."

I helped him into the bedroom and, while pulling the comforter off and the sheets down, realized he was still fully dressed.

He saw me looking at him and seemed to read my thoughts. "Take my clothes off."

"Are you out of your mind?"

"You might've said yes," he said.

"Whatever." I knelt and removed his black boots, then pulled off his socks. "You're on your own with the jeans. You can sleep in them for all I care." I peeled off the pieces of what was left of his shirt. "When I go out tomorrow, I'll get you another shirt. That door goes into the bathroom."

I pointed. "If you need anything, yell."

"Damn doctor. I didn't want the sedative, and now I can't keep my eyes open. Thanks for letting me stay. I'll be leaving in the morning."

"No, you won't. You promised Doc Rivers," I reminded him. "You leave and I'll tell. Besides, it'll give you plenty of time to tell me how you knew Elizabeth and why she would've helped you." I gave him a soft shove, and he sat back on the bed, and I removed his boots and socks. "Now take your pants off and get into bed," I told him. "I'll be right back."

When I returned with some bottled water and a bell for Zach to use to get my attention if he was too tired to yell, his jeans were on the floor, and Zach was lying across the bed, naked but for black boxer briefs. Nice butt, long legs, muscled and tanned. I stood staring at him, smiling.

# Chapter Four

The next morning, I walked into the bedroom with a breakfast tray for Zach just as he came out of the bathroom in his black boxer briefs. I handed him the orange juice and two pills.

"I'm not taking those," he said.

"They're antibiotics, and you damn well will. If not, I can arrange for a shot."

"I have things I need to get done today," he grumbled.

"Breakfast and antibiotics won't get in the way of your day. Stop stalling."

"You're pushy."

"I've been called worse."

He picked up the glass and downed the pills with his juice, then ate the muffin while drinking his coffee.

"Sit on the bed, and I'll change your bandage. Doc Rivers left a sling here if it would help."

"Thank you. I appreciate your help."

"Honestly, after my aunt's death and the funeral, playing nurse for a few days is just the distraction I need."

"I owe you one."

"One? I want a half-dozen."

"That's something I'd expect Elizabeth to say," he said. "Damn, this time… kicked my ass more than…" His voice trailed off, and he leaned back against the pillows.

"What? How many times have you been shot?"

But he only murmured, "I'll sleep for a few minutes, and then I'm leaving."

"I have a few errands to do. Anything you want before I take off or while I'm out?"

One eye opened mischievously. "How about a kiss?"

"I won't be gone long," I said, ignoring his question. But I left the room with a stupid smile on my face.

* * *

I came in the front door with bags hooked over one arm to find Zach lying on the couch, barefoot, wearing black jeans and no shirt.

"How about a turkey sandwich? I stopped at The Bakery Café and picked up lunch. You must be feeling better — you made your way downstairs."

He glared. "Where are my keys?" he demanded.

"In my purse."

"I want them."

"You're not in any shape to drive. You look like crap."

"Gee, thanks."

"Stop fighting yourself. It's only for a day or two. What do you want to drink with your sandwich?"

"Any beer?" he asked.

"Drink this instead." I tossed him a bottle of water and handed him two pills.

He stared at the pills and then back at me.

I rolled my eyes. "Let me guess, more drama about pill-taking?"

He washed them down with the water. "Are these the same pills I took this morning?"

"No, I just picked up this prescription."

His eyes went from deep blue to almost black. "You drugged me, didn't you? No wonder all I want to do is sleep." His face took on a hard look; he was definitely not a man to be crossed.

"Go take a nap."

"Didn't you?" he yelled.

"Didn't I what? Drug you? Yes."

"I *trusted* you."

I dug his keys out of my purse and threw them at him. "If you want to leave so badly, get up and go."

"I can't drive in my condition."

"Doc Rivers left the numbers of two people I can call to come pick you up. Do you have a preference?"

"Fine," he said crushing the water bottle and

throwing it on the floor.

"Then here are the ground rules. Stop whining, you stay till the weekend, and you take your medication."

"Okay."

"No, I want to hear 'I promise, word of honor, and I won't whine.'"

"I promise, word of honor, and I'll try not to do the other."

My cell phone rang. I checked the caller ID, and it was Mother. Unless I answered, she'd keep calling. "Hi Mother, how was your trip?"

"Say hi to Mom for me," Zach whispered loudly.

I put my fingers to my lips.

"What are you doing?" Mother asked.

"Unpacking my suitcases. When I finish, I plan to take a book out by the pool and go for a swim."

"Then I'll let you get back to work. Just wanted to hear your voice."

I barely heard her and didn't remember hanging up the phone. It was hard to take my eyes off my half-naked houseguest.

"Nothing new here?" Zach shook his head. "My mother hates to be lied to, even on the phone."

"Okay, smart guy, what should I have said? That I came home, and a hot guy was lying on a chaise by the pool, bleeding from a gunshot wound? Oh, and wait, the best part is that he's still here, lying half-naked on my couch?" I rolled my eyes. What had I just confessed?

He smiled. "You think I'm hot?"

"I bought you a couple of tee shirts," I said. When I turned to walk into the kitchen, I could hear him laughing.

"What is *that*?" he asked.

Jazz—my twenty-pound, longhaired black cat—had jumped onto the couch, in territorial mode, and was sniffing Zach.

"Go ahead, pee on him. Meet Jazz. He thinks he's a dog, and he's definitely king of the house."

"How old is he?"

"Fifteen. I found him in a parking lot while on vacation in Colorado. He was just a kitten. He came home with us, eating McDonald's all the way," I said, smiling at the memory. "I'll move him."

"That's okay. I like having something soft and purring beside me."

I laughed and walked upstairs to change into my bathing suit.

* * *

With Zach and Jazz asleep on the couch, I took my aunt's letter and settled into a chaise by the pool. I sat staring at the white envelope for a long time. I was anxious to read what she wrote because I wanted to feel connected to her. But I kept putting it off because I knew once I did, it would make her death final.

Instead, I lay back against the cushions and thought about Zach. So many intriguing people in Elizabeth's life, none of whom she'd ever mentioned. I wondered why. And what her relationship was with Zach. I replayed his kisses over and over in my mind, fantasizing about taking advantage of him while he was drugged, then laughed at the absurdity of anyone taking advantage of him, no matter what state he was in.

"What are you doing out here?" Zach appeared in the doorway.

"I guess you dozed off. I'll get you a chair," I said, starting to get up.

"This is a double chaise. There's plenty of room for me," he pointed out.

"What are you up to?"

"Sitting next to you so we can talk." He smiled.

"Talk? What man wants to talk?"

"I want to know more than a woman's name before we have sweaty sex."

I tried to maintain eye contact, but it was hard. "I'm playing nurse, that's all." The mental image of rolling around naked with him made me hot all over.

His finger traced my cheek. "At least give me a chance to change your mind."

I pushed his hand away. "You've wanted to leave since you got here. Get your stuff."

"No, I'll stay till the weekend. Doctor's orders." He looked pleased with himself. "Besides, Elizabeth would never throw me out."

Playing the Elizabeth card was a good move on his part, but truthfully, I didn't want him to leave. My cheeks burned as I pictured him naked. Talk about jumping into the frying pan. I'd made that choice before, and surely I'd learned something. Yes, I'd learned that hot, nasty sex could be amazing, but there was always a price.

"What are you thinking about?"

I changed the subject. "I have good news and bad news. The good is you can stay. The bad, but not *so* bad, is I want my IOU's in writing."

"In writing? Sounds like you don't trust me." He sounded more than a little offended. "Elizabeth never asked for hers in writing."

"What was your relationship with my aunt?"

"She hired me to handle a problem for her."

"What kind of problem?"

"One of her girlfriends got involved with a swindling playboy. When their romance ended, he helped himself to several pieces of expensive jewelry. Elizabeth and I got to know one another during the investigation and became friends. Then there was the time or two she saved my butt."

"How did she do that?"

"Long stories. Elizabeth was a woman you wanted in your backup arsenal; she never said no to helping me. I wish I'd gotten to talk to her one last time."

"You don't get off that easy."

"Another time. Over dinner?" He smiled at me.

I was learning things about my aunt that I'd never known. I'd drifted away from our relationship during my marriage—it was hard being married to someone no one liked—and only now realized how much I'd miss what I could never get back.

"Elizabeth told me you were coming for the summer. I know she had plans to talk to you about staying in the Cove. She was also going to introduce you to all the crazies around town, myself included."

I sighed and, with a tinge of sadness in my voice, said, "We were close my entire life. She was an amazing aunt, and we got to be best friends when I was in college. I loved her so much. We drifted apart over the last few years, and that was my fault."

"Elizabeth wanted you to take over management of The Cottages."

"I'm looking forward to it," I told him. "Mostly because no one expects me to step up and do the job. I've changed a lot. The new me likes to act and then think about it later. I'm trying to remember that that doesn't always work out so well. I want to think carefully about the decisions I make."

"What would your family be most surprised about?" he asked.

"Probably that I enjoy a certain amount of crazy and living on the edge." I could see my answer surprised him.

"You seem like a straight arrow, a by-the-rules kind of girl." He reached out, pulling on one of my red curls.

"A by-the-rules girl doesn't take in a complete stranger with a gunshot wound," I said. "Don't get me wrong — I'm well aware of where the line is; I just want to kick it around a little. What about you?"

"I'm thirty-eight years old, six feet tall, and one hundred and eighty-five pounds. Italian on my mother's side and Portuguese from my father. I'm the oldest, with two younger sisters and a brother, and as the oldest, it was my responsibility to make sure they both stayed out of trouble. After a year of college, I got bored and left, joined the Navy, and became a Seal. I'm very good at being a tough guy."

His fingers were tangled in my hair. "You said you met Aunt Elizabeth when she hired you. Did she find you in the yellow pages?"

"We knew some of the same lowlifes. One of them recommended me. I'm the owner of AZL Securities, a private investigation firm that specializes in security for large and small companies."

He began massaging the back of my neck and

head. I wanted to close my eyes and concentrate on how amazing it felt. "Does everyone call you Zach?"

"My parents call me Anthony and so do the people I grew up with, friends from childhood. When I'm in trouble, my mom calls me Antonio, usually followed by *now*. She's not a woman to ignore, especially when she's mad." He laughed. "My mother rules the family, and my father lives to make her happy. If you seriously want to piss off my father, upset my mother."

"Who shot you and why?" I reached out, touching his arm.

"You get straight to the point, don't you?" He pulled my hand into his.

"No misunderstandings that way."

"I'm working on a case for one of my largest clients, and it took a turn I didn't expect. Getting caught by surprise can be deadly. When I leave here, I figure I can wrap up the loose ends in a couple of days. No drugs, okay? I need a clear head."

"I want you to promise you'll at least take the antibiotics."

He pulled me to him, wrapping his arms around me in a hug. "Thank you for all this." I was content to have my face pressed against his bare chest. I could smell my bath soap.

I pushed away from him. "How about a swim?"

"Sounds good." He stood up and began

unzipping his pants. "You're staring." He smiled.

*Please don't let me embarrass myself.* "What are you doing?"

"I'm not swimming in my jeans, and I didn't bring a bathing suit."

He stripped to his underwear and jumped in the pool. I was so happy I had my bathing suit on and wouldn't have to come up with a reason why I wouldn't swim in my underwear. I dove in after him.

# Chapter Five

When I woke up and opened my eyes, Jazz lay stretched out on the other pillow, staring at me. He stood, arched his back, and meowed in my face, clearly translated as "Get up and feed me."

"Where's our houseguest?" I asked.

It was another humid day outside, and my reasonably straight hair had turned into a big curly mess. My attempt to blow-dry it straight failed miserably. Looking in the mirror, I shrugged and added a touch of makeup, having no patience for something I wasn't skilled at.

Zach was sitting on the couch and watched me as I walked down the stairs wearing a full white skirt and green sleeveless top and carrying a pair of sandals.

"Do you ever wear a bra?" he asked.

"I wore one to the funeral."

He just sat there with a stupid grin on his face.

"What are you, my mother? I have a camisole on."

"Can I see?"

"No."

"One of these days, you'll say yes." He winked.

I followed the smell of coffee into the kitchen. Barefoot and bare-chested, Zach walked up behind me and stood extremely close.

"What's for breakfast?" I asked.

"There's not a lot of food in this house. All I found were some raisin muffins and cereal."

"In case you're not aware, a lot's been going on around here. You're lucky I'm good with take-out."

"I *am* lucky." He smiled.

I wondered what he'd say if I told him, *I've rethought the sex thing — let's do it now, right here in the kitchen*. He looked at me, still smiling. I had a feeling he'd read my mind and knew I'd been fantasizing about him naked again. "Coffee's good."

"What are you doing today?"

"I'm going to The Cottages to have a look around and introduce myself to the manager. I'll bring something back for dinner."

"Would you get a charger for my cell? Does Elizabeth have phone service here?"

"No, but Aunt Elizabeth had the same cell you do, and I got her charger out. Your phone's in the office, plugged in, and probably ready to talk on by this time."

"I'm surprised the damn thing hasn't been ringing like crazy."

"I didn't turn it on."

"Did you think I might get a lot of calls?"

"No, not really, but I thought your recovery

should be top priority. And you're welcome."

"You remind me of someone." He laughed.

"If this is where you tell me I'm like your mother, keep it to yourself."

"I've noticed that women don't like being compared to good ol' mom."

"You think?" I laughed.

"I like that I can make you laugh."

We locked eyes. It was definitely a moment. "Anything I can get you before I leave?"

He crooked his finger. "Come over here."

"No." My cheeks turned red. "Jazz, make sure he behaves, and no wild parties," I said, closing the front door behind me.

* * *

Tarpon Cove was an unpretentious beach town full of old rambling houses and wide porches that had survived the ravages of weather. I loved driving through town, especially on a morning with little traffic.

The Cottages, a ten-unit property, faced the Gulf of Mexico. There were five units on each side of the driveway, in addition to an office, pool, and barbecue area. The beach was just beyond the access gate at the end of the drive.

As I turned the corner onto Gulf Boulevard, I questioned the impulse to come here. But this was my property now, and I wanted to learn everything so I could make good decisions about it. I wasn't a person to sit around and wait for things to happen.

I parked in the space reserved for the office. Elizabeth had always had a manager who lived locally and worked days, but Tucker had told me the new manager, Will Todd, lived at the property. Another person my aunt had never mentioned.

A sign on the office door said "Closed," with a handwritten note that the manager was located in Cottage One. The two waterfront units generated the most income and were reserved for short-term guests. Why was Will living in one of them? Why would my aunt allow that? It didn't make smart business sense.

I walked to the manager's unit to introduce myself and knocked. Someone shuffled around inside and then nothing. I knocked again. How strange—no one was in the office, and no one answered at the manager's unit. When the vacancy sign was turned on, who rented out the available units?

The place to get answers would be at Joseph's. He'd lived there forever, and nothing happened at The Cottages that escaped his notice. The truth was, if you needed any information about what went on in the Cove, he either knew or could find out.

Joseph was a Vietnam War veteran with myriad health problems he kept at bay by smoking weed and drinking beer, but it was too early for him to be drunk. He had two sides — the one that would give you the shirt off his back and his drunken side, when he was mean, surly, and loved to start fights, pitting people against one another, stepping aside, and cheering on the brawl.

The door to his cottage stood open, and Joseph was sitting on the couch, feet up, drinking a beer and watching General Hospital.

"Joseph, how are you?"

"About time. I was wondering when you'd come by. The place is going to hell."

"You're looking good," I told him. In truth, it was a bold lie. He looked sick. "Mind if I sit?"

"You want a beer?"

"No thanks, I'm here for conversation."

"I feel like crap, but only some of the time, so that's not bad." He shook his head. "I went to the funeral, but I left when that ass Quattro went up to the podium. Who had that stupid idea? Did Miss January really get up and speak?"

"Oh yes, she did."

"Gossip has it you let little Dickey what's-his-face plan everything."

"I had zero input. Tucker did all the planning."

"Why would you hire a slimy weasel like him? You'd better watch your back."

"You're not the first person to tell me that."

He stood up, stomped on his beer can, threw it in the trash, and walked with a slight stoop into the kitchen to get another.

"Aunt Elizabeth chose Tucker to be her executor," I said, shaking my head, making it clear I didn't understand the choice either.

"For the most part, Elizabeth had good sense," Joseph said, popping the top on his beer. "Not so much when it came to certain people. She was too nice for her own good. Nice in this town gets you walked on."

"You may have to remind me of that. What's going on here? Why's the office closed in the middle of the day? And there's no manager on the property. Does that happen a lot?"

"Willy-boy's around. He doesn't miss a trick. Don't tell him anything we talk about. I don't want to get kicked out." Talking about Will made Joseph angry. Clearly, he didn't like the man.

"Calm down. No one's kicking you out. You've lived here for as long as my aunt has owned the property, and I promise you'll continue to live here now that I own it. Don't worry. Keeping secrets is a specialty of mine."

He stared at me for a long moment. I could see he was trying to decide if he could trust me and knew it wouldn't be easy for him.

"Well?" I said.

"Even as a kid, you never went around blabbing," he conceded.

"What we talk about will be kept between us. And this no-blabbing thing goes both ways."

"Will and his boyfriend showed up several

months ago. They were regular tenants at first, but Will was forever kissing Elizabeth's ass, always Mr. Helpful. Slowly, he got all the tenants to come to him when they needed something, and anyone who crossed him was kicked out. Since Elizabeth died, he's gone all over town, telling anybody who'll listen that he owns the place."

"How did he become manager?" I wondered why Tucker hadn't mentioned any of this.

"All I know is that whenever Tucker came around, they always had their heads together. The day Elizabeth died, Will moved to the waterfront unit and began calling himself the manager."

"You're telling me he's been manager for less than two weeks?" I asked, shocked. "Why would Tucker do that?"

"Will and your lawyer are thick. When Will's flashing that fake smile, you better check your back and remove the knife before you bleed to death. I've shaken some cages, and no one knows anything about him or the boyfriend. In a town where dirt is easily available on anyone, that right there is suspicious."

He paused to light a cigarette.

"The boyfriend keeps to himself," he continued. "No one even knows what his real name is. The first time I met Will, he referred to him as Pete, and then when I met Pete, he told me his name was Forrest. I said to him, 'I thought your name was Pete.' He got right up in my face and told me I was wrong, and I backed off. He gives me the creeps. Besides, I don't think he'd hesitate to kick this old ass. Piss him off, and in my opinion, he becomes dangerous. I'd bet money he's done time."

"What makes you think that?"

"Trust me."

"So Will and Forrest are a couple?"

"Oh yeah." Joseph laughed. "When they first got here, they told everyone they were brothers. Then I saw them kissing."

"Some relatives are friendly."

He really laughed at that one. "I need another beer," he said, walking back into the kitchen. "Sure you don't want one?"

"I'll take a bottle of water, if you have any."

"Will's always sneaking around here," he said, handing me the bottle. "He's into everyone's business, goes through the units when no one's around. He wanted mandatory inspections, and I told him he could kiss my ass."

"Inspections? Was this before or after Aunt Elizabeth died?"

"Two days after your aunt died, Will passed out a letter signed by Tucker saying he was in charge. He made it clear that if we had any problems, we were to come only to him and not to contact Tucker or you."

"I wonder why he didn't want you talking to me."

"Tucker told Will you were inheriting the property and wouldn't be interested in day-to-day operations. He also told him you'd be selling. Want a smoke?"

"Smoking will kill you."

"I also have a bad liver. Which one do you think will kill me first? They can fight it out and let me know who wins," he joked.

"So, who's living here now?"

"There's four regulars: myself, Miss January, Julie and her kid, Liam, and Creole."

"Creole? Where does he live?"

"In the end unit. Totally keeps to himself. I rarely see him. When I do, he's either coming or going—comes out his door and disappears. Will doesn't rent any units out daily anymore."

Will Todd was one big surprise after another. "Why not?"

"Don't know. I do know he has a night job as a private nurse for some paralyzed millionaire. His boy pal is a construction worker. Forrest leaves for work in the morning and comes back in the afternoon. He never hangs out with anyone and does most of his prowling around in the middle of the night."

It was a lot of information to consider. "As usual, you always have the best info. Here's my phone number. If you have any problems, or if there's anything I should know, call me anytime." I stood up and gave him a hug. Outside, a man walked across the driveway.

"Who's that guy?"

"Local drug dealer."

"Drug dealer? What's he doing here?"

"He comes to see Creole. I don't know what's going on, but I'm pretty sure it has nothing to do with drugs."

"I have zero tolerance for drugs." I'd already been down that ugly road with my ex-husband. There's a situation where I learned from someone else's mistakes. "What makes you think that about Creole?"

"Instinct," Joseph said matter-of-factly.

"Take care of yourself. I need a friend." I smiled.

"Come back anytime." He turned the sound up on the television as I headed out the door.

\* \* \*

Outside, I sucked in the fresh air, happy I didn't smoke. A police car was parked in front of Cottage Four. I walked across the driveway, raised my hand to knock, and the door flew open.

A man in a deputy's uniform stood in the doorway. "What do you want?" he asked. Tall and clean-cut, he would've looked like a cop in or out of his uniform.

"Is everything okay?"

"Everything's fine here; move along."

"Kevin," Julie called out, running to the door,

"I want you to meet Ms. Westin, Elizabeth's niece and the new owner."

"Hi, I'm Madison," I said.

"This is my brother, Kevin," Julie introduced.

He looked at me closely. "Nice to meet you," he said. But he didn't sound as though he meant it.

"I'm happy there's no problem. Say hi to Liam for me. I enjoyed talking to him at the funeral," I commented. They both stood in the doorway and watched as I waved, turned, and walked across the driveway to my SUV.

I was reaching for the door handle when I saw a reflection in the window of a man standing behind me. I yelped and jumped back.

"This is private property," he growled. "What in the hell are you doing going door-to-door?"

He was in his late twenties, rather ordinary — a man who wouldn't attract much notice. "Who are you?" I asked, taking a step backwards.

"None of your business. Get in your car, and don't come back or I'll have you arrested."

"I think calling the police would be a good idea." I sounded more confident than I felt.

He took a step forward. "Get out of here. Now."

I jumped into my SUV, locked the door, and glanced in the rearview mirror, seeing Joseph walking up the driveway. I waited until he was at my driver's door before I rolled down the window. "Who the hell is this guy?"

Joseph snorted. "You haven't met? Well, let me introduce you two." He turned to the man. "This is Madison Westin, the *real* owner of the property. Madison, meet Will, the manager," Joseph said. "I don't need to tell you to play nice, do I?" he said, looking at Will.

Will stepped forward quickly and extended his hand. "Good to meet you. I thought you were a salesperson, or maybe saving souls, and I have a strict no-trespass policy. I'm sure you'd agree."

"You're the manager," I said, with a bit of an incredulous tone, staring at him.

Finally realizing that I wasn't going to shake hands, he pulled his arm back and glared at me. "This is obviously not the ideal way to meet," Will said. "Why didn't you come to my cottage first, instead of walking around banging on all the doors?"

"I did knock; there was no answer."

"I must have stepped out."

"Really?" He was a slick one.

"What can I help you with?" He stood there smiling, but his expression simmered with anger.

I remembered Joseph's warning about checking my back. "I came by to introduce myself and say hello to Joseph. I should've contacted Tucker to schedule this meeting."

"That would've been a good idea," he said, giving me a tight smile.

"I'll contact him and have him arrange a meeting for the three of us."

"In the meantime, if you have any questions, call first, and if it's something I can't answer over the phone, then I can be here when you arrive."

"I'm glad we met," I said, turning to Joseph. "Thank you for the intro."

He threw back his head and gave a high-pitched cackle. He'd always enjoyed this kind of drama.

"Oh yeah, nice to meet you," Will said. With a backhanded wave, he turned and disappeared down the drive.

Joseph whispered, "That went well." He walked across the street to where a neighbor stood drinking a beer, listening to every word.

I decided to take the long way home, go by the beach and calm my nerves after the confrontation with Will. *As first meetings go, that was terrible*, I thought. It had been a day of surprises and more eventful than I could've imagined when I started out that morning. The transition wasn't going to be an easy one.

The idea of spending the evening with Zach brought a smile to my face.

# Chapter Six

Everything was quiet at home—too much so. Curled up on the chaise, Jazz lifted his head and meowed at me.

"Is Zach sleeping?" I asked him, but he'd already tucked his head back into his belly.

Intuition kicked in—Zach had left. I ran into the house, looked around, then headed upstairs. The bed had been made, leaving no evidence he'd ever been there. I walked back down to the kitchen to get a glass of wine, trying hard not to cry. What did I expect? Of course he'd leave this way, with no awkward good-byes.

A note lay on the counter. I didn't want to read the damn thing because I already knew it wasn't going to say "I'll be right back."

*Thank you, Madison. I had to leave. Catch up with you later.*

I tossed it into the trash. "That was nice and short," I told Jazz, who'd followed me inside and sat meowing.

I went upstairs to change into my bathing suit. There was nothing a long swim couldn't cure. The truth was, I wanted to keep Zach. But he wasn't some lost puppy. He was a full-grown man. A hot man. Now would be a good time to read my aunt's letter. I'd run out of excuses now that Zach had taken his drama and left.

I felt like a new woman when I stepped out of the pool, wrapping myself in an oversized beach towel. I sat down on the chaise, slowly opened the envelope, and pulled out a hand-painted watercolor card of a white sandy beach. Inside were several sheets of paper.

*Dearest Madison:*

*If you're reading these words, then I'm no longer here. I love you as if you're my own daughter. I appreciate that when you became an adult, we stayed the best of friends. You're a courageous young woman with a wicked sense of humor. Those are terrific qualities, and you should never sell yourself short or accept less than your worth.*

*You and your brother turned out amazingly well, considering the hell-children you both were. I enjoyed every moment of watching both of you grow up. Sometimes when you two got into trouble, I had to try hard not to laugh.*

*I especially liked the time you and Brad went house-to-house early on a Sunday morning, taking everyone's newspaper and redistributing them to the people who didn't take the paper; it was old man Simms who called your mother. What a snoopy old man, always looking out his windows and lurking around. Madeline made me promise not to tell so you two would think her spies were everywhere. When she talked to him, he told her that if she didn't want him* telling everyone in the neighborhood, he wanted a basket of her baked goods at Christmas every year. Can you imagine him blackmailing her? The funny part was that she'd never baked anything in her life. She bought the cookies from a local bakery and passed them off as homemade.

Don't think I short-changed Brad. When he moved to Florida, I couldn't have been happier... unless, of course, you'd moved here too. You know Madeline wouldn't have been far behind. Brad and I had many adventures that weren't only fun, but prosperous. We own several businesses together, and I left him my interest in all of them.

I think you'll enjoy managing The Cottages. You're the best woman for the job. But in the end, it's not about what I want; you have to make the decision that's right for you. My hope is you'll make Tarpon Cove your home and start a new life here. Explore all your options, take as much time as you need, and make the right decision for yourself.

There are two men in town, Zach Lazarro and Luc Baptiste, who'll help you anytime. They're trustworthy men with integrity. You'll like both of them. As you know, I love to collect IOUs having nothing to do with money. Zach and Luc both owe me, and I leave my markers to you. My best advice is to start collecting your own.

If you ever need any information about what's going on in the Cove, Jake's Bar is the place to go. Nothing happens in the Keys that Jake doesn't know about. In my personal box is an envelope for him. Jake and I were partners, and I'm signing over my interest *to him. Do you know how much fun it is for this old woman to own a piece of a bar? My game of pool has improved immensely, not to mention darts. Please give him the letter with my love.*

*In the same box are other letters. One is for Madeline. Give her a hug and a kiss for me. Make sure she doesn't get into too much trouble.*

*There are also envelopes for Luc and Zach. Honey, they're both incredibly sexy men, and I don't think either one has a girlfriend, hint, hint. The three of us had the best adventures. They kept me young at heart.*

*Walk on the beach, collect seashells, and open your heart to all that is new. You deserve lots of happiness. I love you, Madison. Enjoy every day. Live with no regrets.*

"I love you too, Aunt Elizabeth." I wiped the tears from my cheeks. "I'm making Tarpon Cove my home," I said to no one. "How about you, Jazz? You like it here, don't you?" He snored so loudly, I assumed the answer must be yes.

In truth, I wanted to take control of The Cottages and run them in the same manner as I'd watched my aunt do all those summers. And I wanted to make my own mark.

# Chapter Seven

Another scorching day in South Florida, with the ceiling fans working overtime in every room of the house. In the kitchen stood a floor fan that blew on Jazz as he lay stretched out on the cool ceramic tiles. I loved to watch the fan blow his black fur straight up as I bent over the counter, enjoying the air up my skirt. At a noise behind me, I turned to find Zach leaning against the doorway, an amused smile on his face.

"Honey, I'm home," he said.

"How'd you get in? I put a lock on the fence to keep bleeding people out." I knew I sounded whiny and didn't care. Seven days had passed since he vanished. But who was counting?

"I have a way with locks." He smiled and walked towards me, pulling a beautiful bouquet of white tulips from behind his back. "Thank you for being the best nurse," he said, handing me the flowers. He leaned in and kissed me.

Giddy but trying to sound nonchalant, I said, "They're beautiful. I'll put them in water." I walked over to the kitchen sink. "Can you reach the vase for me?"

He'd come up behind me when I turned my

back, and I could feel his body heat. He pushed me against the counter until our bodies molded together, wrapping his arms around me, vase in hand. I exhaled slowly, not wanting him to realize I'd been holding my breath.

As he turned the water on and filled the vase, I stood there, the flowers in my hands, my mind blank.

"You need to take the cellophane off," he whispered in my ear, his breath warm against my cheek. He took the scissors from the chopping block, handing them to me.

Flustered, I pulled on the wrapping and tried to cut it at the same time, getting nowhere. He took the scissors back, unwrapped the flowers, and handed the stems to me one by one. Somehow, I managed to get them into the vase without mutilating them. I was so hot for him that I didn't trust myself to speak. "They really are pretty," I told him, moving the tulips to the counter.

"The flowers aren't the only thing that looks good." He turned me toward him, his hand on my cheek, and pulled me in for a long, slow kiss.

There was no forgetting him now. When we pressed our bodies together, we were a perfect fit.

"You forget about me?"

I was so lost in the kiss that it took me a minute to realize the voice came from inside my house. Zach and I were no longer alone.

I pushed away. "Who are you and how did you get in?"

"He's with me," Zach said. "My partner, Axe."

Axe looked like he'd just walked in off the beach, his sandy brown hair a mess, chin stubbled.

"Meet Madison, the woman who saved my life."

"Pleasure, ma'am." He winked.

"Doesn't anyone use the front door?" I asked. It was a legitimate question.

Axe laughed, pointing to Zach. "Hey, I just followed him."

"I need a favor," Zach said to me. "I have to go out of town for a couple of days. I scheduled my car for some repairs, and it takes forever to get an appointment. Would you drop it off for me? Jimmy Spoon, the guy who owns the place, had a few problems last night and won't be opening until this afternoon. I could do it myself, but I'd have to leave it out front and it's not the greatest neighborhood."

"Another IOU?" I smiled.

"You already have six."

"You agree to seven, and you've got yourself a deal."

Zach stepped back, dug the keys out of his pocket, and tossed them to me. "Good catch."

"Didn't you two just meet a week ago?" Axe asked. "How'd you manage to get six IOUs?"

"Nursing care. Doesn't seem like a lot for

saving his life, wouldn't you agree?"

"I'm staying neutral," Axe said, a big smile on his face. The man oozed charm.

"Too bad, we already agreed," Zach said.

Axe picked my cell phone up off the counter, and Zach and I watched while he programmed it. "What are you doing?" I asked.

He gave me a lopsided smile. "I put in my number. You never know when you might need help."

"Put my info in too." Zach glared at him. "You need help—" He turned to me. "—*I'm* your first call. If I need Axe's help, I'll call him."

Axe laughed.

"I appreciate your taking care of my car. I'll pick it up from Spoon when I get back." He wrapped his arm around my neck, pulled me to him, and kissed me again before they both disappeared out the French doors.

* * *

Outside, a black 1957 Thunderbird hardtop with portholes, perfection outside and in, sat in the driveway—a complete work of art, and I couldn't wait to get behind the wheel.

When Brad and I were kids, our dad owned a 1957 T-bird convertible. My favorite family picture was of the four of us, dressed up for Easter, standing in front of the car.

The address Zach had given me was down by

the waterfront, where the fishermen brought in their catch to sell to the seafood brokers. He was right about the neighborhood. There were lots of rundown buildings, but the area nevertheless had plenty of history and character. If someone took an interest, restoration of the docks would be beneficial for the Cove.

The sign JS Custom Auto was what stood out. If the gates hadn't been open, I'd never have guessed how large the business was. It had the appearance of a normal car repair place, but where were the customers? The cars in the lot were in various stages of repair, but there was no sign of any employees. Then the side door opened, and a familiar skinny, fierce-looking man in his mid-forties, with dirty brown hair and a hard edge to him, walked out.

He wiped his greasy hands on his pants. "Jimmy Spoon," he said, extending his hand.

"Madison Westin." I presented my dog paw handshake and forced myself not to look for dirt on my hand afterwards.

"Zach said you'd be dropping off the car. Leave it parked right there."

"You don't seem to be very busy," I said, looking around.

"I'm always busy. That's why you only get in here with an appointment." He closed the gates, locking them with a chain.

I had a hard time believing he had any break-ins. His business had electric fencing, with barbed wire at the top, and two German shepherds.

"Weren't you at The Cottages the other day?" he asked.

"Yes. Word has it you're the neighborhood dealer," I said, remembering what Joseph told me.

"People are full of shit. Besides, that would be a violation of my parole," he stated evenly.

*Parole*! I'd always been good with follow-up questions, but I shut up instantly. This was a good time to mind my own business. So I ended with a lame, "Well, there you go!"

"Zach said you'd need a ride. My car's outside." He gestured toward the building. "We'll go through the office so I can set the alarm."

"You have a lot of security. Is the neighborhood that bad?"

"Despite the way it looks, it's quiet. Security keeps the kids out. Anyone with a brain knows if they steal from me, I'll kill them."

What do you say to that? Nothing. Nothing would be good.

We walked through the side door to where a silver Mercedes convertible sat parked. "Great car." I'd expected a pick-up truck complete with a gun rack in the back window.

"This is my babe magnet."

"Do you really want women who're only interested because they're hot for the car you drive?" I laughed.

"When I have sex on my mind, who cares if she's thinking about me or my car?"

His smile made him look even more dangerous, if that were possible. "You can drop me at The Bakery Café," I said.

He squealed out of the driveway, burning rubber. I grabbed the armrest and held on until I thought my fingers would break, my other hand clutching the seat. "Slow down," I squeaked.

He rocketed down the street, showing no signs of slowing for the approaching corner. How the hell was he going to make the turn? I squeezed my eyes shut and said a quick prayer. *Oh please, I don't want to die.* Spoon jerked on the wheel, and with another squeal of tires, the car swerved back and forth, managing to stay upright as we rounded the corner.

"You're scaring me!" I yelled. "Pull over and let me out. I'll walk the rest of the way."

"Don't worry so much."

"This isn't Talladega, and you're not Dale Jr."

"Sit back. I'll get you to the restaurant in one piece. You know, I wanted to be a pro driver."

"If you don't slow down, I'll puke in your car," I threatened.

He gave me a long hard stare and, mercifully, slowed down. I knew from personal experience that sick stink was a smell you never got out of your car.

Finally, he pulled up in front of the café,

slamming on the brakes, tires squealing. He turned to me and ran his finger across my cheek. "You ever have a problem, I'm your man. Friends call me the problem-solver, big or small. Ask anyone."

I was both terrified and repulsed. He was a man who shouldn't smile. Wanting out of the car, I fumbled with the handle and couldn't get the door open. It was locked, and Spoon controlled them. I couldn't unlock it on my own.

"You're my kind of woman. I think we'd be great together," he said, putting his hand on my arm. "Let's go to dinner and get to know one another better."

I jerked on the door again, blurting, "I have a boyfriend."

"If you break up, give me a call," he said, looking me up and down. "I got a good feeling about us." He pushed a button, and the locks flew up.

I yanked the door open and jumped out of the car. "Thanks for the ride." I forced myself to walk calmly into the café.

# Chapter Eight

That evening I opened my front door and was surprised to see my mother. "You're back!" I hugged her.

"I got home yesterday." She smiled. "I thought I'd drive down and surprise you—take you to dinner. We can catch up, and you can tell me how settling the estate is going."

"Dinner's a good idea. I missed you."

Mother looked summery and cool in a white linen dress and red belt. I got my love of dress-up from my mother—I couldn't remember a time when she wasn't fashionable.

"How'd the move go?"

"Very easy, at least for me." She laughed. "I hired a moving organizer, who supervised all the details. Her men came in, packed up everything, and clearly marked each box. When we arrived in Coral Gables, they unpacked the furniture and boxes and put them in all the right rooms. Having done many moves on my own, I consider this the best one. I kept your things separate."

"I appreciate you doing that for me. I'll get some muscle to come up to your place and move it down here."

"You didn't have very much. What happened to all your possessions? Tell me Dickhead didn't get everything in the divorce."

"It's just stuff, Mother." I'd said those words to myself constantly from the start of the divorce until it was final. It helped that I'd managed to hide away a few favorite items that Dickhead never found.

"You had more going into the marriage," she insisted.

"In the end, I had to decide if I wanted my freedom or a fight."

"I could've gotten you a top lawyer."

"You can't blame my lawyer—he came highly recommended. He advised me of my options, and most of them were dismal. The last thing I wanted was a long, drawn-out fight. Trust me when I tell you that Dickhead would've been willing to do battle over every piece of silverware and would've enjoyed himself."

"You should've let me help you."

"I love you for offering, but I needed to do this for myself." I drew the line at him humiliating me in front of my family any further. Once I made up my mind about getting the divorce, it was all about my freedom. My only regret was that it didn't come sooner.

Changing the subject, Mother said, "I'm going to love Coral Gables. Now that the three of us will be living close to one another again, life is good and we'll be as close as ever. Come on, let's go have some fun," she offered. "My new goal is to encourage you to enjoy life more."

"Don't worry so much. I'm meeting new people, and I think I'll find plenty of excitement."

"Tell me over dinner. I'm hungry."

"Let's go to The Beach House and sit outside overlooking the water," I suggested. "The view is incredible, and they have the best key lime pie in town."

\* \* \*

The hostess showed us to a table outside. "Can I get you something to drink?"

"Jack, straight up," Mother ordered, opening her purse and dumping half of it on the table as she looked for something.

"Iced tea, please." I pointed to what looked like cigarettes. "What are those?"

"Hand-rolled cigars." She held one out. "I wanted a change from regular cigarettes."

"Oh Mother, you're too much." I laughed. "I'm glad you're back."

We gossiped about mutual friends, wondered when Brad would be getting a new girlfriend, and talked over the events of the last couple of weeks. I'd missed Mother more than I'd thought. I promised myself I'd never take one moment of time with my family for granted.

The cool breeze off the blue-green waters of the Atlantic made sitting outside the perfect choice. Waves rolled up on the white sand while egrets and pelicans walked along the shore in search of their own dinner. I noticed my mother focused on something directly over my shoulder, a pleased, cat-like smile on her face, and knew Zach was standing behind me.

He leaned down and kissed my cheek. "How's my girlfriend?" he whispered in my ear.

*Did he say girlfriend*? My cheeks turned red, and I was suddenly flustered.

"Introduce us, Madison," Mother said with a huge smile on her face.

How was I going to explain Zach? "This is my mother, Madeline Westin," I said. "Zach Lazarro, a friend of Aunt Elizabeth's."

"Join us, Zach," Mother said. "How did you know my sister?"

"Elizabeth was a family friend. I'm very sorry for your loss."

"Thank you." Then, after a brief pause, "So, how did you meet Madison?" Mother seemed puzzled. "I don't remember seeing you at the funeral."

"I'm sorry, I was out of town at the time and didn't find out until I got back. I stopped by the house to offer my condolences."

"You're kissing my daughter—there must be more to the story than that."

"Mother, please." But I knew there was no stopping her. "Zach is just being nice."

"Actually, I stopped by to ask your daughter

out for dinner tomorrow night." He rubbed the back of my neck.

"She'd love to go," Mother answered.

"Really, Mother, I can speak for myself." I didn't want to have this conversation in front of her. "I'm busy." I stared at her, willing her to stop embarrassing me.

She shook her head. "You are not. She's just acting shy. She'd love to go."

He winked at me. "I'll pick you up early. We'll take a drive through the Keys."

They were both clearly pleased with themselves. Neither one noticed that I'd said no. I wanted to go on the date, but not with my mother's interference.

"Would you like a cigar, Zach?"

"No thanks."

"At least join us for a drink." Mother motioned to the waiter. "Another Jack, please." Zach ordered a beer, but I passed. I needed to be sober for what I knew was coming next.

"Tell me about yourself," Mother said to Zach.

"Mother, stop."

"I don't mind," Zach interjected.

I shook my head. "You're crazy," I whispered. "Don't say I didn't warn you."

"Madison, please. I just want to get to know a little about the man you're dating."

"One date is not dating. Besides, aren't these questions you should ask *before* accepting for me? When you find out he's homeless and unemployed, will you also cancel for me?"

"Ignore her, Zach. I'm always interested in any man my daughter dates."

"Maybe when I was in high school, Mother. I'm a grown woman, a divorced woman."

"Have you been married, Zach?"

"Yes, married and divorced."

"Look, you do have something in common," Mother said.

"Divorce. That's nice. Does your family refer to your ex as Dickhead, Zach?"

He laughed. "No, I can't say I've ever heard anyone say that."

"What do you do for a living?" Mother asked.

"What she means is can you afford to pay for dinner," I said.

Zach pulled me close and kissed my cheek. "I can answer these questions. Trust me," he whispered in my ear.

We looked at one another and laughed. I relaxed and sat back, resuming normal breathing.

I listened as my mother fired her questions at him. He gave the briefest of responses to each one, giving her absolutely no information. *He's good*, I thought. Way better at the "no info" answer than I was.

I tuned out of the conversation and started thinking about our upcoming date. I was excited. Then I heard Elizabeth's name and realized the personal questions were over and they'd moved on.

When Zach's phone rang, he stepped away to answer the call. He said a few words and came back. "One of my clients has had an interruption in service, and I need to go check on the building. It was very nice to meet you, Madeline." He kissed her cheek and turned to me. "I'll pick you up at six." His lips briefly touched mine.

"I like him," Mother said as he walked away.

"I like him too, but I don't want you accepting dates for me."

"You were going to decline. You know damn well you're not busy, now are you?"

"That's not the point," I said.

She looked at me. "What's wrong with you? You want to go, and you're going. What else matters? I bet you have a good time."

She was right. I did want to go.

# Chapter Nine

I was running behind when I raced through the French doors, rushed up the stairs, hurled myself into the shower, and jumped out in record time. I didn't have the patience to tame my hair and decided on wild curls.

I'd spent the day getting ready for my date, getting my nails done in a French manicure and my toes painted a bright pink, and even managed a quick stop at my favorite clothing store, where I'd found a great black dress. I put on a lacy push-up bra and matching boy shorts, stepped into my dress, and checked myself out in the mirror. I was probably overdressed but didn't care.

I transferred a few things to a mother-of-pearl purse I'd found in a second-hand shop, wondering yet again why anyone would give it away because it was so unusual. I added crystal earrings and a bracelet to complete my look, checked myself again in the mirror, and decided I was definitely overdressed.

I rummaged through the closet and pulled out a flowered green tropical dress, then a black skirt that was far too businesslike. I tried on a dozen outfits, throwing them in a pile on the bed, and ultimately decided to go back to my original choice. I slipped in and out of several pairs of shoes before choosing my favorite black slides.

A friend once told me a great tan trumps average looks. If that was true, then I was well on my way. Though I was allergic to the gym, I did like biking and swimming, and my body looked good.

I heard Zach's knock, and my stomach started doing cartwheels. When I opened the front door, he looked me over from head to toe and gave me a seductive smile. "Very nice," he said, reaching out and pulling me into a kiss.

He looked totally delicious in black linen shorts, a short-sleeved tropical silk shirt, and boat shoes.

"I thought we'd drive down to Sand Dollar Isle," he said, helping me into a black Escalade. "They have an excellent Mexican restaurant there. You'll like the food." He reached across and took my hand in his.

The Tortilla Bar was an old adobe structure that hung out over an inlet from the gulf. The outside had leftover Christmas decorations everywhere, with ropes of lights around the building and in every tree. The bar was loud, noisy, and full of people. To one side were a pool table and darts, and the noise from big-screen televisions competed with a jukebox and a pinball machine.

We sat in front of a large window and ordered margaritas.

"Why does Spoon think you're my girlfriend?" he asked straight out.

The question caught me off guard. "I didn't say *you* were my boyfriend. I just told him I had one. I'd appreciate your not telling him I lied."

"What happened?"

"He asked me out on a date."

Zach rocked back in his chair and laughed.

"I'm glad you think it's funny. I certainly don't. I didn't want to hurt his feelings, but I'm not going out with him." I scowled. "I just blurted out the boyfriend story."

"What's my silence worth to you?"

"Worth?" I said. "I only met him doing you a favor. In my opinion, this is your fault."

"Blaming me isn't going to work. I want an IOU."

"You have to be kidding."

"I'm not."

"I'll cancel out one of mine."

"No way. I want one of my own."

"Fine," I said. "This date's beginning to suck."

"I promise the night will get better. I already took care of Spoon. I told him you belong to me."

"Belong to you? Like a piece of furniture?"

"Relax. He thinks we're serious, so he won't be bothering you. I have to warn you… our being a couple is probably all over town now."

"I'm sorry. I didn't mean to get you caught up in my lie."

"Now that we're in a relationship, can I expect benefits?"

"Sex?" I squeaked. My stomach started doing flip-flops. The idea was a total turn-on. "How are you feeling?" I asked, trying to change the subject.

"Don't think I'm going to forget what we were talking about." He ran his finger across my lips.

"How's the bullet wound?"

"It's healing. My shoulder still hurts."

"And your case?"

"I'm a little frustrated. I expected it to be wrapped up by now, but the team ran into some complications we didn't anticipate. It looks like it'll be a couple more days."

"Be careful," I said softly.

"Are you worried?"

"You can't collect IOUs from a dead man." I did worry, but I wasn't going to tell him.

The waiter appeared with our food. My enchiladas tasted as good as they looked.

"Another round of drinks?"

I did want another, but I'd already had two margaritas. Liquid courage. One more, and I might not be able to walk out of the restaurant on my own. "No, thank you." One drink too many, and who knew what outrageous thing I might do. Zach didn't need to see me dancing on the table on the first date.

"Let's go to the bar," he said. "Can you play pool?"

"I'm not bad."

"You surprise me."

"I play on occasion. You up for a game or not?" I asked, challenging him as we walked to the pool tables.

"Oh, I'm up for it. I just don't think this will be an even match-up."

"You worry about yourself; this won't be as easy as you think. Want to put some money on it?"

"Twenty bucks says you don't stand a chance of coming close to beating me."

"You're so arrogant."

He gave me a long kiss on the lips. "Shut up and break, darlin'."

\* \* \*

"I had you on the ropes a couple of times," I told him. I'd played a decent game, but I was ultimately no match for him.

"When?" He laughed. "Did you actually think you were going to win?"

"Maybe."

"Keep your twenty bucks. I want this." He picked me up, set me on the edge of the pool table, and kissed me thoroughly. One hand was wrapped in my hair, the other running down my back. He nibbled on my neck, kissed the swell of my breasts, then pushed me back and stared at me. "Time for us to leave."

The drive to my house seemed all too short. The double dose of tequila had relaxed me some and I was trying hard not to be nervous, but I definitely had a case of the jitters.

At my house, we walked through the back patio area, stopping beside the pool and kissing. It had been a long time since I wanted to kiss a man, and I enjoyed every moment—the roughness of his mouth, the sensation of his tongue against mine. I was considerably shorter than him, yet our bodies molded together in all the right places.

Was I making a mistake? Too late. I didn't give a damn. There was no bigger turn-on than making love with someone you were hot for.

He slowly pushed the straps of my dress off my shoulders, exposing my breasts. "You're beautiful," he whispered, his tongue caressing my nipples with a great deal of expertise. The sensation of Zach touching me in such intimate ways took my breath away.

Waves of desire overwhelmed me. I hurriedly unbuttoned his shirt, desperate to feel his skin against mine, as his hands moved down my back, unzipping my dress the rest of the way.

"This isn't fair," I murmured. "I'm standing here naked while you're fully dressed."

"You standing there naked has been my dream since the first time I watched you walk across this very patio. I had all kinds of hot thoughts while you nursed me," he whispered in my ear.

"Take off your clothes," I demanded, kicking off my shoes and stepping out of my dress.

"You're so bossy," he said, nipping at my neck. He took his shirt off and let it fall to the ground, then played with his belt, slowly unzipping his shorts.

"You're deliberately taking too long."

He threw them aside.

I stood there, admiring his hard body.

Neither of us was able to hold off another second. He wrapped his arms around my waist, then lifted me straight up and laid my body down on a chaise. At first, he was on top of me, and then we reversed positions, with me astride him. It felt so damn good!

The sex was hot, frenzied, carnal. We were both so into each other. It went on and on before we reached climaxes together.

"You don't disappoint," he said, rolling off me.

"And neither do you," I murmured, every fiber of my body tingling.

He stood, pulling me to him and lifting me up. I wrapped my legs around his waist, and he carried me upstairs to my bed. I couldn't remember the last time I felt this satisfied, my skin still tender from his touch.

"Why did we wait so long?" Zach whispered.

So long and so soon at the same time. I couldn't help smiling. The sex was sensational, and he was easy to be around. Not what I expected. I laid my head on his chest and drifted off to sleep.

# Chapter Ten

When I woke in the morning, instead of Zach stretched out next to me, only Jazz lay there. I felt tender all over, the imprint of Zach's fingers etched into my skin.

I listened to the sounds of the house. It was too quiet; Jazz and I were alone. A piece of paper lay on the pillow next to me. It was a sure sign he'd gone, leaving a crummy note instead of a good-bye kiss.

*Call you later, Zach.*

I started to cry. I wanted morning sex. I wanted to hear I was the best something. And what did *later* mean? An hour? Next month? What a letdown—a fun evening with hot sex had ended with three words. Four, if you counted his name.

I dragged myself into the shower and cried until I got all wrinkly and the water turned cold. Then I put on a sundress with a built-in bra to keep the girls from jiggling. They were sensitive, and I wouldn't have been able to tolerate them moving around.

When I walked downstairs to the kitchen, Jazz

stood there, waiting by his food bowl, howling at the top of his lungs. He wanted fresh water and his bowl of kibble topped off and stared at me with a "fill it up now" look on his face. I knew if I didn't, the howling would never end.

"Sssh, Jazz please. I always feed you. Do you have to do this every morning?" I quickly filled his bowl.

He took a bite, then moved to the water bowl and waited, looking at me. "Meow."

"Okay, okay." I picked it up and gave him fresh water. Jazz had me fully trained — he meowed, and I jumped.

I opened the refrigerator door, knowing I couldn't make breakfast out of condiments. What I wanted was a caramel latte with lots of whipped cream from the Bakery Café. "I'm leaving now," I told Jazz.

He'd gotten what he wanted and already gone back to sleep.

* * *

I was sitting at the curb, listening to a Jimmy Buffett song, when I noticed Zach sitting at a table at the end of the walkway. Beside him sat an attractive woman. They were laughing and talking, and it appeared as though they'd just finished breakfast. She licked her fingers, reached across, and rubbed his cheek.

I sucked in my breath and hunched over the

steering wheel. The whole scene reminded me of my cheating, faithless jerk of an ex-husband. Zach had jumped out of my bed to meet another woman for breakfast. I wanted to cry all over again, but I didn't have any tears left. Last night had been about sex — incredibly hot sex — it hadn't been about commitment.

I'd seen enough. I jumped out of my SUV. On my way across the sidewalk, I saw a pitcher of water sitting on a nearby table, just begging to be used, and two steps later, I dumped it all over Zach's head. "You bastard."

The woman began laughing, and my anger turned to embarrassment as I watched the water drip down his face. As I spun around to leave, I walked right into a uniformed sheriff's deputy.

"You just assaulted Mr. Lazarro," he said. We both stared at Zach, stunned disbelief written on his face.

"Assault?" I protested. "The pitcher slipped out of my hand."

"Zach, you want her arrested?" the deputy asked.

"You're friends?" I said.

"This is a small town, Ms. Westin. Everyone knows everyone else." He returned my stare.

He looked familiar. "Aren't you Julie's brother, Kevin? The same Julie who lives in one of the cottages I own?"

His eyes turned steely. "What are you saying?" He clearly wanted to strangle me, but only if he could do so without going to jail.

"I'm not going to evict her, if that's what you're thinking. It's hard to find a good place to live when you have a child." Maintaining eye contact with him was hard, but I refused to turn away.

"Zach, whatever happened here you probably deserved," Kevin told his friend.

"Kev, you're a big pussy. Have you forgotten we're friends and grew up together?"

"I'm not telling Julie she got evicted because of you, regardless of what this one says she may or may not do." The deputy continued to stare. "Try to stay out of trouble," he said and returned to his car.

As I got back into my SUV, I realized Zach hadn't said a word to me. The woman had sat there and continued to laugh the whole time. Once I started towards him, I wasn't sure anyone could've stopped me. Common sense and restraint had vanished. But throwing water on Zach hadn't been as satisfying as I'd hoped. It was inevitable that he'd meet my other personality: "crazy." But this was definitely too soon.

The morning had gotten off to a bad start. So much for the coffee. The restaurant was a favorite of mine; I hoped I wouldn't be banned.

Adrenaline was still pumping through my body when I arrived at Tucker's office. I hadn't given a lot of thought to my plan to try to talk to him. I hoped that going in person under the pretense of making an appointment would get him to take a few moments and talk to me. The man needed to know I had every intention of taking over the management of The Cottages.

Eventually, I'd get rid of Will, but at this point, I needed to be reasonable. In the meantime, I'd tolerate him. First, I wanted to go through all of Elizabeth's files. Since I'd been unable to find them in her home office, I assumed they must be in the office at The Cottages. I knew her to be detail-oriented, so everything should be well-documented and in order.

"I came to make an appointment with Mr. Davis," I said to the receptionist. "Or, if he has a few minutes, could I speak to him?"

Ann appeared instantly. "You don't have an appointment." Her face was drawn into an annoyed smile.

"No, I don't. I was just telling your receptionist—" I began.

She waved her hand, cutting me off. "I heard everything you said. What's this about?"

"I have a few things I'd like to go over with Mr. Davis."

"What things?" she demanded.

"The Cottages."

"I'll tell him you came by. He can call you and schedule something if necessary. Good management is already in place at The Cottages. Please don't stir up problems where none exist. I assure you, Mr. Davis is looking after everything."

There was a long pause while we stared at one another.

"Here is Mr. Davis's card." She handed it to me. "Call next time and save yourself a trip." She walked to the front door and held it open.

"Thank you," I mumbled, shocked speechless. The receptionist kept her eyes glued to her desk.

*What in the world*? Maybe I'd overstepped, but I was anxious to get started. Frankly, I didn't understand the resistance. I was the beneficiary. No one was contesting.

* * *

I loved coming home. I lived in a tropical paradise. A fence ran the entire length of the house, and within the gates was a courtyard filled with plants and flowers. I could either walk across the courtyard and enter the house through the front door or go around the back and in through the French doors by the patio. On the first level were the living room, dining room, and kitchen, all looking out to the pool area. Upstairs were two bedrooms and two baths.

I went around back. I always loved seeing the pool before going inside. As I walked by the kitchen window toward the French doors, I saw that the woman who'd been with Zach at the café was standing in my kitchen. She gave a friendly little wave. *This day just keeps getting better.* I certainly didn't want to face what's-her-name.

"Is Zach here?" I demanded when I got into the kitchen.

"No, he's not. I came on my own."

"How the hell did you get in?"

"That was the easy part. I picked your lock."

"Is that how Zach gets in?"

"Probably not. His lock-picking skills aren't as good as mine." She smirked.

It was hard to find anything wrong with her — a dangerously seductive woman with the bluest of eyes, full sensuous lips, a tangle of waist-length brunette hair, and a dark tan. She wore a white skirt and a tank top that was molded to her rock-hard body.

She extended her hand. "My name is Fabiana Merceau, but please call me Fab."

"I apologize for my rude behavior earlier," I began.

"That was pure entertainment. I came by to tell you that Zach and I are friends. Occasionally, we work together. We met this morning to discuss a case."

"Oh great, that makes me feel worse." I closed my eyes for a second, the beginnings of a massive headache banging my temples. "Emotion overcame good sense. Zach and I are... I have no idea what we are. Seeing him sitting with you... oh, I don't know, reminded me of another time, and I took it out on him."

"Did I mention I enjoyed every minute?"

We stared at one another for a moment, and then we started laughing.

"Why are you here?"

"Whatever your relationship is with Zach, I'm not 'the other woman' and never will be. I'm more of an associate."

"An associate? What does that mean?"

"Zach and I work together on cases. He lacks my special skills."

"Lock-picking?"

"That would be one."

It was hard to believe they didn't have a personal relationship.

"Zach and I used to be lovers," she said candidly, "but our relationship has been over for a long time. Now we're friends. We work well together, know each other's style. You need a person you can trust to watch your back. Zach and I are both intense people," she continued, "which doesn't translate well to a personal relationship."

"Did he send you here?"

"No, but knowing him, he'll show up soon. I wanted to meet the woman he talks so much about. He definitely likes you. When you poured the water on him, he was impressed. He likes a little crazy in his women. He's pretty sure you like him."

"Men are stupid."

"That may be, but he's right, isn't he?" she

asked, giving me a knowing smile.

I ignored her question. "I try not to do things I have to apologize for later. I hate apologizing."

"Keep it brief." She laughed.

This was certainly an interesting way to meet someone, and I liked her. "How about a lock-picking lesson?"

"Do you have a particular one in mind?"

As if on cue, Axe walked through the French doors. He'd perfected the beach boy persona in his shorts and tropical shirt, but the laid-back attitude was deceptive. He gave us a wink. It was easy to be charmed by him.

"Hey, ladies. Hear I missed a scene this morning at the café. Sounded like fun; I wish I'd been there. Word is you blackmailed yourself out of an arrest, Madison."

"See what I mean?" I said to Fab, then turned to Axe. "Any reason why you can't knock on the front door?"

"This is much more fun."

"What if I'd been doing something… well, uh, private? And what are you doing here anyway?"

Axe arched an eyebrow. "I'll call out next time." Chuckling, he crossed the room and took my phone from my hand. "I'm going to put in Fab's number, in case you can't get ahold of me or Zach."

"You can take his number out. I doubt I'll need it."

"It'll take more than a pitcher of water to get

rid of him," Axe said. "He's interested."

"I told you so," Fab said. They both laughed.

"Those are four very annoying words," I told her.

"Yes, I know, but you have to agree that they're so much fun to say."

Axe cleared his throat. "Zach wants to talk to you. I volunteered to stop by and check to see if the coast was clear for a visit."

"When would this be?"

"Now," Zach said as he walked in through the same doors Axe had just come through.

"Hi," I said, letting out an exasperated breath. "About this morning... that was my twin, Crazy."

"I'm here to reassure you that you have nothing to be jealous of."

*Jealous*? I gritted my teeth. I'd never admit to that.

"We should leave, Fab," Axe suggested.

"No one's going anywhere," I said, and turned back to Zach. "Axe just told me you wanted to talk. Another cool car needing to be serviced?"

"I need a favor."

"Are you using an IOU?"

"No. I want to keep the one I have."

"IOUs? How many of his do you have?" Fab asked.

"Seven."

"Very nice," she said. We looked at each other and laughed.

97

The guys appeared confused by our private joke. "Girl thing," I told them.

"Back to my favor," Zach said. "This is about a case we're working on. My company's investigating the theft of millions of dollars of inventory. Without going into a lot of detail, my brother, Dario, is involved, and I need a place he can stay for a couple of days. I'm hoping he can stay here."

"Would I be doing anything illegal?"

"No. He'll keep out of sight, stay in the house, and won't be any trouble."

"When is he coming?"

"Axe and I will bring him here later tonight."

"I have to go," Fab said. "Nice meeting you." She leaned toward me and whispered, "If that brat Dario gives you any trouble, call me. I'll come over and kick his ass."

# Chapter Eleven

Dario watched me watching him be dragged through the French doors by Axe. He was fresh out of high school, with spiky jet-black hair and an entitled look on his face, unlike the hard-edged Zach. You could certainly see the family resemblance between Zach and Dario, who made the same all-black clothing choices as his older brother but sported a snake tattoo on his left arm.

He crossed the room, took my hand, and pulled it up to his mouth. "Call me Dario."

I jerked my hand away, almost laughing at him. He stared at me boldly, sizing me up and not appearing to come to any conclusions.

Zach walked up behind him and hit him in the back. "Behave yourself. This is my girlfriend." He winked at me.

"She must realize she can do better than you," Dario said.

Zach's smile vanished. "Sit the hell down. Listen up." His voice was hard and unyielding.

"Not going to happen," Dario answered.

Zach yelled, "Sit! Down!"

You could've cut the tension in the room with a knife, and I had an instant stomachache.

Thankfully, Dario did what he was told and sat down.

Zach stuck his finger in Dario's face. "I'm going to say this just once, so you better listen. What you did tonight was stupid. You keep talking about what a big tough guy you are, but the people you're involved with will figure out you're working both ends. Trust me. You're not that smart."

"I wasn't going to tell anyone anything." Dario sounded whiny.

"Shut up. You keep saying you're a man, you can live on your own, take care of yourself, but you're acting like a little bitch. You know what the problem is? The entire family has spoiled you your entire life. Me most of all. Well, I'm done. This is the last time. From now until this is over, you'll keep your mouth shut. Stop disrespecting our family. Stay here, out of sight, and don't even look cross-eyed at Madison. Stand up and tell Madison you won't be a problem."

"Fine." Dario stood up and faced me. "I'll be the perfect houseguest. Where am I sleeping?"

I pointed upstairs. "First door on the right."

Dario picked up his bag, actually seeming contrite. "I'm sorry, Zach. I get that I messed up. It won't happen again." He disappeared up the stairs.

Zach put his hands over his face. "It's up to me to get him under control before he ends up in prison or dead. He believes that no matter what he does, I can get him out of trouble. I have to stop if he's ever to become his own man." He turned to me and pulled me into a hug. "Thank you again. Soon, I'll stop asking for favors and show you how appreciative I am. Any problems, call one of us."

"Stop asking for favors? Oh no, you don't. How will I collect more IOUs?" I smiled.

"I hope you don't cash them in all at once," he said.

"Please be safe. All of you," I said.

"Don't worry about me. I have plenty of backup on this job."

"You mean the gun holstered under your shirt?"

"That would be one. And don't forget pretty boy over there." He pointed to Axe.

"Watch out for Fab."

Both Zach and Axe laughed.

"You don't need to worry about her," Axe said. "She's like a cat; she still has lives she hasn't used up yet."

"Later," Zach said, pulling me into a kiss, and then left with Axe.

Other people's family drama was hard to witness. Totally exhausted, I picked up Jazz, climbed the stairs to my bedroom, and closed and locked the door.

* * *

I lay in bed the next morning thinking about my houseguest and realizing I knew nothing about him and darned little about his older brother. What was Dario's role in this big case? It sounded both criminal and dangerous. I said a quick prayer that he'd do as he promised and not cause any trouble.

Downstairs, I found Dario working on his laptop. He had his feet on the table and looked quite at home on my couch. "Good, you're awake. You don't look all that bad in the morning."

"Gee, thanks."

"There's nothing to eat in this house. I went through the refrigerator and cupboards and made out a grocery list. And there's no sports package on the TV. If you call now, they can get it hooked up and running in an hour or two."

His arrogance knew no bounds. "Try to remember you're supposed to be a trouble-free houseguest. Food is one thing, but I'm not adding anything to my TV."

"Aren't you a self-righteous bitch? I don't need you reminding me of how to act."

"Let's get something straight," I said, simmering with anger. "You're not going to stay in my house and yell at me and call me names. Make an effort or go somewhere else."

An expression of utter contempt crossed his face.

"I'll call Zach; he can find you another place to

stay." I pulled my phone out of my pocket.

"Don't bother. I'm sure Super Brother will wrap this up in a day or two." His voice dripped with sarcasm.

Suddenly, I realized there was no meowing, no big ball of fur walking between my legs. "Where's Jazz?"

"Who?"

"A big black long-haired cat." I noticed his food bowl was almost empty.

"I threw it outside."

"You did what?" I yelled.

"The thing was meowing and wouldn't stop. How do you stand the racket?"

"Where?" I demanded.

"Out the back." He pointed to the closed French doors.

I raced to the doors, and as soon as I opened them, I saw Jazz asleep on a pool float on the patio. I walked out, picked him up, and carried him inside. "Don't you ever touch my cat." I kicked his feet off the table. "Don't even look at him funny or I will personally kick your ass."

"Okay, calm down. I'll never look at him again."

After feeding and petting Jazz, I walked up the stairs to get dressed for my meeting with Tucker, who'd finally called and set up an appointment.

\* \* \*

After showering, I looked in the mirror and laughed. My hair was bigger than usual, and I lacked patience when it came to taming my red curls, so I twisted it up into a clip. I did the minimal makeup thing, satisfied that I appeared presentable for a business appointment, then slipped into a linen dress that was a bright shade of lime green—my new favorite color since moving to Florida—and matching slides. If I hadn't needed to appear professional, there was no way I'd have put on a bra.

"Dario," I said as I came down the stairs, "I'll be back later. My cell phone number is on the counter."

"Whose bright idea was it to make a dress the same color as baby puke?" He laughed, enjoying his own humor.

"See you later." I closed the front door, happy he wasn't my brother.

# Chapter Twelve

I made the short trip to Tucker's office in record time. "Hi, Ann," I said as I walked in the door. "I'm here for my meeting."

She had an odd way of pinching her nostrils together and looking down her nose at a person. "Mr. Davis likes his clients to be on time," she said, glancing at her watch.

"I don't believe I'm late."

"This way." Ann led the way down the hall to Tucker's office, where she gave a short knock and opened the door. "You can go in," she said, never making eye contact.

I was surprised to see that Will Todd had been included in the meeting. "Hello, gentlemen." They both turned in my direction, but neither stood up.

Tucker gave me one of his weasely smiles. "Take a seat." He gestured at a chair. "I understand there's no need for introductions." He started shuffling through paperwork. "We're not here to discuss the unfortunate situation that took place at The Cottages. I wish everyone had waited for me to bring the two of you together for an official introduction and avoid any misunderstandings." I opened my mouth to defend myself, but he cut me off. "I'll take comments and questions later."

I wished I'd come better prepared, with my own notes in writing rather than in my head. I felt defensive and talked down to. Not a pleasant way to start.

"I'll spell out how everything will proceed. Elizabeth hired me to draw up her will and named me executor. She thought a strong hand would be needed to make the transition go smoothly. This process doesn't happen overnight." He stopped talking and pushed the intercom button. "Ann, would you bring me some coffee?"

He didn't bother to offer Will or myself anything to drink.

"The estate is under my control until everything is finalized. I make all the decisions. Let's face facts, Madison—you lack managerial experience. In fact, I'm not sure what your background is. At the end of the meeting, I'd like to talk to you about other options. Before Elizabeth's death, she appointed Will to be the manager. She trusted him and was satisfied with the job he was doing, and he's proven himself more than capable. As such, he'll continue as manager, reporting directly to me, until the estate is transferred."

Joseph had told me that Will hadn't become manager until after my aunt died, and there was no reason for him to lie. Why would Tucker?

"The court dictates the timeframe, which can fluctuate depending on any claims made, and frankly, how backed up the court is. Elizabeth bequeathed you her entire estate, other than the measly bequests she left to your mother and brother."

I couldn't believe what he'd just said. The bequest to Brad hadn't been measly at all. I knew for a fact that wasn't true; Elizabeth had said so in her letter. If it'd been his intention to embarrass me, he'd succeeded.

Tucker turned to Will. "Are there any specific issues you wanted to go over today?"

"I agree with you that day-to-day management is going well," Will preened. "I think it should be made clear that I'm the only person in charge. No problems or misunderstandings that way."

"I'm sure Madison doesn't plan to interfere with the running of the property," Tucker said, looking at me.

I nodded, a stupid smile planted firmly on my face, feeling overwhelmed and dismissed.

"I think I deserve some job security in exchange for my loyalty," Will continued. "While I admit that I didn't handle our initial meeting very well, Madison just showed up one day and began agitating the tenants with endless questions." He glared. "You could've stopped by my cottage and introduced yourself and avoided any unpleasantness."

Tucker waved his hand, cutting off my response. "We already agreed your first meeting could've gone more smoothly," he said. "Madison, what are your objectives today?"

"My running The Cottages is clearly what my aunt wanted. I have my own resume of education and training, and my expectation is that I'll start to learn the day-to-day operations. My intent was never to jump in immediately as a full-time manager. In fact," I continued, "I plan to operate the property as Elizabeth did, with a day manager who reports to me. If Will and I work well together, there's no reason he can't be that person. I guess I just don't understand why my request to learn about the running of the property is so unreasonable. I'm the beneficiary, and no one is contesting."

"Are you sure?" Tucker questioned. "As you now know, there's a statutory waiting period, and we need to be certain no one is contesting. Once your mother and brother have had time to think about how unequally the estate was divided, they may feel slighted and challenge the will."

I sat in silence.

Will spoke up. "One more thing. I think it would be a good idea if Madison stayed away from the property. Then the tenants would see that I'm in charge. If anything needs your attention, you'll be contacted."

"I will come and go as I please," I told him. "I have long-standing relationships with a couple of the tenants that I plan on continuing."

Tucker cleared his throat, and Will and I turned to him. He looked amused by the power struggle.

"Now that I've heard from both of you, I see no problem in accommodating you both. I think this meeting ended up being very productive. Will, finish updating the records and preparing the reports for the accountant and, before sending them to Whitman's office, make a copy for Madison."

Will nodded. "They should be done shortly."

"And since Madison wants to learn about the inner workings of The Cottages, perhaps you can arrange a time to take her on a little tour."

*A tour? He must be kidding. I know my way around.*

"She can call me anytime to set up an appointment," Will offered.

"At this time, we're in agreement that Will will continue to act as manager. A letter will go out to the tenants making this fact clear."

Will nodded, and I sat speechless, blindsided. Nothing about this meeting had gone as planned. I looked at Will, who had a big, confident smile on his face.

Tucker asked, "Any more issues? Good," he went on without waiting for an answer. "I'd like to end the meeting. There's no reason for the three of us to get together again. If you have any questions, Will, you can direct them to Ann, and I'll get back to you." He stood up and extended his hand to Will. "Thank you for coming. If anything comes up, call me."

Will thanked him, gave me a half-smile, and left.

"Madison, I want to update you and give you a tentative timetable. I've opened up probate and filed numerous documents with the court. In the coming weeks, more will follow, but none of these proceedings will require your involvement. Ann will send you a letter periodically to keep you informed."

"Do you have any idea of the timeframe?"

"The whole process takes about a year, as long as there are no unforeseen problems. If anything changes, I'll notify you. I realize you wanted more involvement with the daily operations of The Cottages," he continued, "but my duty is to the estate and the court; the letter of the law has to be followed. A year isn't a long period of time. You can use it to decide if motel management is what you're really interested in."

Tucker never noticed that I had little to say, and I was positive he wouldn't care to hear it anyway.

"I want to ask that you keep your visits to the property to a minimum, to give Will the security he's earned."

*I don't care about Will's security.* My cheeks

were cramped from my phony smile.

"During this finalization process, take the time to determine your long-term plans. I realize you think you can run this property, but you should think about that carefully. I'm certain Elizabeth would rather you sell The Cottages than mismanage them into financial ruin. I've had inquiries regarding whether you'd consider selling or not, and I urge you to do so. You'd have the financial security without the responsibility. One last thing," he continued. "I checked with the county clerk, and you're on the title to the Cove Road property, showing right of survivorship. So the house will be excluded from the probate process."

I wondered why he didn't believe me. Did Tucker actually think I would lie about Aunt Elizabeth putting me on title?

"Should you decide not to stay in Tarpon Cove, I'm sure I could find a buyer for both properties: a package deal. Questions? Good," he went on, again without giving me a chance to answer, "so if there's nothing more...

"Mr. Davis, you've made it very clear that your client is the estate; I think my interests would be better served if I had my own attorney. In my opinion, oversight of The Cottages without any family input for possibly a year, or more, is not a good idea." I amazed myself at how calm I sounded.

"I realize you're unhappy, but you don't need

to hire another attorney," he said. "I'll look out for your interests. Truly, my hands are tied. The law is very explicit about what can and can't be done. Another attorney will only cause additional delays."

I stood up. "If I have any questions, I'll call." I'd just spontaneously brought up the notion of hiring an attorney, but the more I thought about it, the better I liked the idea.

"Thank you for coming. This was quite a productive meeting, don't you think?"

"Thank you for arranging the meeting." Good manners prevailed, but what I really wanted to do was scream my frustration in his face.

I was happy Ann wasn't at her desk when I walked out of Tucker's office. I had a headache and wasn't up to seeing her sour face again. I had no doubt that both men had agendas having nothing to do with my best interests.

# Chapter Thirteen

I decided to call Elizabeth's CPA, Ernest Whitman III, affectionately known as Whit. He'd been friends with my aunt forever and her accountant for about the same length of time.

"Madison, how are you?" He sounded happy to hear from me.

"I'm fine. I'm sorry I didn't get a chance to say hello at Aunt Elizabeth's funeral."

He chuckled. "Ridiculous, wasn't it? I can just imagine Elizabeth laughing, asking 'what in the hell's going on here?'"

"I'm sorry. The funeral plans were out of my hands." I didn't know what else to say.

"Oh Madison, I didn't mean to upset you. I know you had nothing to do with the planning. Dickie what's-his-name told me it was all his 'inspiration.' I believe that was his exact word. He used it as a selling point to solicit my future business." He snorted. "I wanted to ask him if I looked close to death."

"He's too much."

"What can I do for you? I've been wanting to contact you to let you know I'm here if you need help with anything."

113

"Do you have time to talk? I'd like to stop by your office sometime."

"Can you come right now?"

"I'm less than five minutes away."

* * *

His office was also located in a converted house. An expansive porch wrapped around both sides, and on it were several colorful Adirondack chairs with cushions. I wanted to curl up on one of them and listen to the wild parrots as I drifted off and took a nap.

Inside, the rooms were decorated in a relaxed tropical decor, complete with an enormous fish tank. My efforts at keeping fish alive were abysmal. I either overfed them or underfed them and hated looking in the bowl to find another one dead. Then the crucial decision: flush or bury?

The best part of coming to Whit's office was the snack bowl that sat in the center of the coffee table, filled with candy, cookies, and crackers. Nearby was a small refrigerator that was always stocked with a dozen different kinds of sodas and bottled water.

I grabbed a bag of Oreos—just looking at them made me feel better—and waved hello to Helena, Whit's assistant, who was busy on the phone. She smiled and waved me back to his office.

He looked up when I got to his door, then

stood up and came around his desk to kiss my cheek. "We lost Elizabeth way too soon. She was a good woman and well-loved."

"Thank you. I always liked to come to your office with my aunt. Today, I went straight for the snack bowl and then the refrigerator." I laughed. "Just like always!"

"The snack bowl is the number one favorite among our clients. On the rare occasion when we run out, they complain loudly." He joined me in laughing. "So, Madison, how can I help you?"

"I just came from a meeting with Tucker Davis and Will Todd, the manager of The Cottages."

"Now there's a sleazy pair." He shook his head. "In my younger and more principled days, I'd never have gossiped, but I don't like either one of them. I'm more than happy to help you with anything I can."

"No wonder my aunt liked you so much," I said. "I'm sure you're aware Elizabeth left me The Cottages. When I met with Tucker and Will today, my plan was to start learning about the property. Tucker essentially told me to butt out. He even directed me to stay away from the property."

"You're kidding," Whit said.

"No, I'm not. Tucker informed me that probate could take a year, and until everything was final, he didn't want me to even go to The Cottages. Zero involvement."

"Tucker's well within his rights as executor to

limit your access to the property, but why would he choose that tactic? He's a smart lawyer; he should know he could alienate you and lose out on any future business dealings."

"What's your professional opinion of Tucker Davis?"

"He's an a-hole." Whit roared with laughter. "He has a questionable reputation, personally and professionally. He'll take anyone for a client, criminal or not, as long as they're able to pay his fees. The sad part is that he usually gets them off; his win record is near perfect. He thinks that somehow makes him legitimate, but most people around here think Tucker is as big a crook as those he represents. Although he primarily handles criminal cases, he never turns away a client who can pay, no matter what the case."

"Why would Aunt Elizabeth hire a criminal lawyer to draw up her will and then appoint him executor? He's the reason the funeral was a circus. He refused to allow any family involvement and just kept saying Elizabeth left him in charge and he was only following her wishes."

"I was aware she used him to write her will but making him executor came as a big surprise. She went to Tucker because her previous attorney retired, and I believe he referred her."

"What do you know about Will Todd?"

"The first I heard of him was when Tucker called needing updated financial records. During the call, he told me he was named executor and also informed me Will Todd would be the new manager at The Cottages."

"Interesting because, in today's meeting, Tucker said Will had been acting as manager since before Elizabeth's death. I wonder when exactly he was put in charge?"

"He informed me of the same thing. I didn't believe it then, and I don't believe it now. Elizabeth never said a word about a new manager, much less that she'd hired one. Cynthia, the previous one, left to have a baby, and I got the impression she'd be coming back," Whit said. "In the few dealings I've had with Will, he hasn't given me one straight answer, just one excuse after another. I don't trust him."

"Someone else made an observation about him to me," I said, unscrewing the top off my water. "They thought he acted like a man with something to hide. That same person thought he'd done prison time."

"Will missed the deadline to turn over The Cottages annual financial records," Whit said. "I had to file an extension. Frankly, I don't understand the hold-up. He hasn't been in charge long. What surprises me is that he has control of the records. I find it difficult to believe that Elizabeth would give him access to all the financial information. She certainly didn't with the last manager."

"Does the fact that Will missed the deadline

raise a red flag for you?"

"Not yet. I'll give him a couple of days and then call him again. When I receive them, I'll let you know."

"What's your opinion of my hiring another attorney to handle my interests? I tossed the idea out to Tucker in frustration. He didn't like it and didn't want another attorney in the mix."

"I'll bet. He's not a team player," Whit said. "You're already having problems dealing with him, so I think your idea is a good one. He represents the estate and has no obligation to you, legally or otherwise. The fact that he even breathes is suspect to me. I'm not sure it was smart to warn him you were thinking of hiring your own attorney."

"Actually, I blurted it out without thinking."

"Tucker's acting within his rights as executor in not allowing you access to the property, but my question is why wouldn't he? In my opinion, he hasn't given you any choice but to hire someone else to look out for your interests."

"I appreciate the advice."

"I'll do what I can to help. I can contact Howard Sherman, another probate attorney, if you want." He walked me to the door. "By the way, I hear you and Zach are a couple. Elizabeth would've been ecstatic. She liked that young man a lot."

I gave him a little smile and a hug. "Thank you for making time for me on such short notice." I was about to tell him Zach and I were only friends when someone called my name. It surprised me to see Jimmy Spoon walk into Whit's office. "Hello, Mr. Spoon."

He cleaned up well. He was wearing tan linen slacks, a short-sleeved silk shirt, and Gucci loafers. His hair was tied back, there wasn't one speck of dirt or grease on him, and I'd have sworn he'd had a manicure.

"Call me Spoon. Still with Zach?" he whispered in my ear.

"I see the two of you have met," Whit commented. "Jimmy's one hell of a mechanic. He found a part for my Jaguar even the dealer couldn't get."

So Whit called him Jimmy. "Nice to see you again, *Spoon*," I said.

# Chapter Fourteen

I drove down the Overseas Highway, thinking about the transformation of Jimmy Spoon, who'd gone from looking like a hard-core criminal to a solid citizen, despite the fierce tattoos. No wonder women were attracted to him.

The news of my relationship with Zach had obviously traveled all over town. I wanted it to be true. And absolutely the last thing I wanted was for anyone to find out it had started as a made-up story. In a small town, a story/lie would haunt me forever.

I drove reluctantly towards home, the idea of spending the rest of the afternoon with Dario making me queasy. He didn't inspire confidence, and I had a suspicion he'd make things worse if he could. I wanted to ask him a few questions, to find out what was actually going on. I should mind my own business and go for a swim.

Everything appeared quiet. In fact, too quiet. I sighed and hoped for an uneventful evening with Dario.

As I walked into the house, a door closed upstairs. Jazz meowed from the living room. "Where's Dario, Jazz?"

"I'm right here," he grumbled from the top of the stairs. "I feel sick. I'm going to bed and watch a little TV." He disappeared into the guest bedroom.

"Hope you feel better," I called, trying not to jump up and down at the prospect of a Dario-free evening.

\* \* \*

I opened my eyes to find that Jazz and I had fallen asleep on the couch watching television. Dario was in the kitchen, banging around and making way too much noise for so early in the morning. I noticed his backpack lying on the floor in the entryway.

He came into the living room, holding a cup of coffee and wearing the same clothes from the day before. The big question: was he coming or going? The question gave me a bad feeling.

"You must be feeling better. Are you going somewhere?" *What now?* My gut told me he'd been out wandering around all night.

"I've had enough. I'm not staying," he whined. "I'm not sitting here for days, doing nothing."

"You promised Zach." *Just perfect. I get to start the day with this stupid drama.*

"Zach needs to be reminded I'm all grown up. I admit to a couple of mistakes, but I can take care of myself."

*He's so full of himself. The little punk is out of his mind.* "Call Zach and let him know you're leaving."

"Later."

"Where are you going? How will Zach get ahold of you?" How was I going to explain to Zach that Dario had up and left?

"I'm out of here." He picked up his backpack, then dropped it on the floor again. "Forgot something," he mumbled and raced up the stairs.

What was I supposed to do now? No one would be able to get here in time to stop him. Getting the Lazarro brothers to stay in one place was impossible.

Dario came back down the stairs with his laptop. "Don't worry so much. This will work out."

"Please call Zach," I begged. *Little brat.* "Can't you stay another day or two?"

"I'll catch up with him later," he shot back as he headed for the door.

I picked up a vase sitting on the counter and hit him over the head. He dropped to the floor like a sack.

I stooped to check if he was breathing. "Thank you," I said to myself and the universe, "he's not dead." Then went in search of my phone, no longer annoyed that everyone's numbers had been stored in it. Fab would know what to do. Thank goodness I could call her for help—I couldn't imagine calling Zach and telling him I'd brained his brother with a vase.

"Fab, it's Madison," I said when I heard her voice. "I hit Dario over the head."

She laughed. "Is he alive?"

"He's breathing. He was on his way out the door, and I didn't think about what I was doing, I hit him over the head with a vase. I didn't know what else to do." I was almost yelling.

"Breathe," she said. "Calm down. I had a feeling he'd start causing problems, but I figured we had a couple of days. Keep him there until I can come take him off your hands."

"What if he wakes up?" I asked. "I can't continue to hit him over the head."

"Listen to me. Go out in the garage. Elizabeth has a cool work area. Open the tall cabinet by the window and find some rope or zip ties. She kept everything pretty organized."

"When were you in the garage?" I asked as I made my way out the door to the garage.

"The other day when I stopped by."

"I didn't even notice." I wasn't sure what I thought about the fact that Fab knew more about what was in my garage than I did.

"Another one of my talents."

"Okay. I'm here, standing in front of the cabinet." I opened the doors and started pushing things around on the shelves. "I found some zip ties. Now what?"

"Wrap a tie around each wrist. Pull his arms behind his back. Take another tie and hook the two together. Do the same with his ankles, and he won't be going anywhere. I'm on my way."

I raced into the kitchen. Dario was groaning. I grabbed his hands, securing each one, and then I worked on his feet. He made noises the whole time but didn't move. I'd totally lost my mind. Wait until he woke up and realized I'd cold-cocked him and then tied him up.

Dario began wiggling, trying to move his arms, and I knew he was coming around. He banged into the bar stool, and it fell over on him. "What happened?" he moaned.

"You weren't supposed to leave," I said, trying to sound calm.

He rolled back and forth on the floor. "What the hell did you do to me?"

"I couldn't let you walk out the door," I reminded him. "All you had to do was call Zach, and you refused."

"You bitch," he ground out.

"That's the second time you've called me a bitch, and I'm tired of it." I kicked him hard in the ass.

"Oww. What are you doing?"

"Call me that word one more time, and I'll kick the crap out of you. Now be quiet."

"You psycho!" he yelled.

"Quiet!" I yelled back.

\* \* \*

When Fab finally came walking in, she was followed by one of the biggest guys I'd ever seen.

"This is Slice," she said.

He nodded in my direction but stayed silent. He stood well over six feet tall, a two-hundred-fifty-pound wall of solid muscle. His long blond hair was tied back in a ponytail, and a nasty scar ran from his forehead to his collarbone, disappearing inside his shirt. He stood against the counter, his massive arms crossed in front of him, with a "Do Not Fuck With Me" look on his face.

"Where's Dario?" Fab asked. "We're going to take him with us."

"Tied up on the floor." I pointed behind the island.

"This isn't the first time he's gotten into big trouble. Zach comes to his rescue every time. We can't have him running around town making things worse."

"Hey, I'm right here. Get these ties off me!" Dario yelled.

Slice smiled. "I'll help him." That smile made the hair on the back of my neck stand up. "Roll over, Dario." Slice jerked him up and slammed him down on the barstool. Dario toppled sideways, landing on the floor, the barstool falling on top of him again.

He tried to pull away. "Take your hands off me, you ugly bastard."

A knife suddenly appeared in Slice's hand. He

used it to remove the ties around Dario's ankles.

"Nice work," I whispered to Fab.

"Dario, I'm going to make you wish you'd kept your promise." Fab grabbed him by the hair, forcing him to face her. "I have a special babysitter in mind for you," she said as she yanked him to his feet. "I'll tell you this once, and trust me, you'll do exactly as you're told." Her voice was ice-cold, and I now believed Zach and Axe when they said she could take care of herself.

"Another crazy bitch," Dario spit at Fab. "I thought my brother dumped your ass a long time ago."

With lightning speed, she kicked his legs out from underneath him, and he hit the floor again.

Slice picked him straight up in the air and shook him until I thought his teeth would fall out. "Keep your mouth shut, you little bastard, or I'll shut it for you."

Fab turned to me. "Don't worry about this. I'll see you in a couple of days. No worries on the Zach front, I'll bring him up to speed."

"Nice meeting you, Madison Westin," Slice said.

He dragged Dario out the front door with Fab following. I leaned against the wall and took a deep breath, relieved Dario was headed elsewhere.

# Chapter Fifteen

Several peaceful days passed, and I was having a quiet morning when my phone rang. I glanced at the display screen and answered the phone. "Hi, Mother, what are you up to?"

"I'm driving down to the Cove, and I want the two of us to go out to dinner. Let's meet at The Crab Shack around six. Dress up a little."

"Are you okay?" She sounded excited about something, not her usual self. "Stop by, and we'll drive over together," I suggested.

"No, I need to make a few stops along the way, so I'll meet you there. Wear a dress and some of your cute jewelry. I'll see you later."

Mother seemed to be acting weirder than usual. She was clearly up to something. But good food and company were what I needed. I'd been obsessing over Zach, and I was exhausted. My eyes turned to the French doors several times a day, waiting for him, Axe, or Fab to appear in my living room. So far, nothing.

I walked into the restaurant right on time, wearing, as instructed, a red strapless sundress dressed up with a fun necklace, gold bracelets, and earrings. Tired of the never-ending fight with my hair, I'd pulled it up off my neck and put in my usual clip.

Mother sat at a table overlooking the water, looking fabulous in a classic black-and-white dress with red leather pumps. When she made plans to go out, she always effortlessly made the right clothing choices, while I stressed continually over my decisions. "Jack, straight up," she told the server.

"I'll have a glass of white wine." I looked at Mother. "What brings you to the Cove? Besides dinner with me." I suspected another agenda.

"You, actually. I haven't heard from you very much."

"I'm sorry." Now I felt guilty that I'd been suspicious. "Are you feeling neglected?"

"Even Brad says the two of you have only talked once. What's keeping you so busy? Zach?"

*Oh brother.* "Did Brad happen to mention he's never home? He and his crew are always out fishing; making the most of grouper season, I presume. Tucker and I finally had a meeting."

"Anything new with Zach?" Mother asked, seemingly oblivious to my attempt to change the subject.

"Mother, we had one date, and we had a lot of fun." I wondered if I should mention the night of hot sex and almost laughed at what her reaction would be.

"Are you going out again?"

"I hope so. Can we please change the subject?"

"I planned a surprise for you," she said with a slight smile.

"What are you up to?" *I knew it*. The phone conversation had been unusual, not like her at all.

As she was about to answer, a man approached our table.

"Madeline," he said and bent down to kiss her cheek.

He was in his thirties, with a medium build, brown hair, Dockers, and a golf shirt. He had a look that broadcast "uptight" and that he'd never done anything wrong in his life. I had an uneasy suspicion the two of them were up to something, but what?

"Connor, I'm so glad you were able to come," Mother said, giving him a big smile and kissing him back.

"Oh Madeline, of course I came. I'm looking forward to tonight."

I sat there listening, my lips turned up in an attempt at a smile. I knew it made me look like a crazy person.

"This is my daughter, Madison. Madison, Connor Manning." She waved her hand at an empty chair. "Please sit down."

My mother wouldn't do this to me, fix me up without telling me.

"Nice to meet you, Madison," he said, extending his hand.

"I told Connor all about you, honey." Mother smiled.

"Funny," I said. "I never heard of you, Connor."

Mother kicked me under the table.

"Oww." They both stared at me. "I hit my foot." Mother gave me a *you better behave* look that was all too familiar.

"I met Connor at a party my old friend Jean threw, and when I realized that the two of you had interests in common, I decided to get you together. This beautiful restaurant is a good place for a first date, don't you think?"

I was so shocked that I didn't trust myself to speak. My face heating up, I stared at my mother. What the hell was she talking about?

"Your mother told me you were having a hard time meeting acceptable people. She thought you needed a little push to get out into the world again. Don't get me wrong; I understand the divorce wasn't your fault."

"A date? Now?" This was one of those moments when anything I said would sound rude.

My mother stood up. "Honey, I'm going to leave. You and Connor enjoy your evening. Call me in the morning." She leaned over to kiss my cheek. "Don't embarrass me," she whispered in my ear and beat a hasty retreat to the door. I wanted to chase after her and wring her neck.

"Well, this is awkward," I said, smiling with

fake sincerity.

"I had no idea our date would be a complete surprise to you," Connor said, looking me over intently. "Mothers always know best, don't you agree? I insist we have a good time."

"So you met my mother at a party at Jean Stewart's?" I would have thought her social set was a little old for him.

"I'm an architect." He made some sort of sound I assumed was laughter. "I designed Jean's new house, which is being built out on Fisher Island."

"Sounds interesting." I wondered what my mother had told him. "You'll have to tell me about yourself." My plan was to keep him talking, eat quickly, and get out of here.

The waitress came to take our orders and ask if we wanted more drinks.

"No thank you, we've had enough," Connor said, then turned to me. "I don't believe in drinking. I make an exception when I'm out to dinner but limit myself to one. I don't keep alcohol at home."

It irritated me that he didn't ask me what I wanted. "How do you feel about smoking?"

"You don't smoke, do you? That's another nasty habit."

"My mother does," I baited him.

"Your mother and I had a long talk about her smoking. On my advice, she started using the patch. It's helped her to stop," he said, obviously pleased with himself.

If I'd had liquid in my mouth, I'd have spit it all over the table. No wonder my mother practically ran out of the restaurant — she needed a cigar. Give up smoking? She might hoodwink this pompous ass, but not me.

"So you're an architect. Do you live and work in the Miami area?" I held onto my wrist so I wouldn't be tempted to check the time.

"I live in Coral Gables, not far from your mother. But I also own some undeveloped waterfront property here in the Cove."

"Are you designing a house for yourself?"

"No, I'm planning a condominium and shopping mall complex."

"A shopping mall? Condos? In Tarpon Cove?" I was horrified. "Your plans would change the community forever. We'd lose our small beach town charm."

"Every parcel of land should be built to meet its highest and best use standard," he pointed out. "I think Tarpon Cove is ripe for updating." He talked like a true outsider, with revenue his only interest.

"When are you starting this project?"

"I still need to acquire a couple more parcels, but final plans are at the City Planning Commission awaiting approval. There have been some stumbling blocks getting the project approved, but no one can stop progress forever."

*What an ass*, I thought. His ambitious idea

would strip all the character from the Cove and create another beach town full of second homes. I hoped the Commission would never approve the plans. "I'm very surprised."

"This is all about the best use of my investment dollar." Connor smiled smugly as the waitress brought our food.

"I should've ordered for you," he said, staring at my plate. "The shrimp is so high in cholesterol. Wasn't there a brown rice substitution? An order of double vegetables would have been a healthier choice."

"Thanks for the tip." I wanted to tell him that the double vegetables would ruin my order of cholesterol. "I eat what I want when I go out to dinner."

"You're in pretty good shape." He didn't sound as if he believed what he said. "I'd hoped that wasn't an exaggeration on your mother's part. I work out every day. A person who lets themself go lacks discipline. You should work out with me sometime. I can get you in much better shape."

I didn't work out in the traditional sense, but I swam and biked and made it a habit to steer clear of a real gym. "Next time I'm at my mother's, the three of us should work out together — she loves to exercise," I said, knowing how much she hated it. As much as I'd love to get back at her, I wasn't doing it just for that but because insisting she go to the gym would mean a second anything with this idiot would never happen.

"In fact, I think bad habits, in general, are just a lack of discipline," he went on.

"What are you talking about?" This conversation was exhausting.

"I set strict standards for myself and would expect my girlfriend to follow them too."

*Girlfriend? We're two strangers sitting here having dinner.*

"You should be well groomed and in appropriate attire too. I like your dress, but the color is a bit bold and you need shoulder straps or a sweater."

"A sweater? It's nine hundred degrees outside!"

"I did say I liked your dress." He smiled. "I'd also insist on punctuality. And no vulgar language."

"Those are a lot of rules." Just how well did Connor Manning know my mother, who smoked, drank Jack straight up, was usually late, and freely used the f-word?

"Your mother assured me you could be the woman I'm looking for and that we share the same values."

"What happens if the rules are broken?" This had gone far enough, whatever it was. I refused to call it a first date. He totally creeped me out.

"One or two reminders would be sufficient." Anger briefly crossed his face. "We wouldn't want to disappoint one another."

Now I was beginning to feel afraid and made a mental note to never be alone with him. It was time for me to make my escape.

An expression of disapproval crossed Connor's face. I turned in my chair, and big, gorgeous Zach stood behind me. Wearing navy silk shorts and a tropical shirt, he looked like an advertisement for Tommy Bahama, a short beard making him seem more ferocious than usual. I flushed, remembering our night together, getting aroused just looking at him.

"Hi." I gave him a big smile. I wanted to talk to him, ask questions, but not in front of Connor.

"Madison," Zach said, leaning down to kiss me. He stood next to me, his fingers pulling my hair from the clip, and exchanged hellos with Connor, whose face turned red with anger.

"Are you two friends?" I asked.

"Not exactly," Zach said. "I'd join you, but I'm here on business. I'll call you later." He walked away.

I wanted to scream *come back!*

"How do you know Zach Lazarro?" Conner asked.

"He's a family friend," I told him.

"He's a criminal. You need to end any association with him."

"You don't get to pick my friends."

"I'll speak to your mother. When I explain to her the kind of man Zach is, she'll encourage you to make the right decision."

"No, you will not." Now was the time to execute my plan for an early exit—go to the bathroom and pretend to get sick. The threat of vomit always made a man run.

"I don't mean to upset you." He backed down slightly. "I don't mean to upset you. I just thought you should be aware of his bad reputation, one you wouldn't want to be associated with." Connor's cell rang. "Excuse me, but I need to take this." He stepped away from the table and went out to the patio.

Maybe he'd come back and say *he* was sick. I couldn't get that lucky, could I? I realized we hadn't shared a single joke. Whatever the sound he'd made earlier was, it wasn't a laugh.

"Why would you go out with him?" Zach asked, returning to the table, pulling up a chair, and sitting down.

"This is your fault," I said.

"Mine?" He was clearly amused.

"We didn't get married and have children fast enough for my mother, so she sets me up without telling me... and with *that*."

Zach threw his head back and laughed. "Ah, Madeline. She's something, isn't she?"

"That's one way to put it. I don't mean to be rude, but you need to leave now, before he gets back. I'm planning my exit strategy."

"Be careful. I miss you." He ran his finger across my lips. "Manning has a nasty temper. If you need help, I'm sitting over by the far window. If he touches you, I'll break his arm and shove it up his butt."

"That's so sweet." I laughed. "Go. Don't worry about me."

Zach pushed back his chair and stood up. "We're here if you need us. Soon," he whispered in my ear and kissed me.

*We?* I glanced around and spotted Axe sitting at the bar. He waved and smiled back. Why would Zach be sitting in the restaurant and leave Axe at the bar? What were those two doing?

Connor returned to the table. "Sorry for the interruption."

"Excuse me," I said. "I'll be right back." I walked in the direction of the restrooms, taking a detour through the middle of the bar.

"Hey, Axe." I smiled without stopping. "Are you the cavalry?"

"Yes, ma'am." He smiled back.

On my return, I went back through the bar. "Hey Axe, call me on my cell when I get back to the table."

Sure enough, just as I sat down, my phone began ringing. "I'm not sure what you want me to say, but I'll go along with it," Axe said when I answered.

"You're not interrupting. Is there a problem?"

"What are you doing with an asshole like Manning?" he asked.

"I'm glad you called. Don't worry, I'll take care of it. Thanks for calling." Plan B would be easier than Plan A.

"Is there a problem?" Connor asked after I hung up.

"Something's come up at a property I own, and I need to take care of it."

"I can go with you. You shouldn't be going out in the evening by yourself."

*Can you say control freak?* "That won't be necessary. I can take care of this myself." I stood up. "Thank you for dinner."

"I'll walk you out. I got your phone number from your mother and will be calling you soon," he informed me. "I look forward to our next date."

Except that there would be no more dates. I was leaving without making a scene, and that made me happy.

I noticed that Axe had followed us to the parking lot and stood a couple of cars away, watching. As I drove out, I rolled down the passenger window and waved.

# Chapter Sixteen

I'd just left the parking lot when my phone started ringing. One of those "unknown caller" numbers appeared on the screen. "Hello?"

"Madison, it's Joseph. I need a favor right now." He sounded frantic.

"What's the favor?"

"I was just released from Monroe County jail, and I need a ride home. I'm standing outside at the pay phone. My only option is to walk if you can't come get me."

"I'll be right there. Where will you be?"

"Out in front of the jail is a bus stop. I'll be sitting on the bench."

This night would go on record as being one of the weirdest ever.

Twenty minutes later, I pulled up in front of the jail, and there was Joseph, a lone figure sitting at the bus stop. The sign said that the bus had stopped running hours ago. I powered down the window. "Hop in."

"Thanks for coming and getting me. It's a long walk," he said, opening the door. "I would've had to sleep in the bushes and hitch a ride in the morning." Joseph was pale, his ankles more swollen than I'd ever seen them.

"How did you end up in jail?"

"Drunk in public. I was walking home from the Back Room Bar, and less than a block from home, a deputy pulled up."

"Why would they do that? Don't they all know you?"

"Yeah, but they're still pissed off about before."

"Before?"

"I got popped for DUI and not having registration or tags. I claimed bad health to get a shortened sentence, and they gave me probation and revoked my license. The cops knew if they charge me with drunk in public, I'll also get charged with VOP."

"Won't a violation of probation get you sent to jail?"

"Probably not. My probation officer is a good guy. He's a vet too."

"I don't want to lecture, but Joseph, a DUI is not cool." I pulled into the driveway of The Cottages, where several people were milling around drinking beer, and stopped in front of Joseph's door. "What happened to your car?"

"The one I got arrested in wasn't actually mine. It was sort of borrowed. The police towed it to impound. No one will ever make a claim. Too much paperwork and too many questions."

I smiled at him, amused by his explanation.

"Thanks for the ride," Joseph said, getting out of the car.

"Stay out of trouble." I backed out of the space. The people who'd been hanging around had disappeared, vanished like roaches when the lights go on.

Something banged on the passenger window. I screamed and turned to find Will standing there. "What?" I shouted through the closed window.

"Why are you here? Is there a problem?" He motioned for me to roll down the window, which I reluctantly did.

"No problem. I saw Joseph walking and gave him a ride."

"Joseph is trouble."

"He has a few problems, but who doesn't? Do I need to remind you he's lived here a long time, one of my aunt's first tenants?"

"He either gets his act together or he can find a new place to live."

"I don't know what trouble you're referring to, and I don't care. You will *not* evict Joseph."

"Do you need to be reminded that I'm in charge? He gets drunk and starts fights. It would be in everyone's best interest if he moved."

"So what? He doesn't start them here. Leave him alone. It's none of your business." I rolled up the window.

"I can't believe you said that!" he yelled.

At the end of the driveway, someone

appeared to be lying in the bushes. *Who's that? Miss January?*

I parked, got out, walked over to her, and called her name a couple of times. She moaned, drunk. "At least she's not dead," I mumbled to myself.

Up the driveway, Will stood staring at me, hands on his hips. "Now what?" he called. He certainly acted as if he had no job security worries, not even bothering to hide his contempt. His attitude was hard to take.

"Miss January has fallen into the bushes."

"She's another big problem, nothing more than a damn drunk."

"Will you help me get her on her feet and back to her place?"

"Are you out of your mind? I'm not touching her drunk ass. Do you think this is the first time she's spent the night in the bushes?"

"I can't leave her here."

"That's up to you. This is another ongoing problem that could be eliminated if she moved out."

"Stop with all the threats. Do you plan to evict everyone?"

"How about I turn the property over to drunks and drug addicts?" he shot back.

"Need some help, Miss Madison?"

"Hello, Mr. Spoon." I smiled. He'd appeared out of nowhere, dressed in an expensive black silk suit with a diamond in his earlobe bigger than anything I or anyone else I knew owned.

He took my hands in his, pulled me to him, and kissed my cheek. "Just call me, Spoon, remember?"

"Yes, I need help."

"I'm calling the police," Will interrupted.

"The police? Why?" *What now*?

"Spoon's a criminal."

"You wouldn't help me, and he offered. Go back to your cottage and mind your own business. The sooner we get Miss January out of the bushes, the sooner we leave."

Will stomped off but stopped a couple of cottages away to spy from the shadows.

"Can you help me with Miss January? I need to get her back to her cottage. She's drunk, and I don't want her sleeping on the lawn."

"Stand back," Spoon said. "I'll carry her." He picked her up effortlessly. "Lead the way."

"This way." I motioned. "She lives in the middle cottage."

Thankfully, the door was unlocked, so I didn't need to ask Will for the key. "Put her on the bed, and I'll take care of the rest." Her bedroom opened off the small living room. I went in after him, took her shoes off, pulled the sheet over her, and turned off the light. "I appreciate your help." I started to lock the door, then spotted her cat sleeping on the couch. "Hi, Kitty. Let me just check the cat's food and water."

"That cat's dead," Spoon said.

"Dead?" I reached out to pet her. She was hard as a rock. "Ooh!" I jumped.

He came over and examined her closely. "No, it won't be needing any food or water. She had the damn thing stuffed. But whoever she went to didn't do a good job. It's lumpy." He chuckled. "That cat's been toes up for a while."

"Let's get out of here." The gruesomely stuffed cat was more upsetting than finding Miss January in the bushes.

Spoon walked me out to my car.

"Once again, thank you. I couldn't have moved her by myself."

"I noticed your SUV parked here and stopped. I meant to tell you the other day how sorry I was that Elizabeth died. I liked her."

"Thank you." I turned and noticed Will still lurking and listening from the shadows.

"I need a favor."

"From me?"

"Your aunt owes me. And since I can't collect from her, I'm going to collect from you."

I laughed at his brass. "What exactly did you do for her?"

"One of her girl pals from the poker group went through a late-life crisis and got herself arrested for shoplifting. Elizabeth asked for my help."

"What kind of help?"

"The kind where the charges get dropped."

"How'd you accomplish that?"

"I introduced myself to the owner of the liquor store, and after a short conversation, he couldn't remember the details of what happened."

"You're telling me one of my aunt's friends robbed a liquor store?" I laughed. "So you went there, scared the hell out of the guy, and he conveniently had a memory lapse?"

"Elizabeth's friend made a bad choice. As for the owner of the store, I didn't scare the hell out of him, as you put it. We had a conversation about how much better it is to have me as a friend than an enemy. Win-win." He smiled.

The all-dressed-up Spoon was extremely appealing. "So, what's the favor?"

"One of my boys is getting released from prison and needs a place to stay for four months. It's one of the conditions of his parole, plus having a job. I'll guarantee the rent, and there won't be any problems. Ask anyone but that rodent manager of yours, and they'll tell you I'm a man of my word."

"Why did he go to prison?"

"He stole a few cars."

"A few?"

"He was good at his craft. Now he's getting a second chance; already has a job waiting. One where he won't walk around with one eye over his shoulder and feel inclined to run when he hears a siren."

I liked Jimmy Spoon, and that surprised me. Would I regret this? I sighed. The question had dogged me a lot lately. "He can stay here at The Cottages on two conditions. One, he doesn't tell anyone he's on parole. And two, if asked, he's a friend of the family."

"Done. Liz said you'd keep her word."

Liz again. She'd certainly known some interesting people. I wondered why she'd kept so many secret.

"When we first met, why didn't you mention that you and my aunt were friends?"

"Because I had kissing you on my mind. Then you broke my heart, telling me you were in a relationship with Zach."

I smiled at him. "I'm sorry."

He reached in his coat pocket and pulled out his wallet. "Here's my card. My cell number is on the back."

"One more thing," I said. "Rodent over there isn't to know anything about this. I'll call you in the morning after I get a set of keys."

"I like you." Jimmy Spoon laughed. "Call me anytime, Madison. And keep an eye on that manager of yours. Word on the street is that he has a big deal brewing. I'm sure it won't turn out well for anyone involved. He's stupid and arrogant. Not good qualities for a con man."

As I drove through the deserted streets of Tarpon Cove, I thought about Spoon's warning and my options. Will needed to go, and sooner rather than later.

# Chapter Seventeen

Rain beat hard against the windows. A summer thunderstorm had rolled in, the kind that dropped inches of fat raindrops before moving on down the Keys, leaving another sizzling day.

Jazz had his head on the other pillow, asleep and softly snoring. All I wanted to do was stay in bed, listen to the rain, and read. Or go back to sleep.

Instead, my phone rang. "Hey Jazz, who's calling us this early?" The screen showed Zach's number.

"Are you awake?"

"Barely. We both just woke up."

"Both?"

"Jazz says good morning."

"He's a lucky cat, getting to sleep with you. I wanted to check on you after last night. I thought Axe would follow you home."

"As it turned out, I didn't come straight home. I had to run by the county jail."

He laughed. "You're going to make me ask, aren't you?"

"One of my tenants needed a ride after being released."

"Let me guess… Joseph?"

"Never mind him. Were Jimmy Spoon and Elizabeth friends?"

"Spoon? Where did you run into him?"

"At The Cottages last night."

"You had quite a night." He laughed. "Well, I saw them together several times. I heard he helped her out with a problem, but she never gave me the details."

"You pretty much confirmed what Spoon told me."

"Why was Spoon at The Cottages?"

"He saw my SUV and stopped. When I was leaving, I found Miss January lying face down in the bushes, drunk. Spoon carried her back to her cottage. I couldn't do it by myself."

"Spoon's an okay guy. He walks a grey line most of the time."

"Most of the people I've met here walk that grey line, myself included."

"So your mother fixed you up on a date and didn't tell you." Zach laughed again.

"Did you just call to amuse yourself? Honestly, it's not funny yet. My mother and I need to have a chat, because this will never happen again."

"Go easy on her. Her intentions were good."

"Whatever. Thanks for the warning on Connor Manning. Halfway through dinner, I had a bad feeling about him. I was happy to get away."

"He likes to control everything in his life,

women in particular. He also has a bad temper. How are you going to get rid of him?"

"I'll start by not taking his calls. I hope he'll get the message and go away on his own. If not, I'll make my mother tell him to take a hike."

"Don't worry—if he doesn't leave you alone, I'll personally feed him to the alligators and consider it a public service."

"Poor alligators. He'll probably be hard to digest." I laughed.

"We're wrapping up this case of ours, and I'll be back to spend some quality time with my girlfriend. Miss me?"

"Sort of."

"I miss you. See you soon." He hung up.

I lay in bed, staring at the ceiling, smiling, and playing over and over in my mind the part where he told me he missed me. "Are you ready to get up, Jazz?"

* * *

At The Cottages, everything had been washed clean by the rain, and the flowers and tropical plants were thriving. When Elizabeth had shared with me her idea of painting each cottage a different color, resembling Miami art deco, I was skeptical, but all the color made the property stand out.

The office was closed, and this time, there was no sign taped to the door. The overhead vacancy sign hadn't been turned on either, and I knew there were available units.

I knocked on Will's door. I listened for movement, and though all was quiet, someone was definitely standing behind the peephole. I debated creating a scene, knowing whoever was inside would be out in a hot second.

Joseph's door stood open, and I called out to him.

"Hey girl, come on in. Thanks again for the ride."

"How are you doing?"

"I'm not in jail."

"I came for some gossip." Behind me, I heard a door close. The man in Cottage Four had just walked out. He briefly looked my way, then disappeared around the corner of the building.

"Was that Creole?" His skin was the color of a caramel latte, his dark hair slicked back.

"That was him. Disappears fast, doesn't he? That's the most anyone ever sees of him."

"I need to talk to you, and I want your word you won't tell anyone, especially Will."

"Word. What's up?"

"Smart-ass. Bet you've been told that before."

"Whatever. What secret am I keeping?"

"If Will tries to evict you or Miss January, you let me know immediately, and I'll handle him."

"Did he tell you he wants me out? If his grand plan is to get rid of everyone who was here when Elizabeth ruled, the place will be empty."

"My hands are tied until the property is legally transferred to me, but some things, I'll derail, even if I have to make a nuisance of myself at Tucker's office. I can't fight every issue, so I need to choose my battles."

Joseph gave me an assessing look. Clearly, he hadn't decided if he could trust me or not.

I continued, "How much do you know about Tucker Davis?"

"I know he's a real dick," Joseph said. "Most of his clients are criminals. Hardcore, not like the bullshit I get myself into."

"What about the relationship between Will and Tucker?"

"Tucker's been here twice, maybe. He stands out in the front, never sets foot on the property. He came by right after Elizabeth died. Will jumped in his car, and they drove off. An hour later, Tucker dropped him back off."

"Interesting. I knocked on Will's door, and no one answered. I can't be positive, but I thought someone was looking through the peephole."

"Sissy boy left a while ago and hasn't come back. It was probably Forrest." He laughed.

"I haven't met Forrest yet."

"And you won't, if he has his way. He leaves for work every day at the same time, and when he comes back, he stays inside and never talks to anyone. The only time he comes out is late at night. He walks around the neighborhood, his baseball cap pulled down low. He's stupid if he thinks no one recognizes him."

"He sounds a little odd."

"My opinion is he's wanted and keeping a low profile."

"What's his last name?"

"No idea. I think Forrest is a nickname. He's a mean-looking bastard, thin and well over six foot. Scarred face like he's been in a few too many fights. Don't go around asking questions about him," Joseph warned. "You'll piss him off, and he might pay you a visit like he did me. He scared the hell out of me."

"Do me a favor and keep an eye on Miss January. If Will bothers her, call me."

"She's an old drunk."

"People say the same thing about you. But you can stick up for yourself, and she can't."

"Want some free advice?" Joseph asked. "Be careful where Will's concerned. He came out of nowhere and got in tight awful damn quick. Both he and Forrest sneak around at all hours."

"He's certainly a piece of work."

"One night, Will and Creole got into a fight in the driveway because someone had gone through Creole's cottage, and he pointed the finger at Will."

"Thanks for the info," I said, turning at the sound of footsteps. "Isn't that Will walking down the drive?"

"Don't leave until he gets inside. He knows you're on the property, and I don't want him to see you coming out of my place. Letting him think you were here is one thing, but he doesn't need to know for sure."

"You hear anything, I'm your first call," I said, getting up to leave.

"Will and Forrest are bad news, and this ain't the ramblings of a crazy old man."

"Just remember this is a 'no blab' conversation."

Joseph grunted, and I left with more questions than ever. I needed someone to talk to. Brad would go into over-protective mode. Mother would be here in a hot flash, trying to kick ass.

I knocked at Will's cottage for the second time. He opened the door slightly, a smile firmly planted on his face. "Did you need something?" He walked out, closing the door behind him.

I guess he wouldn't be inviting me in. "A family friend is coming to town and needs a place to stay for a couple of months. I'd like the key to Cottage Ten. What's the rent?"

"Everything will be in the reports I give you," he said.

"When? I assumed I'd have them by now, since we agreed in Tucker's office."

"When I get them done."

"Could you be more specific? You told Tucker and me they were completed."

"I've been busy," he muttered. "I'll have them done by next Monday. You and that accountant of yours will be getting your reports then."

"I'll call you on Monday to set up a time to come by and pick them up."

"You do that."

"As a personal favor to me, please do not evict Joseph or Miss January. My aunt rented to them and they've lived here a long time, and I want to respect that."

"I thought that after a night's sleep, you'd come to your senses. Guess not. Even you have to realize they're crappy tenants and make it impossible to get good ones."

"We can figure this out later, when things are more settled."

"Anything else?"

"The key to Cottage Ten. Then I won't need to bother you again. And when you give me the reports, I'd like an entire set of keys."

"Keys!" He stopped short of yelling. "Why do you want them? I'm responsible for the keys, and I'm not comfortable with anyone else having a set. I'd insist on Tucker's written authorization to protect myself."

"Fine. Check with Tucker. I'm sure it won't be a problem. Today, I want a key for Ten."

He stomped into his unit and slammed the door. I waited and waited. I wasn't leaving without the key. Two more minutes and I was pounding on the door.

Finally, he opened the door and handed me the key. "I'll need the relative's name."

Oh no, I'd forgotten to ask Spoon. "I'll give it

to you when he gets here." As I walked back to my SUV, I saw Miss January sitting on her porch, snoozing with Kitty in her lap. She was sleeping, anyway; I refused to think about that cat.

I called Spoon. "What've you got for me, Miss Madison?"

"The key to Cottage Ten for your friend. I'll drop it off."

"I'm in Miami for a meeting and won't be returning until late tonight."

"I'm going to stop by Tucker's office, and afterwards, I'll drive to the body shop and put it in the mailbox."

"Girl, you need a better attorney."

"So I've been hearing."

"Watch yourself," he said, still laughing when he hung up.

# Chapter Eighteen

When I arrived at Tucker's office, I was surprised not to see Ann. She must have left for the day, but I could hear Tucker's voice from down the hall. I took a seat in the waiting room. I scanned the back parking lot and realized Tucker and I were the only ones there.

I could hear him speaking to someone, but I didn't hear anyone respond. I was about to knock on his office door to let him know I was there and would be waiting in the reception area when he yelled, "You better listen up! If you want to get the most out of your divorce, you'll do exactly as I say. Make a list of all the items in the house you want and where they're located. Take your wife out to dinner. I'll have my man parked outside, and as soon as you leave, he'll go in and retrieve everything. When you get home, call the police, report the break-in, and make sure you get a report number."

My legs buckled, and I leaned against the wall. Tucker was planning a crime. I wished I hadn't heard anything, and I certainly didn't want him finding out I was there.

"Who's the lawyer here? Do you think this is my first divorce?" he yelled. "You worry too much. No one will connect you to anything, especially if you keep your mouth shut and do as you're told." His voice had gone ice-cold. "Calm down. Don't overreact. Forget murdering your wife. Why do that when you're going to get everything you want from the divorce? Besides, it's much more satisfying to screw her over and leave her with nothing." He laughed.

His laugh chilled me. I needed to get out of there. What if he found me listening?

"Looks like my original plan for acquiring the property we need isn't going to work. We have to discuss other options, figure out another strategy. I could easily kill the bitch myself. She'd already be dead if it would get us what we want, but I need her alive. I'm thinking of a two-pronged attack. We terrify the hell out of her and, at the same time, throw some complicated legal issues her way."

He was suddenly silent. Whomever he was talking to was finally getting a chance to get a word in.

"In the end, hopefully she'll give us what we want, and at a bargain price. If she's lucky, I'll just run her ass out of town. Every time I see her, she's a bigger pain than the time before. After we're done with her, there are a couple of other people that'll need persuading, but they'll be the easy part."

That was the last I heard before slipping quietly out of his office. Safe in the car, I took a deep breath, my hands shaking, and forced myself to drive calmly away.

# Chapter Nineteen

I'd ignored my mother's calls for two days, and it was time to forgive her. She'd spent the morning psycho-dialing me, and I was tired of hearing the phone ring.

"Hello, *Madeline*."

"Don't call me that. On the other hand, at least you're finally speaking to me."

"Don't ever, ever fix me up again."

"He's young, good-looking, and successful. What's not to like? Besides, when we started talking about you, he insisted on meeting you."

"Good grief, Mother, he's creepy. Thank God he hasn't called me."

"That surprises me."

"I'm pretty sure Zach had something to do with it."

"Zach?" Her radar had obviously kicked into high gear.

"Yes, Zach. He didn't think much of your choice of a blind date. In fact, he warned me about Connor's bad temper."

"I thought you two would make a good couple," she insisted.

"Mother, he's a control freak with a temper," I said, exasperated. Did she think I'd change my mind? "By the way, he said he'd talked you into quitting smoking. According to him, you're on the patch."

"Well…"

"Well what? You're smoking now. I can hear the sucking noises."

"Honey, I did listen when he talked about quitting. Why does it matter that I smoke? You don't smoke, so I didn't see a problem."

I laughed. "Mother, you're hilarious."

"What can I say? I like a good cigar. How did the date end?"

"I left him at the restaurant, he went wherever, and I came home. End of story. So far, no calls, and if it doesn't stay that way, you're going to be the one to tell him to take a hike."

"I'll do better next time."

"No more fix-ups," I told her. "I can find my own dates. You do that to me again, I'll walk out, and it'll be a long time before I speak to you."

"What do you know about Zach?"

"I know I like him, and I enjoy his company."

"We should invite him to dinner."

I rolled my eyes. "Mother, maybe we could wait to see if we become a couple. This discussion of my love life is over."

"Honey, I need a favor. Can you come pick me up and take me to Mr. Spoon's? My car's ready, and I'm not exactly sure where he's located."

"You had car trouble? How did your car get to Spoon's?"

"If you'd pick up your phone and talk to me once in a while, I could tell you what's going on. I got in the car the other morning, turned the key, and nothing."

"Okay, Mother. I feel bad now. What happened with Spoon?"

"I called him, and when he found out I was your mother, he went out of his way to be helpful. He sent out a flatbed to pick up my car."

"That's some service. I'll be over in an hour to pick you up." Wait until Mother met Jimmy Spoon.

* * *

The traffic in South Miami was killer. Whichever way you were driving, all the cars were always going in the same direction. I was happy to be on the freeway headed out of town on the Overseas Highway, back toward the Keys. This time of the year, the landscape was lush and vibrant green from the summer rains.

Mother turned to me. "Has he done work on your Tahoe?"

"He comes highly recommended," I said, explaining how I met Spoon, omitting all references to Zach.

"He asked me to put in a good word with you. He obviously likes you."

*Just great.* I wondered what else those two had discussed.

I drove through Tarpon Cove and took the last street off the main highway, then a short drive down to the docks.

"Where are we going?" Mother asked.

"Spoon's place is on the water."

The area was a mixture of old abandoned buildings and warehouses. No new construction down here. Everything standing had survived the ravages of hurricanes, Mother Nature at her fiercest.

"It would've taken me awhile to find this place. Really, Madison, this is a terrible area."

"It's not so bad. Besides, Spoon is the law back in here. Nothing's going to happen to us."

Spoon's business was located on an inlet off the Atlantic Ocean in the heart of the fishing district, where the boats unloaded their catch and sold it to nearby seafood houses. Businesses along there were primarily family-owned, passed down generation to generation. What they all had in common was electric gates and fencing. From the street, it was anyone's guess what went on behind the gates. In this tough area, people minded their own business and expected others to do the same. Not doing so wasn't worth the trouble.

"Don't worry so much." I patted my mother's arm. "We'll be fine. Besides, we both know finding a good mechanic can be as hard as finding a hairdresser. And he has a superstar reputation."

I parked in front of the plain two-story brick building Spoon and I had come out of when I dropped Zach's car off. We both got out, and I rang the bell.

"I don't think the bell works," Mother said, sounding doubtful.

"He knows we're here. Trust me."

"Hello, girls," Spoon said as he opened the door.

"Spoon, this is my mother, Madeline Westin."

"Nice to meet you, Madison's mother." He leaned in and kissed my mother's cheek. "Your daughter broke my heart."

My mother looked at me. "When did that happen?"

"Enough, you two. We're here to pick up her car."

"My guys are finishing up the detailing. Give them five minutes. Can I get you a drink?" He led us into a reception room with comfortable leather furniture and a small kitchen. Not your typical body shop waiting area.

"I'll have Jack on the rocks," Mother said.

"Mother, really?" I shook my head.

"Jack it is." Spoon winked at my mother. "I have a fully stocked bar. What about you, Madison?"

"I'm fine."

"Cigar?" My mother held out her silver case.

"You're my kind of woman, Madeline Westin," Spoon flirted. And she was enjoying herself, giggling. I poked her in the side.

Spoon's phone rang. "I need to take this call. I'll be right back." He walked out into the work area.

"What are you doing? You're flirting with Spoon?"

"I like a man who smokes and drinks."

I rolled my eyes. "You're too much. Please try to behave yourself." I had to admit it bothered me to watch my mother flirting, and with Spoon of all people. I needed to chill; it was harmless.

"How did you break Mr. Spoon's heart?"

She never forgot anything. "I didn't break his heart; he's being dramatic."

"Okay ladies, your car is ready," Spoon said when he walked back in. "Any problems, call me, and I'll fix you up."

"Thank you, Spoon. I appreciate your looking after my mother."

"Anytime, Madison," he said.

When Mother and I returned to our cars, she asked, "Do you like him?"

"Yes, I do. Now stop, there's nothing going on. How about I take you to dinner?"

"I can't. Poker night's at my house tonight. I need to pick up the food before the deli closes. Why don't you come over?"

"Next time." If these women were anything like the last bunch, they'd be ruthless. "I'll call you tomorrow."

Mother flew out of the parking lot and down the street like a crazy woman.

I sat in front of Spoon's, trying to decide what I should pick up for dinner. My only other choice was to go home and cook. Who was I kidding? Cooking for me these days consisted of buying something that I could easily heat up in the microwave.

A black Escalade with dark-tinted windows and a big antenna on top blew by. Had to be Zach; no one else in town had an SUV like his. What was he doing down here? I hesitated, then rolled out of the parking lot and followed him.

In the distance, he slowed to make a right turn, and I followed. Before the electric gates closed, I caught a glimpse of the Thunderbird.

What the heck was this place? From the exterior, it appeared to be a pair of run-down warehouse buildings. I looked for a sign, but I already knew the businesses down here weren't much for advertising. I made a U-turn in time to spy Zach walking up the stairs. He opened the door at the top and disappeared inside. The security gates were the only way in, with no buzzer, no intercom. Every corner of both buildings sported security cameras.

I wanted to make another U-turn, but I didn't want to get caught on one of the cameras, so I drove home. His offices? Who was this guy? It wasn't fair—he knew a lot about me and felt free to walk in and out of my house at all hours. Where did he live? I had a pretend boyfriend who had no time for a pretend girlfriend, let alone a real one. One evening out, one sexual romp—what was that, anyway? One thing for sure, it'd begun to feel like a one-night stand.

In my driveway, I remembered that I'd forgotten all about dinner. Yay for frozen waffles.

# Chapter Twenty

After dinner, I floated around in the warm water on a Styrofoam noodle. Nothing was more satisfying than a swim on a warm summer night.

"Watching you float naked is better than watching you bent over a fan."

I looked up to see Zach smiling down at me. "I need to stop thinking I live here by myself and can swim naked." I slid off the noodle and into the water. "You come in and out so much, you don't even scare me anymore."

"When did I scare you?" He looked amused.

"Turn around so I can get out."

"I've seen you naked."

"This is different. Toss me my towel."

"No, I'll hold it for you. Maybe I'll even close my eyes."

He held the towel out and, as I stepped out of the pool, wrapped it around me. All the while, he had a grin on his face.

It took a lot of courage to come out of the pool like some kind of sea nymph. I hadn't reached that level of comfort with him. "What's up?" I tried to sound casual.

Zach straddled the lounger and pulled me

down in front of him. "I came to tell you the case is finished."

"And Dario?"

"Dario stepped so far over the line this time, I almost couldn't save him. Then I had to lie for him. When I told him that I was finished coming to his rescue, he laughed in my face. I wanted to beat the hell out of him." Zach's voice was filled with anger, his eyes turning black. "One of my biggest accounts is security operations for a state-wide chain of home improvement stores. They brought me in to put a stop to the staggering amount of missing inventory," he told me. "The first thing we had to do was distinguish between employee and customer theft. I knew immediately that it had to be an inside job. Next, we needed to know how widespread the theft was and how many people were involved. The easiest part turned out to be figuring out how the inventory left the building. Which left the final question: where were they taking the goods?"

I made a mental note to give my brother a hard hug the next time I saw him.

"My first surprise came when I found out Dario was a relatively new employee there. He'd talked himself into the job of state-wide sales manager, complete with phony resume and references. When I asked him how he had the brass to submit such an application, he said, 'the top is better than the bottom, bro.'"

Zach unscrewed the top of my bottle of water,

taking a drink.

"Then I found out Dario was a member of a local gang of malcontents. Thieves, basically. Five of them were working in several of the South Florida stores, so it was easy for them to coordinate the thefts from the inside. Dario's excuse was that he joined the gang to pay off enormous gambling debts. He planned to rip off the store a few times, pay the debt, and be gone. But he claims that when anyone tried to turn in their gang membership card, there were threats followed by violence."

I kissed his cheek. I couldn't imagine the betrayal he must have felt.

"My guess is that, once they were organized and business was booming for the little thieves, none of them were going anywhere. Each person in the group had their own 'specialty,' so to speak, and any defections would have created a setback to their plans. By this time, greed had overcome common sense, and they weren't about to let anything stop them. One of the guys in the group had worked for an alarm company. He's the one who short-circuited the system. Next, they'd remove the inventory, then re-engage the system, and that way, the break-in wouldn't show up on the security tapes. After the merchandise left the building, they trucked it to a warehouse in South Miami and loaded it on waiting trucks for delivery to their customers. They took orders from small retailers and would steal in order to fill them." He took another drink. "Remember the night you found me here, shot?"

I nodded and remembered touching his scar.

"That night, we had the main location staked out. At that point, we pretty much knew all the parties involved. We'd watched them finish loading their inventory and were planning to follow them. We'd coordinated so that all their locations would be raided simultaneously. I was standing in the shadows, watching, when I heard the gunshot. It took a few moments to realize I was the one shot. Initially, we assumed that *I'd* made a careless move—uncharacteristic, by the way." He smiled. "But later, I learned they'd been tipped off to my exact location. My money is on Dario, though he says no."

I gasped. "Dario would set up his own brother to be killed?"

Zach shook his head. "I found out later that when the police didn't show up and I didn't check into a hospital, they became bolder than ever. We decided to put a crimp in their operation by having Dario arrested for outstanding traffic warrants. We brought him to your house so his crew would think he was in jail. Finally, when it was time to wrap everything up, what does Dario do? He sneaks out of your house and goes gallivanting around town, running his mouth and compromising the whole operation. Damn near succeeded too."

"I'm so sorry, Zach."

He gave me a small smile. "Once we figured out who all the players were, from employees to outside help, and where the warehouses were located, we were ready to go. We worked with Miami police to set up the final sting. On the last night, once the inventory was loaded, the first arrests were made. Our guy drove the truck to the warehouse, where they made more arrests. Anyone who had the night off was arrested at their house."

"What about Dario?"

"For the most part, I covered for him. I downplayed his involvement and told the client Dario's information was instrumental in breaking the case wide open. I never divulged we were related. Dario claims that when he finally decided to leave the group, they threatened the family. I told myself the reason I protected him was because that was what was expected of me. I didn't want to admit to myself that Dario had hindered our progress every step of the way. I never believed his story about the threats."

He picked up my bottle and finished off the water.

"I had lunch with my father to bring him up to speed and made it clear that my days of saving Dario's butt were over. He agreed that Dario needs to grow up and backed me up when I told him I wouldn't bail him out in the future. I can't allow him to trash my reputation, one I worked hard for. My father also needed to know about the real possibility that Dario could bring violence into his home. He always said that only a stupid person associates himself with people who have nothing to lose."

His fingers traced the skin at the top of my towel. He pulled me to him, kissing me. "All of us who worked on this case are getting together for dinner tomorrow night. Job well done sort of thing. Would you be my date?"

"Your date?" I smiled. "Yes."

"We'll be driving down to Kane's."

"I haven't been, but Aunt Elizabeth raved about the place." A real date. I'd get to meet more of the people Zach worked with.

"The plan is to sit out on the deck for drinks and move inside for dinner. I'll pick you up at four o'clock."

"Will you be knocking on my door?"

"Probably not." He chuckled. "I'd like to stay and peel you out of your towel, but..." He pulled me closer, nibbling on my cleavage, then moving up my neck and onto my mouth. "Tomorrow we'll have dinner, and then..."

"Then what?"

"We'll see where the night takes us." He wrapped his fingers in my hair, pulling me to him, and I savored every moment of the consuming kiss. *He's good. Really, really good.*

Then he left.

# Chapter Twenty-One

Arriving at Kane's, we walked upstairs to the third-level deck and into the bar area. Big tables, comfortable seating, and each table had a tropical umbrella complete with its own fan. No matter where you sat in the restaurant, one had a breathtaking view of the Gulf.

Axe stood by the door. "Madison, this is my girlfriend, April," he said. April was a curvy blonde in a low-cut bright-pink dress that emphasized her enormous breasts. You had to concentrate hard not to stare at her cleavage, and she was surely half Axe's age.

Another woman approached, and Zach made the introductions. "Meet Topaz, Slice's wife." She was the exact opposite of her husband in appearance: petite and delicate, with long black hair and creamy smooth skin.

"Hello," she greeted me. Her accent sounded French. As she checked me over carefully, I realized she shared one quality with her husband: intensity.

"Hi," I said, feeling awkward and uncomfortable.

We all moved to a large outdoor table. This

was clearly a close group of people, used to talking about the personal details of their lives. I was the newcomer—the outsider, as it were—and of course everyone would be cautious. When was Fab going to get here? I could use a familiar face.

Another couple approached the table, and Zach made the introductions. "This is our client, Buckshot Jones, and his wife, Cynthia." Buckshot was in his sixties, in terrific shape, tanned and looking as though he'd just walked off his boat. Cynthia, like Axe's April, was much younger than her husband. She looked like a Barbie doll in her yellow silk strapless dress, big diamonds in her ears and a huge rock on her finger. The ultimate trophy wife.

"Hello," Cynthia said, glaring at me.

Buckshot and Zach shook hands. When Zach kissed Cynthia on the cheek, she pressed her body to his. At our table in the dining area, I ended up sitting with Zach on one side of me and Cynthia on the other.

"This is fun, being seated next to one another," Cynthia purred. "So Madison, how long have you known Zach?"

"Long enough to be my girlfriend," Zach answered for me.

"Girlfriend?" Cynthia said, visibly surprised and unhappy.

"Congratulations!" Buckshot boomed from the other side of the table. "Will you be announcing a marriage anytime soon?"

I was glad I didn't have food in my mouth—I'd have choked. "My mother would like that." I turned to smile at Zach.

He winked at me. "You never know." He put his arm around my neck, pulled me to him, and kissed my cheek. Zach was certainly full of surprises. Axe and Slice, though, didn't seem surprised in the least.

April and Topaz quietly sized me up. Usually, I had an easy time meeting new people, but tonight, I was off my game, unsure of what to say.

"Where's Fab?" I whispered to Zach.

"She's waiting on Marco. His schedule is erratic at best."

"We never wait for Fab and Marco," Axe interjected. "Those two show up when they can. Or not."

If I'd had a choice of who to sit next to, it wouldn't have been Cynthia. I judged her to be a woman with an agenda.

"I hope you weren't upset when you found out about Zach and me," she whispered.

"What are you talking about?" I asked, confused about where the conversation was going. Granted, Zach and I had only known each other a few weeks, but he surely wouldn't fool around with a client's wife.

She pushed her chair closer to mine. "Zach and I have been involved for a while now," she confessed. "He's pushing for me to get a divorce, but I don't want to hurt Buckshot. I'm waiting for the right time."

"I guess he got tired of waiting," I said.

"I don't want to hurt your feelings, but you're just a cover so we can be together," she said.

"Excuse me," I said quietly, slipping away from the table and heading to the ladies' room. I'd barely gotten there when the bathroom door opened.

Cynthia entered. "I hope I didn't upset you. I thought it was only fair you know the truth."

"The truth?" I backed away slightly, feeling cornered.

"How well do you know Zach?"

"Well enough."

"That's hard to believe. Has he told you about me, the woman he loves?"

"Why are you telling me all this? You need to talk to Zach."

"You seem like a nice person." She smiled coldly. "I wouldn't want you to get your feelings hurt."

*I'll bet.* "Thanks for the info." Was Cynthia crazy or could she be telling the truth? One thing was certain—I didn't know as much about Zach as I wanted. That would change, or I needed to move on. I didn't intend to be his or anyone else's so-called cover. The rest of the evening was a daze, passed with a smile pasted on my face.

"Fab called," Zach leaned over and whispered

when I returned to the table. "They're not going to be able to make it. Some last-minute call for Marco."

"That's too bad," I said, disappointed. "I hope I get to meet Marco soon."

"He's a lot like Fabiana: dark, intense, crazy. Their intensity keeps them solid; they shield one another from the craziness of their lives. Marco's good for her."

Dinner continued, but the fun had been sucked out of it. With Cynthia glowering next to me, I was relieved when Zach's phone rang. "We're on our way." He hung up and spoke quietly with Slice, then said to the table at large, "We're going to have to cut this short. Slice and I need to run a check for a client."

"We'll take Madison home," Buckshot offered.

I reached around and pinched Zach's butt hard. To his credit, his muscles contracted but he didn't jump or show any emotion.

"I'll take Madison home," Zach told him. "Slice will go on ahead of me, and I'll catch up with him."

"You need me, buddy?" Axe asked.

"You're off the hook. Be at the meeting tomorrow morning."

We said goodbyes all around. Cynthia smiled at me like the cat that ate the entire mouse. When Zach leaned in to kiss her, she rubbed against him. They lingered longer than I thought necessary.

Out in the parking lot, Zach said, "The pinch hurt, in case you care. Was that your way of telling me you didn't want to ride with Buckshot and Cynthia?"

"Thank you," I said, getting into the Escalade. "Cynthia talked all through dinner and was giving me a headache."

"Did you enjoy yourself?"

"Sure," I said, staring out at the lights dancing on the water.

"What are you thinking about?" Zach asked.

"Buckshot seems like a nice guy. Is Buckshot a nickname? Are you friends or is it all business?"

"Buckshot's a nickname. He never tells anyone what his given name is. I know, but I'm sworn to secrecy." He chuckled. "We're friends as well as colleagues."

"Everyone seemed—" I paused. "—very nice."

"It's a good mix. All of us guys are ex-Seals. We're a tight group after sharing the same experiences, and the wives and girlfriends all get along." We passed the rest of the time with small talk or companionable silence.

"Not so fast," he said as I got out of his Escalade in front of my house. He got out, ran around to my side of the car, and followed me to my door.

"Are you coming in the front door?" I laughed. "That would a first."

"Second time," Zach corrected. "I knocked on our first date."

Our eyes locked into a sexually charged moment. He opened the door, pulled me inside, pushed me up against the wall, and kissed me hard.

"Unfortunately, I have to leave," he said, and left after a final nibble on my earlobes.

I could take a cold shower. Or clean the garage. Black fur wound through my legs. "Meow." I reached down, picked up Jazz, and nuzzled his neck.

* * *

I spent a sleepless night trying to talk myself out of my plan to go check the address where I'd seen Zach at the warehouses. The idea could backfire, but I was determined.

The gates were opening when I arrived, and a delivery truck of some sort came driving out. As the truck drove away, I walked in before the gates closed, realizing too late that I was locked in and the only way out was through the gate I'd just entered. So I either had to wait until someone else arrived or left… or go talk to whoever owned the building. The bottom part of the building appeared to be empty. A black BMW convertible was parked in a space outside— probably another car belonging to Zach, since his Escalade was nowhere in sight. What was it with black cars?

I walked up the stairs and stood staring at the

door. Did I knock? Did I walk in? How had I become some oddly disturbed stalker chick? Common sense had been begging me to listen since I left the house, and I'd totally ignored the advice. So much for that. I reached for the doorknob and opened the door.

"I was wondering if you were going to stand outside all day or come in." Fab laughed.

"I've truly lost my mind. How did you know I was here?"

"I watched you on the security camera." She pointed to the screen.

"God, how embarrassing. I need to leave."

"Not until you tell me how you found this place."

"I was leaving Spoon's a couple of days ago, and Zach drove right by me. When I caught up with him, he'd already driven through the gates. What *is* this place?"

"Zach lives in this building, and the building next door is his office. He left the outside looking run-down so it wouldn't attract any attention. He renovated the inside himself, and as you can see, he did a first-class job."

Fab was right. The wide-open space had professionally stained concrete floors, original brick walls, and an updated kitchen with state-of-the-art-appliances and granite counter tops.

I walked across the room to a large island that served as a divider between the kitchen and the rest of the space. "I missed you at dinner."

"Marco got home late. We got sidetracked, and we were both tired." Fab had three guns disassembled in front of her and was cleaning them.

"I ended up sitting next to Cynthia."

"Who?"

So much for any information on her. "Buckshot's wife."

"I haven't met her. She has a serious case for Zach, and he finds her games annoying. At one point, he almost ended his relationship with Buckshot over it. I know he put a lot of distance between them. Zach knows Buckshot loves his wife, and he isn't going to be the one to tell him she acts like a slut."

"Wow. Well, can confirm she's difficult. I was seated next to her at dinner last night, and she wasn't much fun."

"I can imagine. Zach avoids having me around the corporate clients as much as possible. He's afraid I might pick their pockets."

"You're clearly a woman with many talents."

We both laughed.

At least I now knew Cynthia wasn't in a relationship with Zach and never had been. She *was* a crazy one for sure.

I watched as Fab expertly disassembled the Walther in front of her. "Do you take many jobs where you use a gun?"

"I try to use my martial arts skills more than my guns, but I never leave home without my

Glock and a couple of her friends. A few times, I've gotten in over my head, and with no backup, I wouldn't have walked away alive. Do you own a gun?"

"I have a small caliber handgun. But a Glock makes mine look like a toy. Nice Walther."

"You obviously have experience with guns if you can identify them."

"My brother and I enrolled in a gun safety class a few years ago. I enjoyed myself until I got to the part where it was my turn to shoot a bowl of water off a chair. I blew the bowl and chair to bits, but I didn't have complete control, so the gun recoiled and hit me in the face. I had huge bruises on my cheek and arm."

"Sounds like you did a good job to me," Fab said. "What type of gun?"

".44 Magnum."

"I *am* impressed. Where do you keep your gun?"

"Locked away."

"Put it where you have quick, easy access, so if you have an intruder, you'll have the element of surprise. We should go to the gun range and practice sometime."

"Sounds like fun."

"I can teach you to be more comfortable with any size gun." She gave me a slight smile. "Zach will be back anytime."

"I should leave before he finds out I turned into a stalker. I'm just frustrated at knowing so little about him, so I thought I'd do a little investigating on my own. I'll tell you, after I opened the door, I was very happy you were the one sitting here and not Zach."

"In my opinion, he won't be as upset as you think. He likes you a lot."

"And you know this how?"

"He's not as cranky since he met you. When he's around you, he laughs and smiles a lot. Other people get a flash of teeth and a grunt."

"This is over the top, even for me," I said, feeling increasingly nervous. "I'm sneaking out the same way I came in."

"No, stay. Handle it like he would—be confident and offer no explanations."

"Hmm. I'm not sure about this. Let's do lunch sometime? We could go shoe shopping."

"I don't do the girlfriend thing."

"Why not?"

"Women don't like me."

"Because they're jealous!" I laughed. "We could try it once, and if you have a horrible time, we won't do it again. Or we could go to the gun range and then lunch. Zach told me the girlfriends and wives in your group are all good friends."

"What do men know?"

"That's a completely different subject." I laughed.

"Topaz is the head gang member. She thinks I'm unstable."

"Does she? We'll start our own gang. Membership is contingent on how fabulous our shoes are."

Fab laughed and began packing up her guns. "Time to go. A regular client is arriving in two hours, and I'm his bodyguard when he comes to the South Florida area. I'm picking him up at Miami International and taking him to his hotel. You stay and surprise Zach."

"I don't think so. I'm coming with you."

"Don't worry so much. You'll be fine," she encouraged me. "Tell me what happens when we go to lunch."

# Chapter Twenty-Two

I paced Zach's living room, trying to calm my nerves and becoming increasingly convinced that staying wasn't a smart idea. I tried to distract myself by looking around the room. The pool table was the focal point of the large space. On the far wall, he had a top-of-the-line dartboard, and leather furniture was placed strategically around the room. I sat on the couch, then jumped up and began pacing again.

I went into the bathroom and stared at myself in the mirror. My stomach hurt. Despite Fab's encouragement, I decided I was going to make a run for the door before Zach found me here.

I heard the outer door bang shut. Now there was no chance for a clean escape. I reached for the doorknob, preparing to open the bathroom door and say hello to Zach.

"Fuck!" a male voice yelled. That certainly wasn't Zach.

I peeked through the gap in the doorjamb. A large man stood in the living room holding a gun that looked like a cannon. *What the hell's going on? And where can I possibly hide in the bathroom?* Then I noticed the second door. I opened it and quietly slipped into what was obviously Zach's bedroom, rushed across the room, and bolted inside the closet, leaving the door slightly ajar.

"I'm waiting for the son of a bitch," the man snarled to someone. I hadn't heard anyone else come in, so he must have been on his phone. "He'll walk right into my trap. This day has been a long time coming. I'll savor every minute of killing him. What a great day." His laugh was blood-chilling. "I'll call you when I'm done here." I heard him snap his cell phone shut.

How could I protect myself if he were to discover me? *Think, Madison, think.* There had to be a weapon somewhere.

Brad always kept a gun by his bed; maybe Zach did the same. I crept over to the bed, ran my hands between the mattresses, and spotted a cubbyhole built into the side of the end table. A gun lay right there on the shelf. I pulled it out of its hiding place and tiptoed back to the closet. Thank goodness for concrete floors that didn't squeak.

The man, however he was, made another call. "Bitch isn't answering the phone again," he growled.

Okay, so I'd never actually shot anyone. I'd never even given serious thought to it.

I was terrified.

I checked to see that there were bullets in the chamber and the safety was off. Brad had this gun in his collection, a Sig Sauer P228.

I stuck my head out of the closet. The thug paced the living area and kitchen, pulling open drawers and muttering to himself, becoming more and more agitated. I needed to warn Zach. I fumbled my phone out of my pocket, almost dropping both it and the gun, before realizing I didn't dare make a call. He might hear me. And I couldn't text without putting the gun down. I dithered over what to do, hearing the thug pacing the living area and kitchen.

The outer door opened again. "Zach, old friend. Come in," the man said. "You're a dead man, you bastard." I took a deep breath and snuck out of the closet and over to the bedroom door, which was slightly cracked. The man was pointing his gun directly at Zach.

"What are you doing here, Neal?" Zach sounded calm. "This is a death penalty state, and they do execute."

"I went to prison because of you. I lost everything. My wife, my family, my job."

"You and you alone flushed your life down the toilet. No one forced you to deal drugs. You got a sweet deal. You're out now. Move on. Why would you want to end up in Stark?"

"Shut up. I planned every detail of your agonizing death, and I'll enjoy watching you die."

"When did you get out?" Zach asked.

"Two days ago. Don't you want to hear the details of how I'm going to do it?" He fired.

Zach yelled, falling back and clutching his left leg.

*He'd pulled the trigger*! I jammed my hand in my mouth to keep from screaming, instinctively backing away from the door. This guy meant to kill Zach, and if he found me, I'd be next.

"Relax. I'm in no hurry. The good news is that you're not going to die anytime soon, but slowly and painfully. The bad news is you'll be dead, which is my good news."

I took a breath to steady my nerves and inched back to the bedroom door, Zach's gun by my side, and peeked out from behind it.

Could Zach see me? With his back to me, Neal stood yelling at him about the injustices of his life. I raised the Sig fighting to keep my hand steady, and shot him between his shoulder blades. His body jerked, and he crumpled to the floor.

Zach's pantleg was drenched in blood. His lips moved; I think he said he was glad to see me. Then, "Madison," he said calmly. "Put the gun down."

I was only aware of the body, blood everywhere, and the sound of the gunshot echoing in my head.

"Madison!" Zach yelled. "Set the gun on the floor."

I put the gun down, but my legs refused to work.

"Go into the bathroom, get the first aid kit,

and bring it to me. You'll need to wrap my leg. I can't do it by myself."

I managed to find the first aid kit, but I couldn't tear my eyes from the motionless body on the floor.

"Come sit next to me." Zach motioned me over to him. "Look at me, not at Neal. I need your help."

"Doc Rivers?" I mumbled as I managed to get a bandage onto his leg. "I'll call Doc Rivers."

Zach punched in numbers on his cell. "Hey, Kev. You on duty? Can you come over to my place as fast as you can?" He continued, "Remember Neal Cooper? He's lying dead on my floor. I'd like you to investigate and call the report in." He pressed his hand against the bandage, which was already soaked through with blood. "Thanks, buddy."

He pulled me to him and put his arm around me. I hid my face in his chest and started to shake.

* * *

Kevin burst through the door, looked around, then walked over to Neal and bent down to feel for a pulse. "He's dead, all right. A shot to the back?"

"Neal was standing in the kitchen waiting for me. He blamed me for what happened five years ago and told me he was here to kill me and had a leisurely death planned for me. What he didn't realize was that Madison was in the bedroom. She saved my life."

"You need to go to the hospital." Kevin pulled out his phone and called for backup, the coroner, and paramedics. He walked over to the gun. "Is this the gun you used, Madison?"

"Y-y-y-yes," I stuttered.

"What happened?"

"I came by to surprise Zach," I said, stumbling over the words. "I was in the bathroom when I heard the door open. I was expecting Zach, but it turned out to be this guy. He made a couple of calls, telling someone he was here waiting on Zach and planned to kill him. Once he shot Zach, I thought my only choice was to shoot him." My voice was barely a whisper. "I was afraid, because I knew he meant to kill Zach and I'd be next."

The door banged open. A crowd of men—deputies, firefighters, and paramedics—rushed in. One checked Zach's leg while another asked rapid-fire questions. "The bullet didn't exit my leg. It's burning like crazy," Zach told him.

"Bring the stretcher!" the paramedic called, then said to me, "How are *you* doing? Were you hurt?"

"I'm fine, but can I go with Zach?" I asked quietly, still shaking. "I don't want to stay here."

One of the paramedics examined me. "Absolutely. You need to be checked out by a doctor anyway."

Kevin touched my arm. "I'll be lead on this investigation," he said as the medics lifted Zach onto the stretcher. I followed as they rolled him outside and carried him downstairs. Slice stood at the bottom of the steps. "What the hell happened?"

"The dead guy shot him," one of the medics replied.

"I'll be right behind the ambulance," Slice assured me.

* * *

"You're good at saving my life," Zach said as we arrived at the emergency room.

"I won't leave until I know you're okay," I said as they wheeled him away.

Good to his word, Slice had followed. He made a couple of calls, then sat down and put an arm round my shoulders. "Zach wants a doctor to look at you."

"I'm okay. He didn't shoot me. We need to worry about Zach."

Doc Rivers suddenly materialized, sitting down next to me. "I had a chance to speak with Zach before surgery," he said. "He wants me to make sure you're okay. It's not every day you shoot someone."

Tears began streaming down my cheeks. I couldn't stop crying. Doc pulled me out of my chair, put his arm around me, and led me into an examination room. "You did the right thing. Neal Cooper would've killed both of you," he said, helping me onto the table.

"I'm fine."

"You're not fine. I'm going to check your vitals and give you a mild sedative."

"No sedative. I'm not leaving until Zach gets out of surgery."

"You can stay. But it's just not good to be so upset." Doc Rivers was so quick with an injection in my arm that I didn't have time to object again. "Here's a prescription in case you feel overwhelmed. Don't drive. And I think you need to see a counselor to help you deal with what happened today."

I hugged him. "You're the best."

"Call me anytime, night or day, if you need anything, or if you just want to talk. I've got another patient, so I'll stop by later."

The curtain opened, and Axe walked in. "Hey girl, I'm here," he said reassuringly and then put his arms around me. "What the hell happened?"

"Neal Cooper happened," I said and told him the story as he walked me back out to the waiting room, offering no explanation, for why I was at Zach's.

"Neal had a great life, everything a man could want. But he got greedy and decided the easy money was in dealing drugs. He started snorting the profits, which is the beginning of the end for all dealers. He made one bad decision after another, each decision worse than the last, and trashed his once-perfect life. The wife walked out and got full custody of the kids. He was fired from the police force and ended up in prison."

"He was crazy. His big plan was to murder Zach."

"Lucky day when Zach walked onto your patio, Madison Westin." Axe smiled.

Zach's surgeon came into the waiting room. "Surgery's over. We extracted the bullet, a relatively simple procedure. He'll complain about a sore leg for a while, and he'll need to stay off his feet a day or two, but he'll be fine."

"See, he's going to be okay. So, how are you doing?" he asked me.

"Trying to keep my mind blank. I'm afraid to go home and be by myself."

"You're not going to be by yourself," Fab said from the doorway of the waiting room.

"You're in good hands," the doctor said, checking out Fab, and not in a clinical way.

"I thought you were guarding some guy's body?"

"He had an early night." She winked. "So I'm here to take you home."

"I want to check on Zach before I go."

"He's asleep," the surgeon said. "Doped up to sleep through the night."

"I'll only stay for a minute." Following the surgeon's directions, I walked down the hall to

Zach's room and quietly pushed open the door. Zach slept peacefully, his leg bandaged.

A nurse stood by his bed, writing on his chart. "The bullet didn't do any serious damage," she said. "It'll be painful for a few days, and then he'll be running around good as new."

"Take care of him. I'll be back in the morning." I kissed his cheek.

# Chapter Twenty-Three

I woke up late the next morning, feeling slightly hungover. The smell of gunpowder still in my nostrils, I couldn't block out the images of Neal Cooper lying in his own blood. I still didn't see another choice. The important thing was that Zach and I were alive.

In the shower, I started crying all over again and stayed under the warm water until I could pull myself together. I searched through my closet and pulled out my favorite skirt and tee-shirt, then carried a pair of sandals downstairs, following the aroma of coffee.

Fab had Jazz on the counter, feeding him pieces of raisin bagel. "Wow, could you possibly spoil him worse than he already is?"

"What's an animal for?"

"I owe you one for staying here and babysitting me all night. I appreciate it. I really didn't want to be by myself."

"Good job, by the way."

"Every time I think about what happened, I start to cry."

"Look at it this way—if you hadn't stayed there after I left, we'd be sitting here mourning Zach's death."

"That's too sad to contemplate. You're relieved from guard duty."

"I'll stay as long as you need. You might want to call Axe before you visit Zach—the doctor's on his way to sign him out."

"Is that my phone ringing?" I dug through the junk in my purse to find it. Good thing the screen lit up.

"Madison, this is Kevin," he said. "I need you to come to The Cottages." The tone of his voice made me feel sick.

"Are you calling about yesterday?"

"We have a few questions we need you to answer."

"I was going to the hospital to check on Zach."

"You have to come now."

"Is there a problem?"

"Come to The Cottages first," he demanded. *Why was he being so evasive?* "If you need me to, I can pick you up."

"I'm on my way." I hung up and turned to Fab. "What an odd conversation. Kevin wants me to go over to The Cottages right now, but he wouldn't say why. Yesterday, he couldn't have been nicer. When he came to investigate the shooting, he took charge, and various emergency personnel showed up in minutes. Today, he's a different person. Cold and distant. All business."

"Do you want me to go with you?"

"I'll be fine. As soon as I'm finished, I'm going to go see Zach."

When I arrived, I saw that two police cars and a coroner's van were parked at The Cottages. Had Miss January died? I hurried across the parking lot. Kevin met me with an older man in a suit who definitely had the look of a cop. "This is Detective Harder," he said.

"What's going on?" I asked.

"Come over here," Detective Harder directed. "Where did you go after you killed Cooper yesterday?"

My knees went weak. "What's this about?"

He gave me a cold stare. "Did you think of other options before you pulled the trigger?"

"Before shooting the guy who shot Zach? It was self-defense." I really disliked this detective, and I was very confused.

"Where were you yesterday?" He spoke slowly, as though I might not understand.

"I went to the hospital, and then a friend took me home and stayed with me all night."

"Does your friend have a name?" He sneered.

"Fabiana Merceau."

"For someone new to town, you associate with an interesting group of people. All of them criminals." Harder snorted.

"Is there a reason I'm here?" I started to shiver under the hot summer sun.

"We found a dead man in Cottage Nine. I

need you to come with me and identify the body."

"I'm not looking at a body," I stammered. *A dead man? Who could it be?* Hopefully not someone I knew.

"You'll do what I tell you or you'll be arrested and taken to jail. You should be used to this."

"I want to call a lawyer." I tried to sound forceful.

"Of course you do." He snickered. "But first you need to make the identification and answer a few questions."

"I want to call my lawyer now," I insisted.

"Can you explain how you ended up connected to two bodies in two days?"

I glared at him.

"Why didn't you let Zach and Neal deal with their differences? Then they both might be dead." He barred his teeth in a smile, then fixed his gaze on something over my left shoulder. I turned to see Zach limping up the driveway on crutches.

"What's going on here?" He put his arm around me.

"This is an official investigation, and you need to leave," Harder said to Zach.

"He won't let me call my lawyer." I sounded whiny, but I didn't care.

"Did I say you couldn't call your lawyer? No," he said loudly. "The law says you can make one phone call."

"He said I had to identify a body and answer

questions first." I leaned further into Zach.

"Call your lawyer," Zach said.

Tucker Davis was my last choice, but he was also my only choice. It surprised me when he picked up the phone. "Tucker, this is Madison Westin. I'm here at The Cottages. The police found a dead body and are asking me questions, and I don't want to say anything without a lawyer present."

"I heard you blew away Neal Cooper yesterday. Did you kill this one too?"

"No, I didn't. Are you coming or not?"

"I'll be right there. Who's the investigating detective?"

"Detective Harder."

"Don't say anything until I arrive." He hung up.

Harder laughed. "You called Tucker Davis? Are you aware his clients are always guilty? Good choice in your case."

"He said he'd be right over, and he told me not to say anything until he gets here."

"Kevin, put Miss Westin in the back of your car until Tucker gets here. You need to leave," he said to Zach, "before you get arrested for interfering with an investigation."

"You're a real asshole, Harder. I'm not going anywhere until Tucker gets here."

Kevin led me to his police car. "I called Zach as soon as I found out Harder had been assigned to the case," he confided, the sudden change in his attitude making my head spin. "I thought you could use his support. Besides, I knew he'd look out for you."

"Thank you," I said. "What the heck is going on?"

"An anonymous call came in about a horrible smell, and we found a young guy murdered in Cottage Nine."

"Anybody you recognize?"

"Never seen him before. Once Tucker gets here, he'll put an end to this and you'll be on your way. Then get a new attorney." He shook his head.

From the car window, I could see Harder standing by Joseph's cottage, talking on his phone, laughing and looking my way. What was he up to?

Zach was waiting in his car, and his support meant a lot to me. I wanted to close my eyes and forget about the last couple of days. It seemed like I'd been sitting there forever and Tucker still hadn't shown up. I was beginning to think he'd never had any intention of coming.

About a half-hour later, Harder walked to the car and opened the door. "You're free to go."

"Where's Tucker?"

"Busy. He called me to discuss some of the details of the case and arranged to bring you into the station for an interview tomorrow."

"How long ago did he call?"

"A few minutes."

*You bastard. I've been watching you, and the only time you talked on the phone happened a good while ago.* I got out of the police car, walked across the parking lot, and got in Zach's car.

"Where's Tucker?" he demanded.

"He never had any intention of coming." I shook my head. "He called Harder and made arrangements for me to go into his office tomorrow."

"Screw him. You'll have a new lawyer by tomorrow. Cruz Campion is a friend of mine; he'll handle this for you."

"Do you know any of the details?"

"Not much. They found a murdered man and haven't identified him yet. He's been dead for several days."

"Why would Harder want my alibi for last night if this guy's been dead for days?"

"He's jerking you around, furious I wasn't the one to die. Great shot, by the way."

"You were unarmed. What was I supposed to do? Besides, once you were dead, who'd have protected me?"

"I'm happy we're both okay," he said as he hugged me. "How did you find my gun?"

"Crazy luck."

"Did I say thank you?" he whispered in my ear. "I mean really, thank you," Zach pulled me closer and gave me a long kiss, then drove me home. Good thing it was his left leg that was injured. "I need to go by the office and make some calls, find out what's been going on here the last few days. All my guys have police connections, so whatever information Harder has, we'll find out. I'll come by and check on you later."

# Chapter Twenty-Four

I woke up the next morning in a strange bed and was confused before I remembered I'd stayed the night at my mother's house. Jazz slept soundly beside me. I hadn't wanted to stay home alone, so I'd grabbed an overnight bag, packed up Jazz, and flew out of the house.

Damn. Zach had told me that he might stop by, and I'd completely forgotten about him. He hadn't called, so he must've gotten busy. When I checked it, though, I saw that my phone was dead. I must have left the charger on my kitchen counter, and when I arrived, I'd gone straight to bed to escape my mother's million and one questions.

I didn't have the emotional energy to tell her I'd killed a man... or why I'd been at Zach's in the first place. Much less add that a dead body had turned up in one of the cottages. And the lead detective was treating me like a person of interest, which had me freaked out.

There would be hell to pay if she found out from someone else, but I wasn't telling her today. I needed one day to catch my breath and not be afraid. Tucker had called when I was on my way to Coral Gables and informed me that Harder had rescheduled the interview and would call with a new day and time. He'd also told me that if I'd been a serious suspect, Harder would've taken me into custody last night and I should consider the postponement a good sign. I didn't like Harder *or* Tucker. I definitely needed a new attorney.

"I was beginning to wonder if you'd sleep the day away," Mother said as I walked into the kitchen. "I got your favorite — pecan rolls." She pulled out a pink bakery box.

"I'm surprised Jazz isn't in here bugging you for food." I noticed that he was now sound asleep in a chair.

"Your cat doesn't like me."

"It's because you call him hairball. He's sensitive and doesn't like being called names."

My mother rolled her eyes. "I invited your brother to dinner tonight. How long are you staying?"

"One more night. I'll be leaving in the morning."

She came across the kitchen and gave me a hug. "Don't hurry. You can stay as long as you want."

"Thanks. I'm going to eat this roll and go take a nap."

"You just got *up*," she said.

"What time is Brad coming? I'll be dressed and ready for company by then."

Disappointment was written all over Mother's face, but I couldn't take the chance she'd start asking questions again.

"Brad said late afternoon."

I retreated to my bedroom, planning to hide until Brad arrived. I smelled some sort of ambush by the two of them. I turned on the television and fell back asleep.

\* \* \*

I woke up and dragged myself into the shower, still emotionally wrung-out and woozy from one of the pills Doc Rivers had given me.

I only made a half-hearted attempt at my appearance—no need to impress my mother and brother. What I needed was to figure out how I was going to tell them about the shooting and the dead guy. Shocking news isn't always a good conversation starter.

As I walked into the living room, I reviewed my options. *Guess what? I have good news and bad news. The bad news: I shot and killed someone. The good news: I saved Zach's life. Oh and more bad news: a dead body was discovered at The Cottages.* That was enough to make up my mind—I wouldn't be telling them today.

"You never sleep this much. Are you sick?" Mother reached out and touched my forehead.

Saved by the doorbell. "Why is Brad ringing the bell?"

"Stay there; I'll get it."

If I hadn't been sitting on the couch when Zach limped in, I'd have fallen over. "What are you doing here?"

"Madeline invited me to dinner." He smiled.

*No, she did not.* "When?" I whispered as he bent down to kiss me.

Mother had gone back into the kitchen. "When I called this morning."

"Nobody told me you called."

"Didn't I tell you I'd be coming over last night?" He sounded annoyed.

"Honestly, I forgot. When I got home, the thought of being there alone had me running back out the door. I remembered on the drive over and planned to call when I got here, but instead went to sleep. My mother doesn't know what happened," I whispered.

"When I called and it went straight to voicemail, I got worried about you."

"I took one of the pills Doc Rivers gave me and was asleep when my head hit the pillow. I didn't realize until this morning that my phone had gone dead. How'd you find me here?"

"I'm an investigator. A good one," he pointed out. "I went to your house, and when you didn't answer the door, I went inside."

"Are you telling me you knocked on the door?"

"Funny. I walked around and realized you'd packed up Jazz and left. I figured there weren't many places you could go and take your cat. When I called this morning, Madeline confirmed you'd arrived last night, and here I am."

"You should have asked to speak to me."

"Why would I do that? You wouldn't have invited me over."

"I could've warned you that Brad's coming to dinner."

"I want to meet your brother."

I rolled my eyes. "Do you remember the last time you had dinner with Mother? Expect that times two."

He sat down next to me and pulled me into his arms. "I figured Madeline had an ulterior motive—she's your mother." His hand found the deep slit in my dress, and he ran his fingers over my butt. "I can protect both of us. Trust me."

"I hope so. My mother isn't one of your criminals. And she's really good at getting information out of her children."

"I like this dress." He grinned, pulling on the neckline and peering inside.

"Stop that! What if my mother sees you?"

"No underwear. Very nice." He chuckled. "I may not be able to protect you from your mother and brother after all. I'll be distracted with other thoughts. How far do you think I can get my hand up this dress?"

"You definitely don't want to get caught." I laughed.

Mother walked back in carrying a tray of fresh

shrimp and cut-up fruits and vegetables. "What happened, Zach? Why are you using a cane?"

The front door opened. "Brad's here." Mother smiled at my brother.

"I apologize in advance," I whispered in Zach's ear.

"Hey, sis." Brad looked at Zach. "Mike, isn't it?"

"Mike? His name is Zach," I said.

"Whose cane?" Brad asked.

"It's Zach's. I was just asking him about that," Mother said.

"Minor leg injury," Zach answered.

"Ah. The boyfriend." Brad gave Zach a once-over. "Don't you two think the boyfriend-girlfriend thing is a little soon? How long have you known each other? Five minutes?"

"You've been in love, haven't you?" Zach baited him.

"Love." Brad snorted.

Zach and Brad ramped up with the testosterone talk, marking their territory.

"First of all, big brother," I interrupted, "my love life is none of your business. If you and Mother have some sort of good guy, bad guy scheme cooked up, forget about it."

Brad stared at me. "With your history, we just want to make sure he's not a total jerk."

"With my history." I snorted. "What about yours? Let's talk about psycho Patty. Didn't she end up doing a stint in the nuthouse?"

"Behave. Both of you," Mother said loudly.

"Let's change the subject," I said.

"What's happening with the estate?" Mother asked.

"Tucker, Will, and I had a meeting and discussed plans for a smooth transition," I lied.

The buzzer sounded on the stove, and Mother disappeared into the kitchen. "Do you need any help?" I called out.

"Brad can help me."

I laughed as Brad left the room, and he glared.

"Come here," Zach said, pulling me into his arms. I leaned against him, hungry for his kiss. And more. "How much of what you said about The Cottages is the truth?" he whispered, nibbling on my ear.

"None of it."

"You lied to your mother?" he asked, trying to sound shocked.

"Don't go there. If those two had any idea I was having problems, they'd want to micromanage."

His hand slipped inside my dress again, and his fingers moved up and down my back.

"Hey sis, have you forgotten you're at your mother's house?" Brad asked.

"Is dinner ready?" I responded.

"Food's on the table if you two can separate yourselves."

I stood up and handed Zach his cane. He got up slowly. "We haven't talked since Neal

Cooper," he reminded me. "Not really. Come home with me tonight."

"I can't. I told Mother I was staying overnight. I'll be back late in the morning."

Zach sat next to me and across from Mother, which I thought would be safer than having him sit next to or across from Brad. I hoped everyone would be too distracted by Mother's barbequed salmon for anything more than small talk. Secrets were hard to keep in this family. The less talk, the less chance anything would slip.

"I found a guy to work on Aunt Elizabeth's boat," Brad told us.

"That's good news," I said, excited that the boat would be running again.

"Was Mr. Spoon able to recommend someone?" Mother asked.

"Spoon?" I said, turning to Brad. "You know Spoon?"

"Never met him. Madeline gave me his number."

I turned to Mother. "Why does he get to call you Madeline and I don't?"

"He doesn't either." She frowned at him.

"Spoon referred me to a man named Moron who'd worked on the boat for Elizabeth in the past.

"Moron?" I said. "That's awful."

Zach spoke up. "You know how Spoon has a gift when it comes to cars? Moron has the same talent with boats. Moron is a nickname from elementary school. His name is Angelo Marone, and the kids teased him unmercifully. First, they called him Angie, and after a couple of fistfights, it changed to Moron. Trust me, there's nothing stupid about the man."

"Moron asked me how solid your relationship was with Zach here." Brad eyed me.

"Why would he ask about me?" I asked. "I've never met him."

"Well, he seemed to know all about you. He did say he hadn't actually met you but that he's looking forward to it." He glared at me.

"How nice." I glared back.

"He also thought someone should warn you about your friendship with that character, Spoon."

"Spoon's not a bad guy," Zach interjected.

"He did a good job on my car, and I got it back looking like new," Mother said.

"Moron also wanted me to tell you that renting to one of Spoon's parolee friends is a bad idea. Most of them go right back to prison. Why would you rent to someone who just got out of prison? Why not drug addicts?"

"Prison?" Mother said, horrified.

"What would Aunt Elizabeth think?" Brad asked. "I'll tell you what she'd think—that she made a bad decision leaving you The Cottages."

Beneath the table, Zach put his hand over mine and squeezed.

"I can't believe you had a conversation about

me with someone who hasn't met me," I told Brad. "You're making all kinds of accusations without facts. I'd never be so disloyal to you, and I won't sit here while you question me about pure gossip," I added, my voice rising.

Brad turned to Mother. "Have you noticed she's become a master at not giving a straight answer?"

"How's this for clear, Brad?" I said. "Go fuck yourself."

"Madison!" Mother chastised.

The silence around the table was deafening. Brad and I continued to glare at one another.

"So what's a security expert?" Brad asked Zach.

"Stop!" I yelled. In an attempt to change the subject, I asked, "Did you win at poker, Mother?"

"I did, but not as much as I wanted."

"You're a lot like your sister," Zach said. "Elizabeth had a weekly poker group. She loved those games."

"I used to play with them when we came for a vacation. We always had a lot of fun."

"Madison, at some point, you're going to have to let us ask your boyfriend a question or two," Brad continued, intent on forging ahead with grilling Zach now that he was apparently done, for now, with me.

"How's your love life, Brad? Got any more hot psycho babes stashed out in the Glades?"

"Really, you two," Mother pleaded. "You're

acting like children and ruining a family dinner."

I gave it right back to her. "When exactly did you call and invite Brad to dinner? Before or after you invited Zach? When you called Brad, did you tell him Zach would be coming?"

"Madison, there's no need to protect me. Not tonight, anyway," Zach said.

Mother stood up. "Who wants dessert? Crème brulee or ice cream?" The mention of dessert broke the tension.

"Who's going to take ice cream or over crème brulee?" I asked.

"No thank you, Madeline," Zach told her. "I'll share with Madison."

"If he eats more than two bites, he gets his own," I said. He was crazy. No one shared dessert, at least not in this family.

* * *

"Let's go outside and sit by the pool," I suggested to Zach.

Brad, who refused to be left inside by himself, followed. "You never said what happened to your leg," he reminded Zach.

"I got shot. No damage, just hurts a lot."

"Shot?" Mother asked as she walked out on the patio. "Is that part of your job?"

"It's a hazard of the job." Zach tried to sound casual. "Thankfully, it doesn't happen often."

"I'll help you do the dishes," I told Mother.

"Brad can help me. You stay with Zach."

I mouthed a thank you to her.

"I'm rinsing; you load," Brad told her as they walked into the house together.

I looked at Zach. "Let's go put our feet in the pool. We need to talk."

He looked at me, a serious look on his face. "I don't think I can get my hand inside your dress if we sit on the concrete."

"How would you like it if I stuck my hand down your pants?" *Did I really just say that*?

"Yeah. My turn?" His big smile told me he'd remember my suggestion.

"How about if I owe you one?"

"That would be the best IOU I've gotten to date."

"Since we've met, you've been shot twice, I've killed someone, and now a dead body has turned up. Not to mention Tucker, the irritating Will, and let's not forget Harder."

"What's going on with Tucker and Will? I might be able to help. I'll send Slice over," he suggested. "He can straighten out Tucker — he's afraid of Slice. They had an argument once that didn't end well for him."

"Whit recommended a real probate attorney, Howard Sherman. Tucker doesn't know it yet, but I'm going to follow through and hire Mr. Sherman. He can deal with Tucker and handle my interest in the estate. I'm out of my league where Tucker's concerned. He's a master manipulator." I kept quiet about my impromptu visit to his office. I didn't want to admit that he scared me.

"I gave Cruz your number. He can represent you when you go to Harder's office. Unlike Tucker, he has an excellent reputation."

"Aren't you going to ask what I was doing coming out of your bedroom?" I asked.

"At the hospital, Fab began explaining and at the same time yelling that she was glad I was alive." Zach laughed. "I didn't ask her to try to make sense. I learned a long time ago to wait until she calms down."

"She seems like a person who never loses her cool."

"For the most part, she doesn't. When she does start yelling, that's her way of telling you how important you are to her."

"I'm not sure where to begin."

"I wish the first time you came to my place had ended in hot sex, not gunshots."

"My thoughts exactly," I said against his lips.

"I could sneak into your bedroom later." He kissed me back, his finger tracing my neck.

"I hope I'm not interrupting," Brad said, sitting in a chair next to us.

"You are," I retorted.

"Mother's going to bed soon."

I laughed at him. "That's such a huge lie, Bradley."

"I need to leave," Zach said, standing and

pulling me into another kiss. "Come with me," he whispered.

"Can you imagine?" I led him outside. "I don't want to disappoint my mother."

"When do you think you'll get back to the Cove?"

"I'll be home by late morning."

"I'll meet you at the house. In the meantime, I'm going to learn everything I can about The Cottages and everyone who lives there. We'll figure this out."

"I'm sorry my brother was so rude to you," I apologized. "He wanted to make sure you weren't anything like my ex-husband."

"I'd terrorize any guy who liked one of my sisters and chase off any I deemed unworthy. Thankfully they're all married."

"Wouldn't you give the guy a chance?"

"Hell no. I'd check him out every which way, and if I didn't like what I found out, he'd be gone. Your brother doesn't have my resources. We should be happy Moron hasn't heard about the shooting and the body yet. This could've been a lot worse."

"I'll never get used to calling anyone Moron. Mr. Moron, maybe. When I do meet him, I'll make it clear he's not to rat me out to my brother ever again. I'll take Slice along."

"Taking the big guy?" Zach shook his head. "Walk me to my car. Your mother's standing in the doorway giving me the evil eye."

Zach and I walked over to Mother. "Thank you for inviting me, Madeline." He kissed her cheek. "Come down to the Cove for dinner sometime."

"I'd like that. And thank *you* for the hand-rolled cigars. I'm looking forward to sitting out here enjoying one."

"Cigars?" I said, confused.

"A hostess present," my mother answered. "Wasn't that nice?"

At the car door, I grabbed Zach by the shirt, pulling him close and kissing him. "You scored on the cigars. Hand-rolled, very nice! I'm glad you came."

"Kiss me like that again."

And I did. I watched as his SUV took off down the street, wishing for a different ending to the evening.

"Mother, you outdid yourself on dinner," I told her as I walked back into the house. "I'm going to bed."

"You slept all day," she said, frowning. "How can you still be tired?"

"Mostly, I'm tired of the way you two treated Zach. I'm going to my room before I say something I can't take back. Good night."

# Chapter Twenty-Five

As I made my way downstairs, I could smell coffee brewing. "Morning, Mother." I kissed her cheek. "Any pecan rolls left?"

"I went out early and got some more; they're on the counter."

"Where's Brad?" I asked, taking a roll from the plate. If you had a favorite anything, Mother always got it for you when you came to visit.

"Still asleep. We stayed up late talking and sharing a cigar."

"I'm going to shower and head home after breakfast. Zach and I are meeting for lunch. Maybe we'll spend the day together."

"How are you feeling? You look better than yesterday."

"I feel good," I reassured her. "I guess I needed the sleep."

"You are secretive, Madison." She sounded worried.

"I'm going to work on that. Can you keep my secrets and not interfere with my decisions?"

"I can keep secrets. And I can try on the other."

I gave her a big hug. "I'll be back soon. We can

go to lunch and shop."

I put my dishes in the dishwasher, then showered, pulling on a coral smocked summer dress and matching flip-flops that had big flowers between the toes. "Come on, Jazz; time to go home."

Brad sat in the kitchen drinking coffee. "I'll carry the cat and your bag out to the car," he offered.

Mother pointed to a familiar pink box and said, "The bakery box is for you. Do I know my daughter or what?"

"You're the best. I love being spoiled. I have so much more appreciation of it as an adult."

"Promise you'll do this again," Mother said.

"Come and stay with me for a few days. We could do an overnight trip to Key West. Now that would be some *shopping*."

"Sounds like fun. Be nice to your brother on the way out."

I hugged Mother and gave her a kiss on the cheek. "I love you."

"How mad are you?" Brad asked once we were outside.

"Give Zach a chance. He's no Dickhead. You'll like him."

"I figured out pretty quickly that he's no Dickhead. I liked the fact that he took the grilling when he could've told me to stick it. I can see he likes you."

"We need to do the family dinner thing — get

together and barbecue at my house."

"Your house. Now that sounds weird." He seemed a little sad.

"It does, doesn't it? You're welcome anytime. Nothing's changed from the way Elizabeth left everything. Just more seashells."

"You and your seashells." He shook his head. "Keep in better touch and I won't worry so much."

"You too." I gave him a big hug. "Love you."

"Back at you."

\* \* \*

"We're in the kitchen," Zach called out.

We? Now was not the time to ask them to wait to be invited in when I hadn't made an issue of it before, accepting people walking into my house as normal. I walked into the kitchen to find Zach, Axe, and Fab standing around the island.

"Is there anything more to bring in?" Axe asked, heading outside.

"My bag and Jazz's stuff."

"Stay here," he told me. "The food just arrived."

I turned to Zach. "Take-out?"

"From Jake's bar," he said, pointing to the familiar containers.

"Poor guy—aware you're all here and he doesn't have any idea what's going on."

"At least he can keep his mouth shut, unlike

Moron." Fab laughed. "I heard he met your brother and shared way too much information."

"I can't wait to meet this Moron fellow. I thought Brad would have a stroke. Thankfully, he wasn't up on the latest, or it could've been a lot worse," I said.

"What did you tell your family?" she asked.

"Nothing. Although they both commented on how much I've changed since the move. How I've gotten more secretive."

"Their finding out is inevitable. Then what?"

"Lots of hard feelings. I'll think about it tomorrow or the day after. Like Scarlett."

Axe pushed open the door for the second time. "How does the damn cat have more traveling gear than you do?" he asked, coming in with Jazz's stuff.

"Damn cat? I hope he pees on your leg."

"What a nasty smell." Zach laughed.

"Did Jake send over chicken enchiladas?" I asked, heading over to the counter where the food containers were stacked.

"I joked with him about sending your favorite, and he just sent a container marked with your name. So how much time have you spent at Jake's?" Zach asked with a raised eyebrow.

A male voice called out, "Anyone home?"

"We're in the kitchen," Zach yelled.

Kevin came walking through the door. He had on rumpled blue jeans and a white golf shirt, and his hair was messy. Who'd have guessed that under that deputy's uniform, he had such a great body? "Something smells good."

"Jake's. There's enough food for ten people," Zach told him. "Get a plate."

"Hey, Madison, how are you doing?" Kevin asked.

"Not as freaked out as the other day."

"What's happening with the investigation at The Cottages?" Zach asked.

"The dead guy was ID'd as one Oscar Wyatt," Kevin announced. "He got released from a prison in Georgia about a month ago. Theft, burglary—your basic small-time con with a lengthy rap sheet. We're working the theory that he ripped off the wrong guy, who got mad enough to put a .38 in the back of his head."

"Any tie to The Cottages? Any spike in local crime?" Zach questioned.

"No more than usual. Same as always. Auto theft, personal property theft, drunkenness in one form or another—nothing new there," Kevin answered. "We showed his picture around. No one stepped forward to identify him. As a matter of fact, no one admits to having ever seen him in town anywhere."

"What's a low-level criminal with no known associates doing here in the Cove?" Zach looked surprised. "New people always get noticed."

"We couldn't find any information on him after he left prison. He dropped off the radar, which isn't uncommon," Kevin said.

"Why was Harder working so hard to tie Madison to this guy?" Axe asked.

"I've been wondering the same thing," I said.

"It's no secret he hates Zach. Big disappointment to him that Neal Cooper didn't kill you." Kevin laughed, looking at Zach. "The more interesting part is that the manager at The Cottages pointed the finger at you," he added, turning to me.

"Why would he do that?" Zach asked.

"He doesn't like me either, and the feeling is mutual," I said quietly. All eyes were on me. "But I didn't realize he disliked me enough to accuse me of murder."

"Blaming someone for murder goes beyond dislike," Axe said.

"His attitude has never made any sense to me." This morning, I'd been happy to come back home. Now I changed my mind. I should've stayed at my mother's and fessed up. I did crises better in numbers.

"He told Harder you sneak around the property at all hours," Kevin relayed. "Go in and out of your tenants' cottages when you know they're not home."

"Those are all accusations that have been made against Will and his partner." I found it hard to believe all this was happening.

"He also told Harder that you and Spoon have some sort of secret business dealings," Kevin continued. "And that you let an ex-con, who you claimed was a family member, move in and demanded copies of all the keys, and that's when the body showed up. Harder was jerking you around because he could. You were never a serious suspect." Kevin popped the top on his beer. After a swig, he added, "Will definitely hates you; he made that clear. Harder and I figured he took one or two facts and embellished them into a big story. We'd both pretty much discounted everything he said by the time we cleared the doorstep."

"Harder wanted me to come in for an interview, then changed his mind. What happened?" I asked, trying to control my temper and fear.

"Harder and Tucker are not only friends, they're business partners," Kevin answered. "Right now, they're working on some big real estate deal. My informant at Headquarters told me that Tucker wanted you jerked around and out of his hair. He has plans for The Cottages that don't include you running them. Once Harder was notified of the time of death, he verified your alibi and moved on to other leads. I also heard he got a call from the chief, who told him to back off unless he had something solid. Anyone you know call in a favor?" Kevin asked, looking at Zach.

"My attorney, Cruz Campion," Zach answered. "Cruz and Chief Reese play golf together on a regular basis. Cruz called the chief to make him aware he'd replaced Tucker Davis. He requested that Harder call him directly if he needed to speak with Madison again, and he'd set up a meeting."

"What do you know about Will?" Fab asked me.

"Nothing really. Tucker hired him after Aunt Elizabeth died. He threatens the tenants and sneaks around the property and the neighborhood. He got into a fight with a tenant who accused him of going into one of the units. No one at The Cottages likes him," I told everyone.

"What's Will's last name? I'll give the info to my skip tracer and see what she comes up with," Zach suggested.

"Will Todd. Don't forget to run Forrest."

"And who's Forrest?" Zach asked.

"Will's roommate, partner or whatever. Nobody seems to know his last name. Joseph's convinced Forrest is a nickname and thinks he's wanted. I've also heard that Forrest has been seen slinking around the neighborhood and break-ins went on the rise when those two moved in," I volunteered.

"How did you find out all this information?" Zach asked.

I smiled. "People talk to me."

He shook his head and popped open a beer.

"Both Harder and I have been to Will's several times," Kevin said. "We were under the impression he lived alone. We didn't have cause to search the residence, and curiosity doesn't get you a search warrant."

"I wish you'd told me all of this sooner," Zach said to me.

"Told you what, exactly?" I asked. "And when?" I raised my eyebrows. "While you were chasing bad guys and being shot? Is that when I should've casually mentioned that Tucker and Will are a pain in my butt?"

"I still don't understand why this Will guy would go so far out of his way to implicate Madison. He'd have to know that his words would come back to haunt him sooner or later," Fab said.

"At least you're not asking why I didn't tell Zach sooner."

Kevin and Axe laughed.

"Let's run a check on this Oscar Wyatt guy too," Zach said, making a note.

"If anything about Forrest pops up, call me," Kevin said.

"I'm also going to have Anoui check into the business dealings between Tucker and Harder," Zach said.

"Who's Anoui?" I asked.

"A computer whiz who works for me. She does all the skips and can find someone even if they live under a rock," Zach said.

"Your people have the most amazing talents," I complimented him, winking at Fab.

"Careful what you learn from her," Kevin whispered to me, staring at Fab like he wanted to eat her. "You could go to jail."

Fab stared back at Kevin, who reddened. "I heard that."

*He likes her.* I almost laughed. Fab was entirely too much woman for Kevin, even if she were available.

"Axe and I are going to go kick the bushes," Zach told me. "Keep me in the loop if you find out anything new," he said to Kevin, then rose to leave, giving me a quick kiss.

"What do you want Fab and I to do?" I asked.

"You two can clean up," he said as they slammed the door, laughing.

"Funny, ha-ha. Joke's on them. No leftovers for them. You need to take some home, or I'll have to start taking two walks a day. Sorry you got stuck babysitting again," I told her while we cleaned up.

"Zach's worried about you," Fab said, putting the rest of the food in the refrigerator. "It's always worrisome when someone tries to pin a murder on you for no reason."

"He has a reason. But what is it?"

"Good question."

"Well, girlfriend, we could sit here and stare at one another... or we could go to The Cottages and snoop around on our own."

"I think Zach wants us to stay put."

"How often do you do what Zach tells you?

Aren't you the least bit curious about what's going on?"

"Are you sure about this?"

I laughed. "Absolutely."

# Chapter Twenty-Six

Yellow caution tape cordoned off Cottage Nine. "Police tape isn't very good for business," I said. "I wouldn't stay in a place where a murder had occurred, even if it is beachfront."

"Which one is Will's?" Fab asked.

"Last one on the left." I pointed.

"Find out if he's at home," she instructed. "If not, call me, I'm going to do a little snooping." She disappeared down the side of the building.

I walked over to Joseph's and stuck my head in the door. "Anyone home?"

"Come on in!" he yelled, walking into the living room.

"Is Will around?" I asked.

"He drove out about ten minutes ago. Why? What's going on?"

"I'd just like to walk around the place without him following me. Better yet, I don't want him finding out I was here." I pulled my phone out of my pocket. "Let me answer this." I said, pretending to take a call. Instead, I went outside, called Fab, and told her Will had left. "Be careful."

Back inside, I asked, "What's the latest on the

dead guy? Anyone figure out how he ended up in number nine?"

Joseph hesitated. "Nothing new. I never laid eyes on the guy before."

I was surprised. "How did you get a look at him?"

"Harder asked me to see if he was from this area. He hoped I might recognize him. I was relieved I didn't know the guy."

"Good friends with Harder, are you?"

"He's not a bad guy. He just has an unpopular job. You were never a serious suspect."

"Really? That's not the way it felt when I was sitting in the back of a police car," I said, trying to control my anger. "Has anyone said they heard a gunshot? Why the heck was he in that cottage, anyway?"

"All I know is he's an ex-con, no friends, and no one is willing to step up and claim his dead ass. Who believes that bull in a town where everyone knows everyone else's business? Why would they keep their mouths shut?"

Joseph had good questions.

"You want to be mad at someone, be mad at Will. He's the one who told Harder you were a serial killer." He laughed.

"I know. Do you have any idea why?"

"Same old thing. He wants control of The Cottages. For whatever reason, he's obsessed with this place, and with you out of the way, he thinks he can run the property anyway he wants.

As far as I can tell, no one has stepped up to tell him he's spitting into the wind."

"Well, I will."

"First you need to open your eyes and take a good look around."

I shook my head. "Did Will think he'd magically get the property if he got me arrested? I've got news for him—not happening. Not even if I went to jail for life. Anything else going on?"

"The body's pretty much the highlight of the week," Joseph joked. "Miss January and I are the only ones living here now."

He didn't think that was news? "What are you talking about?"

"Creole and Will got into another fight when Creole caught Will inside his cottage. Forest had to break them up. Two hours later, Creole packed his bag and left."

"Damn. I never got to meet him."

"Julie and Liam are staying at Kevin's until the murder's solved."

"I hope they come back. I like them both."

"He's the only kid I can stand. He's entertaining." Joseph laughed.

"What about the neighborhood?"

"There've been more break-ins; they're becoming a regular occurrence," he said matter-of-factly. "It's been going on for a while now. You know, small items that are easy to sell or pawn."

"Someone suggested Forrest could be the one

behind the break-ins. What do you think?"

"I heard the same thing. He's stupid and walks around as if he owns the town, and he's not one bit careful. That untouchable attitude." Joseph shook his head. "Old man Dale caught him sneaking around outside his house about a week ago and confronted him with a double-barrel shotgun. Forrest claimed he was cutting through his yard, going from one street to another. Dale says he turned white and ran off."

"Is Mr. Dale okay?"

"Don't worry about him. He told me he enjoyed himself."

"Did you find out Forrest's last name?"

"Nope." Joseph shrugged. "I'm telling you, Forrest is a nickname."

"Call me if anything happens."

"I'm not sure I want to be involved."

"What the hell are you talking about?" I said, trying not to lose my temper. "Who else would I ask?"

"What's in it for me?"

"Joseph, don't piss off your only ally."

"When you put it that way…"

"Just as long as we understand each other. And don't tell anyone I came by."

"I don't speak to Will. If he comes this way, I close my door and don't answer when he knocks."

"That's funny." I smiled, relieving some of my tension. My phone rang, Fab's number showing up on my cell. I waved to Joseph and left, pressing the button to answer the call. "You okay?"

"I'm fine. Pick me up at the shell store on the highway," Fab said and hung up.

* * *

"What happened?" I asked as she got in the car.

"I started looking around Will's cottage and realized I wasn't alone. Boy, it was creepy knowing someone was watching. I hurried up and left before they showed up holding a gun."

"I'd put money on Forrest being the one watching. Will would've confronted you. I'm happy you got the hell out and nothing happened," I said.

"One or both is your neighborhood thief. A lot of used electronics were sitting around. My guess is they're having a problem moving the stuff— probably worn out their welcome at the local pawnshops. Too much activity raises red flags. I did find a record book marked 'cottages,'" she continued. "He's in the process of creating a double set of books. My guess is he's stealing from The Cottages and is trying to cover his tracks. Why else would he keep two sets of books?"

"No wonder he's been slow to hand over the records." My phone rang. "This is Tucker's office. Should be interesting."

"Madison, this is Ann from Tucker Davis's office."

"Hi, Ann," I said, making a face at Fab.

"Mr. Davis wants you to come into the office tomorrow to discuss your pending murder case."

"There's nothing to discuss. I'm no longer a suspect, and Tucker should know that. I won't need his representation in the matter. You can tell him thank you for me."

"Who told you you're no longer a suspect?"

I ignored her question. "I'm glad you called. I've been meaning to call Tucker, since I've hired another attorney to handle my interests in the estate."

"When did this happen?" she asked. "Who's your new attorney?"

"Howard Sherman."

"I'll convey our conversation to Mr. Davis," she said. "You can expect a bill." She hung up.

"She's always hanging up on me." I shook my head, looking at Fab. "That woman gives new meaning to the word loyalty. No way she doesn't know what kind of man he is and what he's capable of."

"Ann's whole life has been wrapped around Tucker," Fab reasoned. "She's been with him from day one. I respect her loyalty, no matter the situation."

"Really?"

"You've heard the saying 'the end justifies the means'? That pretty much sums up Zach's attitude. He appreciates my talents when we're out of options, such as what I just did at The Cottages."

The ensuing silence was awkward. "I appreciate your going into Will's cottage. You uncovered two more pieces to the puzzle," I said, feeling chastised.

"Before I met Zach, I was a completely different woman. For the most part, I now use my skills to help catch the bad guys." She smiled.

I hit the reject button on my phone. "I guess my phone's going to ring all day. Tucker's office again. It's either Ann or Tucker."

"Tucker likely flipped when she told him you hired another lawyer. Trust me, if he hadn't been in the office, she would've tracked him down," Fab predicted. "Somehow, he's a big piece of this puzzle. We need to figure out how he fits in. Why would he involve himself with a lowlife like Will? I'll make an after-hours trip to his office."

"What if he catches us? It scares me to think about what he'd do."

"Us?" Fab laughed.

"Don't even think I'm going to let you go by yourself," I said stubbornly. "Didn't your mother teach you about safety in numbers? Besides, the only reason you'd go to his office is because of me."

"Zach will kill us both."

"So we don't tell him," I said.

"You won't keep it from him for long," Fab

said, shaking her finger at me. "He always finds out."

"If he does, I'll change the subject to sex," I stated boldly. We'd only slept together once. How could I be sure that tactic would work, and where did I get the nerve to even suggest it?"

Fab looked at me as if I'd lost my mind. I made a face at her.

"Let me know how the sex thing works out for you. If you pull it off, I want details."

We both started laughing.

"Let's not get caught," I said.

# Chapter Twenty-Seven

I felt the bed move. "Come here, Jazz."

A masculine laugh nearly sent me rolling off onto the floor. Zach's arm reached out and caught me before I fell. He lay next to me fully dressed. "Did you... sleep here?" I said, recovering from fear and an adrenaline rush.

"You were passed out on the couch when I came by last night," he said, playing with the ends of my hair. "I carried you upstairs; you opened your eyes, mumbled something I didn't understand, and went back to sleep. Those are some pills Doc Rivers prescribed."

"I'm glad he only gave me a few days' worth. I'm afraid to close my eyes, and I'm tired of dreaming about dead people."

"Where's Fab? She told me she'd be here," he said, giving me a sympathetic smile.

"I sent her home. She doesn't need to babysit me."

"What did the two of you do yesterday?" he asked, looking at me as if he already knew.

"Fab and I went to The Cottages. I wanted an update, so I talked to Joseph. He told me he looked at the body and didn't recognize the guy."

"How did he manage to do that?" Zach wondered aloud.

"Harder asked him. He and Harder are friends of some sort, and Harder hoped he could identify the body... or at least tell him if he'd seen the guy around town."

"Did he have any new information?"

"No, he said he'd call if there was any."

"Anything else?"

"Ann called. You know, Tucker's assistant? I told her to inform him that I hired another attorney. Tucker called back instantly, but I didn't answer. He left a message. I haven't listened to it."

"He's not a man who likes to be ignored." Zach shook his head. "He won't let it go—he'll call again. He doesn't play well with others." Changing the subject, he continued, "I have an early morning appointment." He pulled me into a kiss. "I'm glad you woke up before I had to leave."

"Me too."

\* \* \*

The rain had blown through, and overcast skies had turned an amazing blue with large, fluffy white clouds, the rain-filled morning becoming another hot summer afternoon. I was sitting by the pool, my feet in the water, making a to-do list on my laptop, when my phone rang, displaying an unfamiliar number.

"Is this Madison Westin?" a female voice asked.

"Yes." *Now what?*

"My name is Dee Burke. Your manager at The Cottages, Will Todd, also works for my boss, Gavin Patrick, as a private nurse," she said. "I wanted to discuss Will with you and inform you of what's about to happen. Will's going to be arrested at any minute," she declared.

I was shocked. "Arrested? Why?"

"He's being picked up on an outstanding warrant from Georgia. When he lived there, he worked as a private duty nurse to an elderly woman, Mrs. Leary. Before he left town, he cleaned out her bank accounts, stole her valuables, and took her car. In light of this, the real estate deal is off," she said obscurely, her voice full of contempt.

*What real estate deal? What in the world was she talking about?* I floundered a bit, then said, "I'm at a complete loss as to how to respond. I barely know Will and certainly don't know what he's been up to."

"Mr. Patrick hired Will about six months ago, and we were aware at the time that he'd recently moved to Florida," Dee began, sounding exasperated. "When he interviewed with Mr. Patrick, he found Will's resume and references impressive. Will was hired to take care of Mr. Patrick, who's partially paralyzed and confined to a wheelchair. We did a routine background check, and the report showed no problems—a clean record. We had no way of knowing he'd assumed the identity of a friend, including the man's nursing credentials. Recently, we've found out that Will's real name is Bobby James. Will Todd turned out to be someone Bobby knew in high school. We believe the real Mr. Todd was unaware that his identity had been stolen. Bobby began using the new identity shortly after his release from prison on burglary and drug charges. He's spent his life as a con artist, pulling one scam after another, with a rap sheet a mile long."

"How did you find out Will wasn't who he said he was?" I asked, disturbed that this story was going from bad to worse. "I'm sorry about Mr. Patrick," I added calmly, fumbling for something to say. I wanted off the phone so I could bury my head in the sand.

"I'm the one who figured out there could be a problem with Bobby." She sounded pleased with herself. "Mr. Patrick, Bobby, I, and a couple of other employees were sitting around the pool last weekend, and Bobby made several comments about his background that didn't match the information on his application. In particular, his birthdate. After everyone left, I pulled his personnel file, confirmed my suspicions, and ordered a new background check. I had his license plates run, which turned out to be the break we needed. The car had been reported stolen in Georgia, and when I contacted the police there, they filled me in on his background. How much do you know about Bobby James?" she asked.

"Not a lot. I met him for the first time in the attorney's office after my aunt's death."

"If you don't know him well, why would you let him negotiate a million-dollar real estate deal on your behalf?" she asked.

"What real estate deal?" Panic coursed through me.

"The contract to buy The Tarpon Cove Cottages."

I tried not to yell. "What? The Cottages are *not* for sale."

"They are according to Bobby. From the beginning, he played on the affections of Mr. Patrick, and within a month, they became personally involved. Then Bobby presented him with this real estate deal, and frankly, Mr. Patrick wanted to make him happy."

The whole story made me sick. "How could he have possibly thought he could sell The Cottages without my knowledge?"

"Bobby gave a very professional presentation. He presented Mr. Patrick with the financials and arranged for a tour and for him to be present for the property inspection. After our accountant went over all the records, Mr. Patrick decided the purchase would be a good investment. Key Title has the original signed contract and other disclosures completed and signed by you, along with a sizeable earnest money deposit. The check cleared our account, and we want our deposit returned immediately." Her tone informed me that she didn't believe I was unaware of any of this.

"That crook has been busy," I murmured to myself. He'd gotten very close to pulling off his scheme. What a huge mess that would have been and still was.

"Mr. Patrick is having the entire scam investigated," Dee informed me. "If we find out you're involved, we'll press criminal charges." Her voice was chilly.

"Don't threaten me. Send me a copy of the contract and any other paperwork. I'll turn everything over to my attorney, and I think the best thing would be for your attorney to contact mine."

"I'll call Mr. Patrick's lawyer, and he can contact you directly."

"Do you happen to know anything about Forrest, Will's roommate?"

"*Bobby*," she emphasized, "told us that Forrest was his brother. The police, on the other hand, believe that he's a man Bobby met in prison, Morris Pribble, who escaped two months after Bobby's release. The escape had been well-planned and executed. He had a ride waiting for him, and they're sure Bobby was the driver. Fortunately, this scam came to light before the transfer of the three million dollars."

"Three million dollars?" I gasped, my head reeling at the amount and the rapid-fire changes of direction.

"That was the negotiated price of the property."

"I'm hearing all this for the first time," I told her. "It's difficult to process."

"The sheriff's department is arresting Bobby before he leaves for work today. There will be a no-bail hold until Georgia authorities pick him up," she said. "Mr. Patrick and I decided I should talk to you and determine your level of involvement," Dee continued. "If it turns out you've conspired in any way, I promise you'll be prosecuted alongside him."

"Ms. Burke, kindly stop with the accusations and threats. I realize Mr. Patrick has been through a terrible ordeal, but whether you choose to believe it or not, I had no connection to this scheme. My Aunt Elizabeth recently died, so the property is in probate and not even legally mine. I have no authority to sell it or, for that matter, do anything with it at all."

"Oh really? Well, then perhaps you'd like to explain how Bobby happened to have your power of attorney. The original is in the file at the title company."

*"He what?!"* I came very close to shrieking. I got myself under control and managed to say relatively calmly, but through gritted teeth, "He thought of everything, didn't he?"

"Except how to keep his story straight," she shot back.

"Thank you for calling and informing me of everything. Especially since you don't know me and have questions of your own."

"As I said, you'll be hearing from our attorney. Your cooperation is appreciated," she said in a businesslike tone.

"Would you keep in touch with any updates?" I asked Dee. "And I'll do the same."

"I'll do that."

I hung up, feeling as if someone had kicked me in the stomach. Will had some big balls to mastermind such a massive fraud. There was much more to Will Todd — or Bobby James — than a condescending attitude, and this explained a lot about how he treated me. He needed me out of the way. The fallout from his scheming would have been staggering. I was lucky he'd tripped himself up.

# Chapter Twenty-Eight

I turned into The Cottages as three police cars drove out. Will was likely inside one, but he'd never spot me through the tinted windows. But where was Kevin? Wait until he found out he missed the big arrest.

I went straight for Joseph's. His door was closed, a rarity. The blinds moved a little when I knocked, and then the door opened. "Are the cops still here?" he demanded.

"No, why? You wouldn't be avoiding them, would you?"

"When they pulled in, I about had a heart attack. I haven't been in trouble lately, but I closed my door before they could open theirs," Joseph said as he kicked the door shut and locked it.

"Did you see what happened?"

"You bet," he said, looking insulted. "I went from window to window, watching everything."

"Well?" I asked, impatient for answers.

"I told you those two are bad news," he gloated.

"Skip the 'I told you so' and get to the details."

"I was sitting here, minding my own business like usual, when the cars pulled in. One, okay, but three? I almost fell jumping up to close my door. They went to Will's, and one knocked while the other two stood back with guns drawn. He answered right away. You could see he was surprised, but he didn't resist being cuffed and put in the back of the patrol car. The other two disappeared inside."

"What about Forrest?"

"Funny you should ask. In the middle of all the commotion, he comes walking up the street from work. He hung out across the way, hiding behind that hedge over there, and watched. When they drove off, he looked around, then continued on, all normal-like, turned the corner, and disappeared down the beach. When he saw me peering out the window, he gave me the finger."

"You didn't tell the cops?"

"No way. I'm not getting involved."

"You let Forrest get away," I accused. "What if he comes back?"

"He's not stupid," Joseph said. "He knows the drill. The deputies will patrol the neighborhood for a few days, especially if he's wanted."

"I heard he's been dealing in stolen property. Do you know if the deputies took anything from their cottage?"

"Don't think so. I would've seen them

carrying stuff out, and if they planned to return, the door would be taped shut. Besides, a whole bunch of electronics went out of there last night, fenced to Victor."

"How do you know?"

"What a stupid question. I know everything," he boasted. "Victor liquidates stolen items you can't get rid of any other way, and he likes quantity."

"Do you know why Will got arrested?" I asked.

"No, do you?"

"Apparently, he's wanted in Georgia. He cleaned out the bank account of an elderly lady and stole her car," I said smugly.

"You're pretty proud of yourself, one-upping me," he said. "You're telling me he's been driving a stolen car? That's funny. I told him the other day that his tags had expired. He glared at me and said 'fuck you.'"

"That wasn't very nice."

"What about Forrest?" Joseph asked.

"The police aren't exactly sure who he is. Maybe an old cellmate of Will's who escaped with his help."

"I told you he was wanted," he said.

"By the way, they told other people they were brothers."

"Brothers, my ass." He laughed. "I'm telling you, they were lovers. Don't ask me how I know."

"A little threesome action?" I joked.

"Get out of here," he said, pointing to the door.

"Is there anything else?"

"Where did you get *your* info?" he asked suspiciously.

"His boss's assistant, Dee Burke, called to tell me he was being arrested and related the whole ugly story. She got suspicious of him, did some investigating, and when she found out he was wanted, turned him in to the sheriff's department."

"Who's going to be running this place? I can't see Tucker getting off his high horse to collect rent, and you can be sure his snot-ass assistant won't."

"I'm not going anywhere. And I doubt Tucker will object to my being involved now."

"You're lucky Willy boy won't be getting out of jail anytime soon," he said, shaking his head. "He wouldn't be able to stand you or anyone else taking control. He told everyone who would listen and didn't know better that he owned the property."

"How come you didn't tell me any of this?"

"You didn't ask." He shrugged.

I shook my head in disgust but made no comment because I wanted details. "Didn't your mother ever tell you not to bite the hand that's nice to you?"

"She never mentioned it."

*Oh, brother.* "What happens when someone is arrested on an outstanding warrant from another state?"

"Before the deputies even come out, they call the other state involved and ask if they want him and, more importantly, if they're going to come and get him. If the answer is yes, he sits in jail until the Georgia authorities show up. How long depends on whether or not Will fights the extradition. If he does, he can sit in jail anywhere from days to months. If he's charged with anything here in Florida, he'll have to go to court here first before being extradited to Georgia. A lot depends on which state has the better charges. He won't get bail; he's already established himself as a flight risk."

"I like the idea of never having to lay eyes on him again. Forrest is the wild card."

"Forrest knows the rules of the game—he won't be coming back either. He's probably up in Miami by now, and he won't stop moving. He'll settle in a big city where he can blend in and no one will ask any questions."

"As usual, you're a fount of information."

"I'm impressed you had information of your own. In the future, we'll be trading info for info," he said.

"Just so you know, if I don't have anything to trade, I'll pull the owner card."

"You damn women." Joseph snorted. "Want a beer?"

"No thanks, I'm driving," I said, walking out the door.

"If I hear anything, I'll call." he yelled. "You too," he added.

When I got back to my car, I called Tucker's office, began to leave a message, then changed my mind. My days of dealing with him and Ann were over — my new lawyer could handle them.

I left messages for Zach and Fab, wishing I had Fab's lock-picking skills so I could retrieve the records and all the keys from The Cottages office before something else happened. I needed to figure out everything Will had been doing, and I'd need Whit's help.

While I was on the phone to Fab, Zach had left a message. "I'm on my way to a dinner meeting with a new client. Talk to you tomorrow."

I played the message twice, just to hear his voice. I'd call him tomorrow and fill him in on the latest. Would we ever get to spend a night together without interruptions? Was it too much to ask for a casual evening of nothing but food and sex?

My phone rang again, and I checked the caller ID before answering. "Hi, Axe."

"Zach wanted me to get ahold of you."

"For what?" When he didn't answer I said, "I'm on my way home."

"I can send someone to stay with you if you don't want to be by yourself," he offered.

"Fab's coming over," I told him. It wasn't the truth, but I didn't need a babysitter.

# Chapter Twenty-Nine

"Meow." Jazz sat on the floor by my feet, staring up at me.

My mind was reeling from the events of the last couple of days. I couldn't stop thinking of the conversation I overheard at Tucker's office. He was one scary man. My gut instinct told me I was the pain in the ass he'd been talking about. How much did he know about what Will had been doing? Kevin had warned me that Tucker had plans for The Cottages, and I wondered if they were the same plans Will had had. I didn't have to worry about Will now that he was a guest in the county jail. Tucker, though, was another story.

I called Fab again. I'd already left a message that Will had been arrested and I needed her help, but I left a second one. I needed to locate the record books, and if Fab didn't call back, I'd get into Will's cottage another way, even if I had to climb in the window. Then I called the jail to check on Will's status and found out he'd been booked under Bobby James. He was on a no-bail hold, just as Joseph and Dee had said. My next call was to Whit's office.

"Hello, Madison," he said, abnormally cheerful. "What's new?"

He'd clearly already caught wind of Will's arrest. "You're really bad."

"If I had an office full of people, I would've kicked them out to take your call. What the heck happened?"

"Will Todd cooked up this incredible fraud to sell The Cottages. Thank goodness everything unraveled for him before he could pull off his scam." I quickly related the pertinent details.

"First thing this morning, my phone started ringing off the hook, with everyone wanting to tell me about Will's arrest, but no one had any actual facts."

I repeated the conversation I'd had with Dee Burke.

"I figured he was a weasel, but I had no idea."

"There's more. Will set up at least two sets of books."

"That's not good news. Most likely, he's been stealing from Cottages accounts and wanted to cover his tracks. Alternately, based on what Ms. Burke told you, a well-documented set of records would be instrumental in his getting top dollar. If he made a formal presentation, as you said, another CPA would be involved for certification of the financial statements. My guess is it was both."

"I'm going to try to retrieve all the records today. Once I do, I'll drop them off at your office, and hopefully, you can figure out what all he did."

"Of course! I'll review them and put together a plan to minimize your losses."

"I have a couple of questions I'd like to ask in confidence."

"Anything you say to me stays between us."

"Have you heard of anyone else showing an interest in acquiring The Cottages? Possibly as part of a larger real estate deal."

"That's an interesting question. Why do you ask?"

I told him about Kevin's comment and overhearing the conversation at Tucker's office. "I'm not positive Tucker was talking about me, but the pieces fit, and it makes sense."

"I wouldn't be surprised if he was involved in a scheme like this. If he is, he has to be the principal in the deal. He's smart enough to know that if he did something illegal that was challenged in court, he'd be disbarred if it were found to be fraudulent. The one sure way to keep that from happening would be if he had your consent, or at least could make it look like you were part of the deal. I could see him wearing you down with legal machinations. I'm still bothered by the fact that Elizabeth never mentioned that she named him executor. It's not only that she didn't ask my opinion that surprises me but that she never said one word about her decision."

"Thank you for referring me to Howard Sherman. I hired him to act on my behalf after my last meeting in Tucker's office, where I was clearly outmaneuvered and in over my head. Time to level the playing field. I loathe both Tucker and Will, and I certainly underestimated what they're capable of and the lengths they'll go to."

"Will, or Bobby, doesn't strike me as a man sharp enough to pull off a deal of this size alone," Whit said. "I'll ask around, and if he had any help, I'll find out who. There are no secrets in this town. In the meantime, my dear, steer clear of Tucker and forward his calls to Sherman. He won't be blowing any smoke up Sherman's pant leg."

"I'll take your advice. Tucker is obviously unscrupulous. I hope I can get through the resolution of the estate without him figuring out a way to take The Cottages from me."

"Tucker is in for a rude awakening. He'll never get his hands on the property. I'll help you in any way I can. He's smart enough to cover his tracks, but if we get our ducks lined up, we can force him to resign as executor."

"I'm sorry for dumping all my problems on you."

"Don't be ridiculous." He snorted. "I'm honored. I'll get the financial matters straightened out in short order. Whatever Will's done can be undone. For someone who's only been here a few months, you're well-liked. I know several people who would step up on your behalf. And a couple of your fan club members would happily make him disappear without a trace," Whit joked. "I'm not recommending the idea, although it would be a service to the community. You just get me those books as soon as possible. I'll call Dee Burke and get all the information on the so-called real estate deal. Then I'll call the title company and try to figure out what their involvement might be."

I'd barely hung up before my phone rang again with an unrecognizable number.

"Ms. Madison Westin?"

I hesitated. "This is she."

"Campion here—your hotshot criminal attorney."

"Oh," I groaned. Now what?

"There went my ego." He laughed. "I called with good and bad news."

"Good news first, please."

"Harder won't be bothering you again. He's completely cleared you in the death of Oscar Wyatt."

I exhaled. "That's a relief. I hated being a suspect. And the bad news?"

"My bill won't be as large as I'd hoped," he said with mock seriousness.

"Sounds like a win-win for me."

"I enjoyed sparring with Harder. He was out-lawyered, and he knew it. Keep me on speed dial. You never know when you'll need a good criminal attorney."

* * *

It was another hot, hot day, so I dug around in my clean, but unfolded, laundry pile, finding a pair of black yoga pants and a workout tops. I pulled my hair back in a ponytail and laced up my tennis shoes, dressed for breaking and entering.

It was way past time to tell all to Mother. I called her number, and thank God, it went straight to voicemail. "It's your favorite daughter. How about a girls' dinner tomorrow night? You pick the restaurant, and I'll pay. Love you."

I hung up, thinking a couple of shots of Jack and a cigar would do the trick on her mood. Then I could tell her everything, but a little light on details. The most important thing was that she'd hear everything from me.

At The Cottages, Miss January was bent amongst the rose bushes, weaving around.

"Hi, Miss January. What are you doing?"

"Walking Kitty."

*Oh no.* When she pulled the leash out of the bushes, I was relieved to see that Kitty wasn't attached.

"I haven't seen you in a while." I smiled. "How are you?"

"That little piece of shit told me if I ever came outside of my cottage except to leave, he'd throw me out. I watched them drag his ass out of here," she said, making wheezing noises.

I reached out and put my arm around her. She was all bones. "Don't worry. Nobody's going to bother you again."

"You're nice, like Lizzie."

Fab pulled in. "You're not hard to find," she said, getting out of her convertible. Shorts showed off her long, tanned legs, and instead of looking like a giant knot ball, as mine would have after driving with the top down, her hair simply had that messy, sexed-up look.

"I'm glad you found me, since I have a lot to tell you and I need your services again."

After being brought up to speed, she asked, "Did you call Zach?"

"I haven't talked to him today."

"Too bad that we may never figure out who Forrest really is."

I asked Fab if she could get me into Will's cottage. "That way, I can get the record books and anything else pertaining to The Cottages."

"I'm coming in with you. It'll go faster with both of us."

I was relieved—I didn't want to go in by myself. "I'm looking for the keys and my aunt's original records." We walked over to Will's cottage, where Fab pulled a case out of her back pocket and removed a small tool. The door was opened as quickly as if she'd used a key.

"I'm very impressed." When we walked inside, I gasped, "What the hell happened in here?"

Clothes, shoes, and personal belongings were strewn all over the floor. Every piece of furniture was gone, except for a small loveseat. Trash was everywhere, including food on the floor—five-star accommodations for roaches and mice. Someone had even relieved themselves in the middle of the kitchen.

"I realize I didn't know Will very well, but whenever I had any contact with him, he was always well-dressed. I can't imagine he would live this way. It's nasty. I'm going to get a cleaning crew in here tomorrow."

"All this was done deliberately," Fab said. "When I was in here the other day, the place was neat, clean, everything in order. Forrest was obviously pissed off and served up some payback. What did you ever do to either of them?"

"I was the biggest obstacle in their scam."

"Well, they left in a big hurry," Fab observed, looking around. She pulled a gun from the waistband of her shorts and went room to room. "All clear!" she called.

I walked after her, going into each room. "I guess whatever personal items those two didn't want, they threw on the floor. But what the heck happened to all the furniture? Even the kitchen appliances are gone."

"I wonder when they did this," Fab said. "The furniture was here the other day."

"Will never invited me in, so I have no idea. I got the impression from Dee that the real estate deal was supposed to close soon. Stripping the place suggests they had one foot out the door already. Why would they slow themselves down by moving furniture? That makes no sense."

"You told me Forrest was over six feet tall and Will several inches shorter, right?"

"Yes."

"My guess is that Forrest came back here last night and only took his clothes. If this is all Will had, he traveled light. That Forrest left Will's belongings behind indicates that he doesn't expect him to get out of jail anytime soon. No need to worry about Forrest; he's on to his next con. Since all we have is a nickname, he'll fall under the radar until he gets arrested again. And he will; they always do."

I walked across the room and opened a closet door. "Ah. The record books!" I called to Fab, bending down to pick up the papers.

"These were in the back of the desk," Fab said, holding up a big ring of keys. "I'm sure they're the ones you're looking for. Each one is individually marked."

"Will you come with me while I open the empty cottages? The police tape is gone from Cottage Nine, and I need to see what kind of shape it's in."

"Stay here. I can go do that for you," Fab offered.

"I'm coming with you — I just don't want to do it by myself. Honestly, I'm a little afraid of what I'll find."

Every unoccupied cottage was stripped of furniture and appliances, exactly like Will's. Cottage Nine had also been cleaned out and reeked of dead body stink.

"What am I going to do about the odor?" I asked.

"I have a friend who runs a disaster cleanup service. If he can't help you, he can put you in touch with someone who can."

I groaned as Joseph pulled into his parking space in an old Buick. "I can't believe Joseph's driving again."

"Who's he?" Fab asked.

"Joseph was Aunt Elizabeth's first tenant. He knows everything that goes on around here and in the neighborhood. Keeps his mouth shut, as far as I can tell."

"Maybe he knows something about the missing furniture," Fab suggested.

"Joseph," I called out. He walked over to us. "This is Fab. Did you get your license back?"

"I've got it handled," he said, busy eyeing Fab.

"Did you happen to see Forrest last night?"

"Sure did. He came, got his clothes, and didn't stay long."

"Anyone with him?" Fab asked.

"A couple of big guys and a truck. He left on his own, though."

"What were his two big friends doing while Forrest packed his bag?" Fab questioned.

"It was dark out, so I had a hard time seeing. I assume they were moving Will's stuff."

I sighed. "Why didn't you call me?"

"It was late, and I thought you'd be asleep," he said defensively. "Were you going to come over in the middle of the night and confront a couple of big guys? Besides, Forrest had left by the time I thought to call."

"I wouldn't have confronted them by myself; I would've called the sheriff," I informed him.

Fab looked disgusted and walked off to look around the property.

"She's hot," Joseph said.

"Her boyfriend is a pro wrestler." That sounded nicer than telling him he was wasting his time.

"I wrestle." He smiled.

I couldn't help myself; I laughed. "Do you? Be careful; I wouldn't want you to get hurt."

"Put in a good word for me in case they break up."

"Answer me this—did you know Will and Forrest stripped all the empty cottages of furniture and appliances?"

"I didn't know anything about that," he said, refusing to make eye contact.

"Your info doesn't do me any good if you tell me after the fact, or not at all, especially when I'm being ripped off. Anything weird going on here, pick up the damn phone," I told him. "Stay out of trouble." I walked across the driveway to Fab.

"He's a piece of work," she said, shaking her head. "I wanted to kick his scrawny ass. He knew exactly what was going on here and didn't say a word to anyone. Someone should point out to him that playing both sides is a dangerous practice."

"He thinks you're hot," I said, biting my lip to keep from laughing.

"What did you say?"

"I told him your boyfriend is a pro wrestler and he better be careful."

"That's a good one. If he only knew—I don't need anyone else to kick his ass. I can do it myself."

"What do you do when a man won't take no for an answer?" I asked, curious.

"I pull out my gun and point it at his balls."

What a funny mental image. "You're hilarious. Do you always carry a gun?"

"Yes, I wear it against the small of my back," she said matter-of-factly. "I don't go looking for trouble, but I'm always prepared. You know, like a Girl Scout."

I had a hard time summoning up that image, unlike the gun to the balls. "I still want to go to the gun range and lunch and shopping," I reminded her, reaching out to hug her.

She stood there, clearly assessing me. Whatever her conclusions, her poker face gave away nothing. She hugged me back.

# Chapter Thirty

The next morning, and once on the highway, I kept my eyes peeled for a water view, no matter how brief. I checked my rearview mirror and noticed a car on my back bumper. I hated tailgaters. The driver wore a baseball cap pulled down so low, I couldn't see their face.

I swung over close to the shoulder to let the car pass, and it rammed into my back bumper. A shriek escaped me. I gripped the steering wheel, eased my foot off the gas, and tried to pull off the road. The car hit me again, harder than before. Whoever it was must be drunk. Slamming my foot down on the gas, I shot down the road, simultaneously hitting the emergency button on the rearview mirror.

"911."

"I'm on the Overseas Highway going south, about a mile from Tarpon Cove," I reported. "There's a silver mid-size car behind me that has run into me twice. I think the driver must be drunk."

I kept one eye on my mirror as the car swerved to my left, trying to pull around me.

Once again, I moved closer to the shoulder to let him by.

"What's happening?" the operator asked.

"He looked as though he wanted to go around me, so I moved to the side, but he just ran into the driver's door!" I yelled. "I'm speeding up, trying to lose him, but I can't."

"Slow down and let him pass."

"I tried that, and he ran into me twice, and now a third time! Every time I try that, he hits me again."

"Units are on the way. Try to stay calm. What are you driving?"

"A black Chevy Tahoe. He hit me again!" I shouted, panicked. "He made another attempt to go around me, then hit the rear driver's side. If he keeps this up, he'll spin me out."

"Weave back and forth, and if he gets close, speed up. Help is only a minute or two away."

"I can hear sirens."

"Stay calm. I'll stay on the phone with you."

"Lights are flashing in the distance. The car just turned right onto Conch Street."

"Pull to the side of the road."

I eased over and rolled down the window. Two police cars pulled up behind me, and I was happy to see Kevin step out of one.

"Kev," I called, hanging out the window. "Man, I'm glad to see you."

"What the hell happened?"

"Someone pulled up behind me and started

ramming me out of nowhere."

"You told the 911 operator that it was a mid-size silver car. Do you have a description of the driver?"

"Whoever it was was wearing a hat that hid their face. I couldn't even make out if it was a man or woman. I assumed they'd been drinking."

"Where'd they go?"

"The car just turned on Conch Street."

The other deputy jumped back into his car and went in pursuit. Kevin stared at me. "Is there anyone who would want to run you off the road?"

"Neal Cooper, but he's dead."

"So we'll take him off the list. Who else?"

I thought about Will and what I'd overheard Tucker saying and realized I didn't have anything concrete enough to share. "I honestly don't know. Do you think it's a case of mistaken SUV?"

He stepped back and surveyed my poor car. "It doesn't look like the damage has made the vehicle unsafe to drive. Are you okay to drive home?"

"I'm fine, and it's not far. I'm happy you got the call."

"I'll let you know when we find the car."

As I drove off, I had to talk myself out of jamming my foot on the accelerator so I could get home as fast as possible. When I finally got there,

I jumped out and closed the gates, happy to be home.

When I examined my Tahoe, I found that the driver's side panel had taken the most damage and the rear had the least, despite taking several hard hits. Thank goodness for those oversized bumpers.

I went inside and, after locking the door, leaned against the wall, trying to calm my nerves. Why would someone want to run me off the road? I knew Tucker wanted me out of the way, but what use could it possibly do him to have me killed?

# Chapter Thirty-One

The next morning, I decided on an early morning swim. As I stepped in, the warm pool water felt good against my skin. After swimming laps, I brought my coffee and banana muffin to sit by the pool. Looking around the yard, I realized it had been sadly neglected, as I'd ignored all gardening chores with the exception of watering.

No time like the present. I went upstairs to change into capri sweatpants, a tee shirt, and old tennis shoes. Back outside, I stopped at the garage to pick up a bucket of gardening tools. I began with the hibiscus, dead-heading the shriveled blooms. Each plant had a story. Every summer, Aunt Elizabeth and I had scoured the nurseries in search of a new variety or color. We got creative and added small flowers around the base of each tree, and continued planting even when we'd run out of practical space.

My phone rang as I was busy weeding the overgrown pots. By the time I retrieved it, the caller had hung up. The screen said private caller, so hitting redial wouldn't work.

"I put it back in my sweatpants pocket. As I returned to the patio, Will stepped out from behind a tree and stood staring at me. Pure fear shot through me. "What are you doing here?" I squeaked, trying to stay calm.

"Happy to see me?" he said, pure hate written on his face.

I turned to run, but he grabbed me by the hair and jerked me around to face him, his fingers digging painfully into my arm. I felt my phone slide out of my pocket. "What do you want?"

"Plenty," he shouted, shaking me hard. "You're going to give me everything I want, you bitch," he growled.

I kicked him in the shin as hard as I could. When he yelled and stumbled, I jerked away and raced toward the house.

"You *will* do what I say," I heard him snarl. Then there was a sizzling sound, and everything went black.

* * *

When I opened my eyes, darkness surrounded me. I lay curled in a fetal position, my body needled with pinprick sensations. It dawned on me that I was locked in the trunk of a moving car. Trapped in the enclosed space, I told myself to breathe shallowly before panic set in.

The last thing I remembered was trying to escape from Will while he yelled about wanting something. I didn't remember him putting me in the trunk. How did he get out of jail? The car made a sharp turn onto a bumpy road, throwing me abruptly from side to side.

When it jerked to a stop, I hit my head. The engine cut off, a door slammed, and the trunk opened. Will stood over me.

"Oh good, you're awake." He laughed, sounding deranged. His eyes were black pin dots, making him look like a rodent on crack.

"I'll give you whatever you want; just let me go."

"Shut up." He grabbed my arms and dragged me out of the trunk, dumping me on the ground.

Tall grass grew out of murky water, and it was eerily quiet, except for the loud chirping of the cicadas. Thousands of mosquitoes were swarming around us. We'd come in via a single lane of dirt and rock through thick undergrowth. There was no doubt we were in the Everglades.

"Where are we?" I asked. We stood in front of a rusty run-down singlewide on the verge of falling apart.

"Welcome home." Will laughed. "Stop asking questions." He grabbed my arm and pushed me up the stairs and onto the rotted porch. "Get in."

I had no intention of going inside. I wrestled away, jumped off the steps, and picked myself up. Then, once again, I fell and felt nothing.

* * *

I was lying on a dirty mattress in a dark room

that smelled like dirt and mold. A tiny sliver of sunlight shone through a hole in the sheet covering the window. When I tried to sit up, I found myself disoriented, and the pinpricking, sweating sensation had returned. My stomach was rolling and churning, and it took all my concentration to not throw up.

How could I escape? Even if I managed to get outside, finding my way out of the Everglades would be next to impossible. I didn't want to have to choose between being eaten by an alligator or killed by Will.

Will kicked opened the bedroom door. "Don't you just love a taser?"

"I feel sick," I whispered, head down. "Why are you doing this?"

He pulled it from his pocket and stroked it as though it were a lover. "Makes a person do what you want them to." His smile was evil.

I felt weak all over. "I'm going to throw up."

He kicked a filthy trashcan, complete with dead palmetto bugs in the bottom, toward the bed. I threw up several times before he jerked me to my feet. I swayed unsteadily, my muscles scrambled by the taser. Live palmetto bugs, Florida's version of the cockroach—which, as a plus, could fly—scurried into the corners, and I screamed.

He slapped me hard. "Shut up. Nobody can hear you anyway." His face full of rage, he pushed me back on the bed.

Fear — gut wrenching, cold fear — went quaking through me. Getting out of the Everglades would be impossible unless I had help. I was under the control of a lunatic.

"Get off the bed." He grabbed me, dragged me out to the living room, and threw me on the couch. "If you make another attempt to run, I'll shoot your foot off," he threatened, pulling a handgun from his waistband.

"I won't try to get away," I cried, holding my cheek while tears rolled down my face.

He grabbed me by the hair and shook me. "This is all your fault," he screamed. He hit me a couple more times with his open hand, then with his fist. I rolled away and curled up into a ball.

"Stop!" I cried. "I'll give you whatever you want."

He put his face to mine, nose-to-nose. "You bet you will," he snarled. "You'll do exactly what I tell you to do. When I say jump, you'd better start jumping. Got it?"

I blew my nose in my shirt.

"How'd you figure out my real name and turn me in to the cops?" he yelled.

"I didn't tell anyone anything. Dee Burke is the one who had you investigated and made the call that got you arrested."

"How do you know?"

"She called me the day the deputies picked you up to tell me about it. She was mostly interested in letting me know Mr. Patrick intended to put me in a jail cell alongside you. Your real estate deal is dead; Mr. Patrick cancelled it."

"How in the hell did she find anything out?"

"Apparently, you sat around the pool talking one day and let a few things slip which she knew were inconsistent with your application."

"I don't believe you," he sneered. "I've told the same lie so many times, I'd never screw up."

"When did you get out of jail?"

"Checked myself out yesterday." He snickered.

"What does that mean?"

"You're a stupid bitch. The jail staff messed up. I was scheduled for video court, and instead, they put me on the bus for a personal appearance. I slipped out of custody at the courthouse when the guards had their backs turned."

"The police will turn the city upside down looking for you."

"You think that means someone will be coming to your rescue? No one," he emphasized, "is going to find you out here except the alligators."

"What do you want?"

"Money and lots of it."

I wasn't about to tell him I didn't have *lots* of money. That would get me killed immediately. "How much?"

"One million."

"Dollars?"

"Funny. You want to live? You cost me three mil—one is a bargain." He pulled a pint of spicy dark rum out of his pocket and downed more than half in one swallow.

I needed him to believe that I had the money and he needed me alive to get his hands on it. "I'll make arrangements with my accountant."

"You dumb bitch. What's your plan—have him get you a suitcase full of cash? Like that wouldn't attract attention. Or is that how you plan to get away?"

"I said you can have the money."

"Every detail has been planned, and you're only on a need-to-know basis. You don't get out alive if I don't get the cash," he said, spitting on me.

I'd never realized it was possible to be so scared. My face throbbed with pain.

"You're a clueless piece. You know how many people were lined up to take advantage of you?" He downed the rest of his rum and threw the bottle across the room, sending glass flying.

"What are you talking about?"

"News flash. Tucker knew about my scam, and he didn't give a shit. He figured the worst I could do was create a legal nightmare, and he'd ride in and talk you into selling to end all your troubles. He's partners in a real estate development company, and they need The Cottages for a big project they have in the works—shopping mall and condos."

I massaged my face, trying to digest the news and alleviate the pain.

"The partner, Connor Manning," he continued, "his bright idea was to force a shotgun wedding on you, giving him control. Even though he found you 'totally boring and uninteresting'—his exact words, by the way—he and Tucker would have done whatever they had to to get their hands on your property."

"All this for one piece of property?"

"Manning's a total jerk and I knew he didn't stand a chance, but he planned to continue pursuing you even though your date sucked. Until some big ugly guy—Scarface, he called him—paid him a visit and threatened to kill him if he ever breathed the same air as you." Will laughed. "Connor said the guy scared him so bad he peed himself."

He laughed even harder, pausing only to pull a cigarette out of his pocket, light up, and blow a smoke ring in my face.

"Tucker didn't care what I was up to cause he figured my plan was going nowhere. He'd pretty much dismissed me as a stupid ass, but I knew too much and eventually he was forced to deal with me. You know the old line 'keep your enemies close'? He went ballistic when he found out the deal was done and ready to close. Just my luck that he had connections in the title company I'd chosen. Once I opened the file at the title company, Chandi-the-closer got hot on the phone and informed him. Then he tells me to back off and I'd get my money at the conclusion of the deal." He blew out more smoke. "I agreed to it, making out like I was a team player. If I didn't, I knew I'd end up disappearing. I managed to convince Tucker that I'd cancelled the closing, then went ahead with my plans behind his back. He didn't have a clue. I bribed another closer at the title company to keep her mouth shut. By the time he found out anything, I'd have sold the property out from under you both and been long gone. The two of you would have been fighting in court for a long time, and I'd be happy and comfortable."

He stomped on what was left of his cigarette, then threw it at me. I jumped back, and a couch spring popped loose and hit me hard in the butt.

"Here's a good one. Elizabeth never even *named* Tucker executor. She only hired him to draw up her will. After she died, he changed the will, appointing himself executor. I took the original—my leverage over that fool," Will scoffed, reaching for another cigarette.

*Not another cigarette. There's so little air in here already.*

"I ransacked the old bitch's house the morning before you arrived. When I picked the lock on your aunt's safe and found nothing there but her will and some cash, I was pissed. But the will ended up being a big score for me. Who knew the damn thing would give me power over him? I searched her bedroom too, went through her granny panties and decided she was too cheap to buy any jewelry. That will, though, that was my big score. His days of ignoring me were numbered, because I now had the ammunition to blow his ass out of the water. I'm smart enough to figure out he'd never voluntarily give me a dime. He'd get rid of me somehow."

He took a drag on his cigarette.

"Boy, was he pissed when he discovered your name was on the title to the Cove Road house. He wanted that house bad and all Elizabeth's possessions. He'd figured he could go anytime and get what he wanted; his mistake was thinking it was all his before he had the legal right. He's consumed by everything that belonged to your aunt. When you turn up dead, it'll all be his. But the big prize is The Cottages. You were never going to get control."

He continued, pleased with the story, "Tucker dismissed you before he even met you. You were a puppet with him pulling the strings. After I met you, I realized that controlling you wasn't going to be as easy as he thought. We sat around in his office one afternoon, tossing around ways to get rid of you, and decided if it came to that, there'd be a convenient accident involving your old lady and bro too. All three of you dying together would remove all the obstacles."

If I'd had Zach's Glock, I'd have pulled the

trigger without a second thought, murder or no, blowing that stupid smile off his face. Did Zack know I was missing? Would he be able to find me? As nasty as hearing him out was, if he was talking, he wasn't hitting me, so I asked, "What were you doing last night?"

"Yeah, that was me," he gloated. "I wanted to run you off the road and grab your ass then. You're a better driver than I thought you'd be. Plus, you got the cops to come out in record time."

"What about Forrest?"

"That old whore. He got away. He's got a woman out by the dog track." He shook his head. "No one else would help him. I'm not worried. When I get the money, one call and he'll go wherever I tell him."

"Why did you tell Detective Harder I killed the guy in Cottage Nine? You and I both know I didn't do it. Did you kill him?"

"Oscar Wyatt, the stupid fuck, was trying to blackmail me," he snarled. "I gave him money once, and he came back for more. That's the problem with paying a blackmailer—they don't know when to quit. Forrest is to blame for Oscar. He likes to go out, get drunk, and run his mouth. I wasn't paying close enough attention, and the two of them got too chummy. I don't expect fidelity from Forrest, but I do expect him to keep his mouth shut. He told Oscar about our scam, and then came the demands for money. The one time I let him briefly off his short leash, he blew it. The dumbass."

He reached into a backpack and produced another bottle of rum, taking a healthy swig. "Blaming you for the murder was fun," he sneered, pointing at me with the bottle. "Harder already hated you because of your boyfriend. He was just looking for an excuse to dick you around. Too bad you had an alibi. Even I would've gotten a boner watching you being cuffed and taken to jail—the last obstacle on my way to payday."

"What about Gavin Patrick? Did you have feelings for him?" I felt awful for that man, whom I'd never met, for getting jerked around emotionally by this piece of crap.

"Are you out of your mind?" Will asked. "Gavin had no chance with a man like me. He was a tool. I made him fall in love with me and then used him. He deserved everything he got. He needs to learn to be realistic."

It sickened me that he had no remorse for taking advantage of a man in a wheelchair. Poor Mr. Patrick; he was much better off without Will Todd in his life. "I need some water." My throat was feeling scratchy and dry, making it difficult to swallow.

He got up, went into the kitchen, and came back with bottled water, which he threw right at my chest.

I had to focus, figure out how to escape from

this madman. But one doesn't go wandering aimlessly around the Everglades. My only way out was the way we came in, and it would be child's play for Will to catch me there. Never mind the snakes and alligators and other surprises the tall grasses held.

"Time for bed," he informed me. "Tomorrow, we're going to start putting my plan into action."

Bed? The word filled me with fear.

"Give me your shoes."

I untied my tennis shoes and handed them to him. He threw them outside. "Open the door and I'll shoot you." He pointed his gun at me and pulled the trigger.

I screamed, covering my face. The noise and the smell of gunpowder filled the air.

"That's just a taste. If I'd meant to hit you, I would have."

Shaking, I turned and saw where the bullet was lodged in the wall.

Will grabbed my arm and yanked me to my feet, dragged me down the short hall, and shoved me back in the bedroom. I hit the edge of the mattress and fell on the floor. The door slammed shut, and I heard the lock turn.

I scrambled away from the bugs and cried soundlessly until exhaustion finally overcame my terror.

# Chapter Thirty-Two

"Get up, bitch," Will said, kicking open the bedroom door. He threw a rock-hard bagel and a bottle of water on the bed. "Breakfast, yummy, yum," he sneered before walking back to the other end of the trailer.

Light filtered through the sheet at the window. I kicked away a cockroach at my foot; probably the same one that had run up my leg during the night.

"Get out here!" he yelled. "We have work to do!"

*Now what?* If I planned to outwit him, I'd need to anticipate his moves. But how do you stay one step ahead of a psycho?

He walked into the bedroom and said, "Get up," then kicked me hard several times, jerked me off the bed, and shoved me into the living room.

"Can I have my shoes?" I willed myself not to cry. Every exposed inch of skin on my body was bruised and filthy.

"No, in case you get the bright idea to run.

You'd never make it to the main road. All you'll succeed in doing is tearing up your feet."

By daylight, I could see the place was even dirtier than I'd thought, if that were possible. No one had lived here in a long time. Cockroaches in various sizes, spiders, and rodent droppings were all over the floor. There were two mummified mice in the corner.

Will produced a laptop from his briefcase, connected it to the internet, and pulled up the homepage for my bank. "What's your password?"

"Coveroad," I told him.

"Where in the hell are you going to get a million dollars with only thirty-six hundred in your account?"

"The money's in my trust account. I can transfer it to my regular account, but I need the authorization of my mother and Ernest Whitman."

"Whitman? What the hell does he have to do with any of this?"

"He handles all the family accounts."

"You better not be lying." He kicked me.

I yelped. "He'll do what my mother says."

"Get mommy dearest on the line and tell her she's got twenty-four hours to get the transfer done. If she tells anyone, and I mean *anyone*, you're a dead bitch," he warned. "Understand?" he barked, throwing his phone at me. "Put it on speaker. I'm going to be listening to every word.

Don't say anything I don't like," he said, pointing the gun at me. He pulled the trigger, the bullet buzzing the side of my head, and I screamed.

I ran my hand through my hair, feeling for blood.

"Oh good." He smiled. "Still working."

I punched in the number. "Mother, it's me," I said shakily.

"Where the hell are you? I'm worried about you," she said, sounding frantic.

"Listen to me."

"What's going on?" she demanded. "Are you okay?"

"For now. I've been kidnapped, and the kidnapper wants money. Call Antonio at Mr. Whitman's office and have one million dollars transferred out of my trust account into my personal account. This guy says if he gets the money, he won't hurt me."

"Madison—" she started.

"Mother," I cut her off, afraid she'd blurt something that would tip off Will that I'd been lying. "This needs to be done today. Also, can you go to Brad's place and feed his dog?"

"I'll get ahold of Mr. Whitman right now. Call me later, and I'll update you."

Will grabbed the phone. "Do you want to see your daughter alive?"

"Yes!" Mother gasped.

"Do not call anyone. *Anyone* is the police or that boyfriend of hers or anyone else. If you do,

I'll find out and you won't get a body back to bury," he threatened. "I'm a nice guy, though, so I'd probably send a piece or two." He discharged his gun into the floor and cut off the call.

"My mother thinks you shot me!" I cried.

"Oh boo hoo. Shut up. I'm sick of you."

I sat silently, thinking about the conversation. I hoped Zach had been by her side. He'd call Kevin, and all the best people would be looking for me. I'd given them a couple of clues, if they weren't too obscure. If anyone could find me, it would be Zach.

"Hmmm… I wonder how popular I am?" Will opened his laptop and proceeded to search his name. "Look here, I'm the subject of a manhunt. So far, they have no clues. Dumbasses. Once I get my money, I'll disappear." He packed up his laptop and started for the door. "Take your sweatpants and shirt off." He waved his gun at me.

I stripped down to my underwear, thankful I had on a cami top.

"Toss them over here. I'm leaving for a while," he said, wadding my filthy clothes under his arm. "If you're not here when I return, I'll track you down and beat you till you wish you were dead. And if you don't think I will, just ask Forrest," he continued. "He'll tell you I can administer a beating that'll have you begging to do what I say. I only had to threaten him and he'd straighten up." He threw his head back and laughed, pleased with himself.

After the car took off down the road, I went from room to room, looking in closets. Absolutely nothing that could be used to protect my feet. Everything had been cleared out. Only a couch and chair remained, along with dirty mattresses on the floor in both bedrooms.

I walked outside and looked around. The only living thing around was a big crow, and it was only interested in the dead animal it was snacking on. I knew trying to go anywhere barefoot was a terrible idea. Now was not the time to be stupid. I would stay calm and wait this out. At least I'd get to talk to my mother again in a few hours.

* * *

Bathed in sweat and dirt, my hair-soaking wet, I was wondering if the heat would kill me when the car drove up. Will came through the door looking smug. *Now what?*

"Time to call Mommy again and find out if she got her part done. You better hope so." He tossed me the phone and, after I punched in the number, snatched it back, clicking on the speakerphone. "You keep your mouth shut." When the call connected, he said mockingly. "Hey, Mom. Did you get the money transferred?"

"I want to speak to my daughter. You prove to

me that she's still alive, or I'm not telling you anything."

"I'm calling the shots, bitch!" Will yelled. "You'll talk to me. Being a psycho bitch runs in your family," he spit, throwing the phone at me.

"Mother, it's me. I love you and Brad."

Will grabbed the phone back. "Satisfied? The two of you make me sick. Did you transfer the money or not?"

"I got my part done. Madison needs to go to Ernest Whitman's office and sign the paperwork."

"You lying bitch. You're trying to set me up."

"No, no I'm not," she said. "They won't transfer anything without Madison signing. It takes both our signatures. The paperwork will be ready tomorrow, and you can go in anytime. Please don't hurt her," she pleaded.

"You'd better be telling the truth, or your daughter is dead and so are you," he threatened. "Understand?" Not waiting for an answer, he hung up. "You're going to be sorry if this is a set-up," he said nastily. "Cause I have nothing to lose."

"Mother wouldn't do anything to get either of her children killed. She'll cooperate and do as you ask." It was hard to believe she hadn't called the police. Or Zach. My other wild card was Fab. If Will were holding Fab captive, she would've kicked his ass by now, stolen his keys, and been out of this dump. I almost smiled at the pleasant thought.

"I'm going to walk you into that weaselly bastard's office with a gun pointed at your back."

*Weasel thinks the same of you*, I thought.

He got up and slammed out the door, where he stood on the porch, talking on his phone. I couldn't make out the words. At least I was getting out of here; he had no choice but to take me with him. Then I'd ditch him. Somehow. If he got me back here, he'd kill me for sure.

He came in, a big smile on his face. "I just took out an insurance policy."

"What?"

"I hired a guy to watch your mom. If he doesn't get a call by a certain time, he'll kill her. If you try to get away, you're a dead bitch and so is your old lady."

All he'd done every five minutes was threaten to kill me, and now my mother. What would happen when he found out there was no money? How many people would wind up dead?

"When you get the money, then what?" I asked, keeping up the charade.

"None of your business. Now shut up."

"You're a stupid psycho!" I screamed in his face.

He pulled out his taser, waved it in my face, then reached out and hit me on the shoulder, and my world went black.

* * *

The only way to determine night from day was through the hole in the stained sheet tacked up over the window. It was dark. I rolled over and threw up in the trashcan, having a hard time focusing. The foul smell coming from the can made me sick again. Every muscle and joint in my body ached with every move. The mosquito bites had turned into welts, driving me wild with itching.

"When are you going to stop doing that, Pukehead?" Will said, throwing a bottle of water at me, hitting me in the arm, followed by a cold hamburger in my face.

I tried to sit up, groaned, and collapsed again.

"While you were out, I kicked you a few times, but you disappointed me. Didn't make any noise." He crossed the room, grabbed me by the hair, and shook me around. "Ever had someone beat your face so you can't eat or see? Maybe later." He smiled. "You need to look your best for our meeting at Whitman's office tomorrow." He threw me back, my head hitting the wall so hard the trailer trembled.

My vision blurred. Dried spit was caked on my face. I was afraid to move. What was worse — his evil little smile or the laugh that sent shivers up my spine?

"Eat the hamburger before you're wrestling it away from the roaches." He laughed as he left the room, slamming and locking the door.

\* \* \*

Morning peeked through the hole. I tried to look out, but the glass was muddy with dirt. Today was the day. One way or another, it would be over. Will had put a crimp in my plan to get away when he threatened my mother.

He opened the door and threw a hard muffin at me. "Got you a dress and some makeup," he said as he tossed me a plastic grocery bag.

Inside was a plain brown, tent-style dress with two oversized pockets and long puffy sleeves. I remembered seeing a woman on television in a similar style dress. She was a cult member. I didn't know anyone who would manufacture these. It was the ugliest thing I'd ever seen, and I wondered if he'd stolen it.

"Get dressed and do a good job on your face. You'll still be ugly, but I don't want to see bruises."

I moved slowly into the bathroom. Black and blue marks covered my whole body. The worst were over both legs and arms. The red marks on my face had turned purplish, and the right side bore the largest bruise, which I hoped I could cover with makeup. My hair was a gigantic, dirty rat's nest, matching the rest of me.

Every movement was painful. The foundation did a fairly good job covering the bruises, although I looked like a circus performer. I put on the brown dress, large and baggy, but it concealed the injuries.

When I came out, Will checked me over and started laughing. "Too bad your boyfriend can't see you now. He'd go limp."

I sat quietly in the chair, not wanting to give him an excuse to hit me again.

"Put this in your pocket," he said, handing me a piece of paper. "It's the information you'll need to wire the money to my account. My gun will be jammed in your back the whole time we're at Whitman's office. You want to walk out alive, you'd better play your part well." He threw my shoes at me. "Put these on."

I noticed that he, too, had changed clothes, adding a moustache and glasses. Did he actually think no one would recognize him?

"We're leaving early so I can scope out the area. Try to pull anything and the guy staking out your mom's place will kill her." He jerked me from the chair. "Give me your hands," he directed, zip-tying them.

Outside sat a black Audi coupe, a different car than the one used for the kidnapping. He certainly had excellent taste in stolen cars. He threw me up against the car, turning me to face him. "When I tell you what to do, you do it with no hesitation, or you'll be painfully sorry." He cracked his knuckles. Opening the back door, he pushed me inside. "Lay on the seat and don't get up until I tell you." He turned the car around and bumped down the dirt road, the bushes slapping the sides of the car. The ride to the main highway was a lot longer than I remembered.

My body jerked with each pothole we hit. Finally reaching the paved road was a relief. I started to shake and shiver.

Will held all the cards. He talked like a man with nothing to lose who was willing to do anything to get what he wanted. He seemed to be looking for any excuse to kill someone, preferably me. I thought his plan was ludicrous, but he seemed confident. I mulled over my options and decided that if I had to, I'd run. Better to let him shoot me than beat me to death. I trusted my mother and whatever plan she'd come up with. I wanted her and me to come out alive. If someone had to die, it needed to be Will.

After endless cruising, he suddenly pulled into a gas station. While he pumped gas, he talked on his cell phone. "Everything's in place," he said as he got back in the car. "My man at Whitman's office tells me all's clear. The man who's watching your mom says she's home alone. He's just waiting for my call."

# Chapter Thirty-Three

Will sang off-key the entire way to Whit's office. Once there, he opened the back door, leaned in, and cut the ties off my hands. He dug his meaty fingers into my cheeks and temples and pulled me eyeball to eyeball.

"Do *exactly* as you're told," he warned. Then he jammed the muzzle of the gun into my stomach. "Understand?"

Judging by the parking lot, Whit, Will, and I were the only ones there. Will walked me into Whit's office, his arm around my waist, the gun jabbing into my ribcage.

"Hello, Madison. Will," Whit said as he came walking out. "Come back this way. Antonio is out today, but he left the papers for you to sign." His voice was soft, friendly. *He said Antonio! Maybe my message got through.*

"Thank you for handling the matter on such short notice," I said.

"The transfer documents are ready for your signature. I have a couple of questions, and I need some additional information. Take a seat." He pointed to the chairs in front of his desk.

We sat. Could Whit not see how awkwardly Will had turned his body toward mine to keep the gun against me and hidden?

Whit opened a file, taking out several sheets of paper. "Do you want this wired to your other account?"

"No, I have a different one I'd like it wired to," I told him. I pulled the paper Will had given me out of my pocket and handed it over.

"Sign on all the pages where I placed the sticky arrows. Then I can complete the transfer." He pushed the papers across to me along with a pen.

I signed without even glancing at the paperwork, my thoughts in freefall. What the heck was happening? Either this was a well-organized scam on Will or someone had put up a million dollars on my behalf. No one in my family had that kind of money. My stomach had twisted into a tight knot, and it hurt to breathe. Never mind the gun's painful poke, reminding me Will was in control. I handed the papers back.

Whit began entering information into his computer. In mere minutes, he looked up, smiling. "The transfer is complete."

Will spoke up. "Before we leave, let me check to make sure everything went smoothly. We wouldn't want to have any problems. If there are any, you can handle them now." He took out his phone and placed a call.

Cold fear had settled in; my heart pounded.

Now he'd discover I'd been lying all along. I had to get away. Now. Dumb instinct propelled me out of the chair, but he jerked me back so hard, the chair wobbled.

Will reeled off some numbers over the phone, which I assumed was account information. We waited for what seemed a long time, and then a big grin spread across his face. He'd obviously gotten the answer he wanted: the transfer was complete. I didn't understand, and at that moment, I didn't care. Will had gotten his money, and I wanted out of here.

"Everything went smoothly," he informed us. "We can leave."

"Thank you, Mr. Whitman, for your assistance, and thank Antonio for us," I said, staring at him. Couldn't he see the pleading on my face?

Will stood up, digging his fingers into my arm and dragging me to my feet. He put his arm around me and pushed me toward the door.

"If we can be of any more help, Ms. Westin, please call," Mr. Whitman said to me in a businesslike tone, his smile sympathetic.

*Why isn't someone jumping out of the bushes to save me?* I panicked when I realized no one was coming to my rescue. I dragged my feet, not wanting to leave the building with Will.

"Did you forget about our little talk? Do what you're told. Start walking," Will spit in my ear.

"You got what you wanted. Leave me here."

He shoved me into the side of the car. "Get in the car, lie on the back seat, and don't get up."

I shoved with all the strength I could muster, but I got only a couple of steps before he caught me by my hair and held the gun to my cheek. He opened the car door and whacked me on the temple with the gun. I felt a flash of pain and crumpled to the ground, then passed out.

I came to on the backseat of the car. My head throbbed, and my eye was swollen shut. Blood was trickling down my face. Will was speeding, and veering recklessly in and out of traffic. He'd never intended to let me go, I realized. He'd talked too much about killing me, and always with that smile. A sharp turn threw me violently off the seat, and we were on the familiar bumpy road again, where every pothole sent pain screaming throughout my body.

He slammed on the brakes, came to a stop, threw open the car door, and dragged me to the ground. "Get up!" he screamed.

I stared dumbly at him, numb. No way was I going back into that trailer.

"Are you hard of hearing?" he demanded and kicked me.

I rolled away and stumbled to my feet. Pure adrenaline launched me at him, kicking and clawing, rolling in the dirt. But he had eighty pounds on me and slugged me in the face. Before pulling me up the stairs, he kicked me several more times, then dragged me into the trailer by the hair, yanking out a chunk of it in the process.

"Stop," I whimpered. "I'll do what you say."

He bent down so his face was inches from mine. "I told you so." He spit at me and threw me in the bedroom. I hit the wall and slid to the floor.

"If you make one sound, I'll come in and beat you." He closed and locked the door.

I crawled onto the bed, closed my eyes, and put my hand in my mouth so I wouldn't make a noise that would bring him back. How long before he managed to kill me?

The window suddenly shimmied in the frame, the sheet fell to the floor, and Fab stood outside. A hallucination, no doubt. But she knocked again a little louder, and this time waved. She was definitely real. She motioned me over to where the window didn't quite close.

"Go hide in the bathroom," she whispered, pointing across the room. "Stand behind the door and leave it open. If he comes in, kick it shut in his face. Go. Now."

Leaning heavily against the wall, I concentrated on merely standing, then inching toward the bathroom. Suddenly, an explosion rocked the trailer side to side. The blast threw me across the bathroom as the trailer settled into a tipped position. Someone was screaming. I heard breaking sounds and then silence. Unable to move, barely able to care, I lay on the floor.

The door opened. Zach stood in the doorway.

"You're safe, Madison." He crouched down beside me.

He eased me up, helping me to stand. I tipped a little, took a step forward, and passed out cold.

# Chapter Thirty-Four

An unfamiliar face loomed over me, and I screamed, thrashing away, but my arm was tied to a railing with a tube running to a machine.

"It's me, Axe," he said, touching me lightly. "No one's going to hurt you."

"Where am I?" My eyes were open, but everything appeared blurry and out of focus.

"Miami Hospital," he said, brushing the hair from my face. He had a gentle touch and a cool hand for such a big man. "Zach is outside pacing the hall, driving the doctors and nurses crazy. Spoon took your mother to the cafeteria for tea."

I tried to smile, but pain shot through my face. "She must be upset to agree to tea."

"I think he snuck her in a cigar."

"Did he also sneak in some Jack?"

"Madeline's a handful, all right. She and Zach have been sitting by your bedside this entire time," he reassured me. "Zach's going to be disappointed he wasn't here when you woke up. I came in to give them a break."

"How long have I been here?"

"Not long. Once we figured out you were missing, Zach acted like a crazy person, determined to get you back."

"Will?"

"He's in jail, and this time, he won't be breaking out."

My eyes filled with tears. "I wish he were dead."

"Zach had to talk me out of killing him. He didn't want me to be the one to end up in prison."

I reached out and touched Axe's cheek. "You're a good man. Tell my mother I love her." My whole body hurt, and even talking made me tired. I shifted to my side and drifted off. I didn't want to remember why I was here. Or anything else.

\* \* \*

Someone kept pulling on my arm. "Leave me alone," I tried to beg, but my throat was dry, too dry to swallow. I wanted to stay in my safe place. I opened my eyes slowly. Mother and Zach stood over me.

"Welcome back." Zach smiled, leaning into me. I flinched and pulled away from him.

"Oh honey, I'm so happy you're finally awake," Mother said, beginning to cry.

"Water," I croaked.

Zach took a cup from the bed tray and held it while I sipped through the straw.

"Don't cry." I struggled to get my arm free.

"Why is my arm tied to the bed?"

"When they brought you in, you were so dehydrated and needed an IV to replenish your fluids. When the doctor decided to ease off the pain meds the next day, you became restless, and he didn't want you ripping the line out," Zach explained, untying my arm. "If you start to get agitated again, I'll hold your hand."

The hospital room smelled like disinfectant. There was a small window in the corner, and with the shade drawn, who knew if it was day or night? "Where's Axe?"

"I sent him home. He needed to get some sleep. He relieved Madeline and me for a few hours each night, so we were able to catch a quick nap."

"How long have I been here?"

"Three days. You were sedated the first day, while they determined the extent of your injuries, and then the doctor made the decision to let you wake naturally."

"Jazz?"

"Don't you worry about Hairball," Mother said, kissing my cheek. "That nice girl Fab is taking care of him."

Zach raised his eyebrows and looked at me with a smirk—he'd probably never heard Fab described as a "nice girl." I tried to smile, but moaned instead and put my fingers to my puffy and painful cheeks.

Doc Rivers walked in wearing a white coat.

"I'm happy you're awake, Madison. How's my patient?"

"He shot me, didn't he?" I started to cry.

"No, my dear, he didn't shoot you. I just stopped by to check on you," he said, wiping away my tears. "Are you getting the star treatment I prescribed?"

"Everything hurts. All over. I'm thirsty." I tried to reach for the cup, and my arm barely moved; it felt broken.

"Besides being dehydrated, you'd been severely beaten," he explained. "In spite of the injuries you sustained, there were no broken bones and all your organs are healthy. I promise no long-term damage. You'll need to give yourself time to heal. At first, you'll be a little slow moving around, but the pain should subside quickly. I predict a fast recovery. You'll be good as new in no time." He patted my hand. "I've asked a hospital counselor to stop by and talk to you, to help with your emotional injuries. Talking to a neutral party will speed the healing process. Once we get you up and walking, you'll be allowed to go home. A few days at most. We'll take this on a day-to-day basis."

The whole time he talked, he listened to my heart and checked me over in a general way. He looked at my chart and made notes of his own. "Everything looks good. If you need me, call anytime. I make house calls." He leaned down and tenderly kissed my cheek.

"Thank you, Doc," I said.

"I'm going to talk to the doctor," Mother said, walking out after him.

Zach squeezed my hand. "You're safe now. Will Todd is headed to prison for a long, long time."

"Are you sure he won't get out of jail?" I asked, panic filling me.

"I'm positive. Right now, he's in maximum-security detention due to his escape. Even his court appearances will take place in his tier by video feed. He'll have to serve his sentence on kidnapping and attempted murder charges here in Florida, and then he'll be released to Georgia."

When he reached out to touch me, I pulled away before I could stop myself. "Will killed Oscar Wyatt," I whispered. "Oscar blackmailed him over The Cottages deal. After Will paid him once, he came back for more money."

"That's the problem with blackmailers. It's why a lot of them end up dead."

"And Tucker knew what Will had planned. He only stepped in because Will was getting in the way of his interests." I went on to tell Zach all about Tucker's involvement. We stopped talking when the door opened.

"What are you two doing?" Mother asked, coming into the room.

"Where's Brad?"

"He pulled out on a fishing trip the day before you—" She paused, tears in her eyes. "—went missing. He'll return in a week."

"I'll let you tell him. He can't come visit me until he's calmed down."

Mother snorted. "That's not going to be easy."

"How bad do I look?"

"I wish he were dead," she said.

"I do too." I teared up again.

Zach touched my cheek, dabbing my tears. "We're all happy you're alive. Are you up to telling us what happened?"

"I think Madison should wait until she's back on her feet. There's no hurry," Mother said.

"I don't mind." And I told them. I started from the beginning, when I was gardening out by the pool, and took them through all the events I could remember. My voice was emotionless until the end. "He planned to kill me, to beat me to death." Tears spilled down my cheeks.

It was too much for my mother, who had to leave the room. Zach struggled to control his anger. "You gave me good clues."

"It's hard to think when you're scared. I had a difficult time coming up with what I did, and I could only hope Mother already had you involved. I had to be careful choosing my words because Will was listening. If he'd any idea I was trying to send you a clue, he would've ended the call and slapped me around some more. Or worse."

"When Madeline asked who Antonio was, I remembered telling you about when my mother called me that and knew you were in big trouble," Zach said. "Then she told me that Brad didn't have a dog. I remembered you mentioning he lived in the Everglades and thought, okay, she's trying to signal that she's out there."

"In the end, I'd already given up, and then somehow you found me," I said, nearly in tears again. "He'd been threatening to kill me nonstop. After he got the money and refused to let me go, I knew he'd follow through."

"It's over now."

"Are you looking inside my hospital gown?" I tried to look shocked.

He ran his hand gently across my shoulder and nibbled on my ear. "Look, easy access."

"There's something very wrong with feeling up a woman in a hospital bed," I said.

He pushed me gently against the pillows, kissing me tenderly.

"How did you figure out I was missing and in trouble?"

"Fab went by your house and was surprised when you were nowhere around, especially with your Tahoe parked in the driveway and your keys and purse on the bench in the entry. Like me, she knows you wouldn't leave without Jazz, and he was asleep on the couch. She called your cell and heard it ringing outside. When she found it lying under some flowers by the pool, she became worried and phoned me."

*Thank goodness for Fab, she'd come to my rescue a*

*couple of times now.*

On my way over to meet Fab, I called Madeline, and she told me you'd invited her to dinner and she was on her way to your house. Right after I hung up, Kevin called to inform me that Will had escaped custody the day before. He also let me know that someone had tried to run you off the road the previous evening. Why weren't you the one to tell me about that?"

"I'm sure I had a good reason at the time. Who knows now?"

He arched his eyebrows and continued. "It took a couple of hours, but they found the car that tried to run you off the road abandoned in an overgrown field, and by then, it had been reported stolen. I was sure Will had abducted you, and my guess was that he blamed you for The Cottages deal going south."

"He stole some fancy cars, but I spent most of my time in the trunk or on the back seat. Between you and me, I prefer the back seat to the trunk because it's so cramped back there." I tried to smile, but my face ached.

Zach turned away and coughed. I wanted to tell him that his laughing would make me feel better. When he turned back, he was serious again.

I touched my head and felt a bald spot. Zach and I looked at one another. "Will pulled my hair out. Thankful for the adrenaline pumping through my veins. I didn't realize it at first."

"It doesn't look bad."

"That was a nice lie. Were you the one who told Mother that I was missing?"

"When she arrived at your house, the last thing I wanted to tell her was that you were missing and we had no clue why or where you'd been taken. I was certain Will's motive was money and he'd have to contact her. From what we'd learned, he couldn't have financed a life on the run." Zach then continued, "Your mother is one tough cookie. We waited for the call to come, and I had her prepped, and when the phone rang, she did exactly as we rehearsed. Followed the game plan to a tee."

"My mother is amazing in a crisis and very protective of her children. I need to tell her how lucky I am to have such a great mother."

"I know she was relieved to hear your voice and terrified at the same time."

"Just hearing her voice brought a ray of sanity into an unreal situation," I confided to Zach. "Will honestly believed I could write a check for a million dollars, and I let him. I told him whatever he wanted to hear."

"You did the right thing."

"Where did the money come from?"

"Anoui has connections I don't question. They helped her wire the money to his account. Once we got confirmation he'd verified the deposit, she reversed the transaction."

"Very impressive. I'd like to meet her and say

thank you. If the money hadn't been there, Will would've killed me first and then Whit. The whole time I sat in Whit's office, I was hoping he'd pull out a gun and shoot Will."

"He felt like he let you down when Will drove away with you."

"When the deposit was confirmed, I thought I'd be able to get up and leave. How did you find me?"

"The Glades are so vast, we had to draw him out. I had a man staking out your house, one at The Cottages, and Spoon stayed with Madeline. It surprised me to find that Will had his flacks in the same locations. They were so stupid, they never figured out we had them under surveillance. Slice put a couple of men out on the Tamiami Trail, which we thought was a long shot, but we covered it anyway." Zach rubbed his neck. "Kevin had issued a police bulletin, and the cops were on alert. The original plan was to grab you once the two of you arrived at Whit's, but we realized he had a gun on you and we had to hang back. When you and Will walked into Whit's office, Fab placed a GPS device on the underside of his car. Fab's motto is 'always be prepared,' girl scout that she is." He laughed. "I didn't expect him to get out of the parking lot. I thought he'd release you, and once he did, the deputies were waiting to take him into custody."

"Yeah, me too." I sighed deeply, trying to shake off the dark memories.

"I'll tell you the rest later. Your eyes are going to close any second."

"No, I want the details now. Don't keep anything from me." Worry lined his face, but I needed to know.

"I wanted to kill him when I saw him coldcock you with his gun and throw you in the back of the car. The four of us followed him in separate cars, trading off so he wouldn't see the same car in his mirrors. I was behind him as he pulled off the highway. We regrouped at the road and hiked in so he wouldn't suspect we'd tracked him to his hiding place. When we found the trailer, Will was pacing in and out, drinking liquor straight from the bottle."

"He's a big fan of dark rum. Didn't smell as bad as the cigarettes."

"Fab crept around the perimeter to locate you while Slice rigged a small explosive device to create a diversion. When we were ready, Fab had you move into the bathroom. We waited for Will to come back out on the porch, then detonated our surprise. Although it wasn't a major boom, it was big enough to catch him off guard and get him cuffed and hauled off in the police car Kevin had waiting at the turn-in."

"The explosion knocked me off my feet."

"Slice dragged his ass off, and I ran in and picked you up. Fab and I drove you up to the highway, where paramedics were waiting. They loaded you in the ambulance, and we followed you to the hospital."

"Did you blow the trailer to bits?"

"No, but local law enforcement is demolishing the old relic and hauling away the pieces. No one will be able to use the place for hiding out in the future. I'd like to know how he found it in the first place. That land is highly restricted. No one's ever been given a permit to live back in there."

"What happened to Forrest?"

"He's long gone, not a single sighting of him. We circulated an old booking photo. Turns out his real name is Morris Pribble. He and Will were a match made in criminal heaven. Long criminal histories, Pribble's more violent."

"Will told me he had a woman friend out by the dog track that helped him."

"We'll continue to show his picture around, but I don't expect a sighting. He's smart enough to be long gone. This scam was all Will's. He's the brains, if you want to call it that, and Forrest the muscle. His only motivation was profit, and when that vanished, he vanished too. He knows if he comes back, he'll be caught."

# Chapter Thirty-Five

When I woke next, Mother was sleeping beside me, her head on the mattress of my hospital bed. I lightly stroked her hair.

"I willed you not to die," she said, lifting her head, looking tired. "Zach promised to get you back alive, and I had to trust him. I also believed him when he assured me he'd find that nutbag and make sure he never got out of jail."

"Zach's a good guy. I'm glad you let him help."

"He told me he owed you for saving his life and that he wasn't going to let you down. Something about IOUs. I had no idea what he was talking about." She stared at me. "Imagine my surprise when I found out you killed a man who was trying to kill him."

"I was going to tell you all about that during our dinner. So Zach told you what happened?"

"No, I tricked Slice."

"Does he know that?"

"No, he doesn't, and you're not going to say anything. I talked to him as though you'd confided in me and found out all sorts of interesting things about your life. He's quite a fan of yours."

"I won't tell him," I said.

"The foursome of Zach, Axe, Fab and Slice work well together," she said. "They were committed to finding you, with the help of a couple of other odd ones."

"They're an easy bunch to like," I said, trying not to cry.

"When you get out of here, you can tell me about how you zip-tied Dario. And how you became so friendly with Mr. Spoon."

"Spoon was a friend of Aunt Elizabeth's." I tried to laugh, and instead started coughing.

"He never said one word about knowing Elizabeth. How did she meet him? Do you think they had anything personal going on?"

"Mother, he's a little young."

She raised her eyebrows. "Elizabeth liked men."

I was speechless. "He told me he helped keep a friend from her poker group from going to jail. Apparently, she had a bad day and decided to rob a liquor store. Spoon was vague on the details."

"I wonder why he didn't mention any of this to me. She was my sister. I did ask if he had another diamond to match the one in his ear. Have you ever seen anything so big?"

"Mother, you did not. What did he say?"

"He told me he could read my mind and that he had only one, and no, I couldn't borrow it. I really hoped he would tell me he had two. He was right; I wanted to wear them to my next poker game." She winked. "Zach sent Spoon over to stay with me while I waited for the phone to ring. He was positive Will would call. I wasn't so sure. Zach wanted me at home in case that bastard had someone watching me, and he turned out to be right. Skinny little dude, full of energy. He twitched around—never stopped moving—and chain-smoked."

"Spoon, hmm. Did you enjoy yourself?"

"He stayed by my side and was quite reassuring," she said. "I like him."

That was enough for now. Details could wait for another time.

Fab walked in holding a gigantic shopping bag. "You look like crap," she informed me with a smile.

"That good?" I groaned. "I'm hoping to go home this afternoon."

"I'll let you two catch up. I'm going outside. I need a cigar," Mother said. She gave Fab a hug and left the room.

I wasn't sure what surprised me more—the fact my mother hugged Fab or that Fab didn't seem to mind. They'd become friendly, and I wanted details. But which one would I ask?

Fab held up the bag. "I brought a gift."

"I love gifts. Especially big ones."

"I wanted to be here sooner, but I had to finish this first."

"You *made* me a gift? You're full of surprises. It's heavy." I pulled out the tissue paper, and Fab helped me take out a wooden stand. She set the miniature door, complete with doorknob, on my hospital bed.

I stammered, "Uh, thank you?"

"There's another present in the bag to open. Maybe then the whole thing will make sense." She laughed.

I ripped the paper away from the smaller package. Inside was a small black leather case containing eight chrome tools. "A lockpick set?"

"Yes, and there's a lock to practice on. I'm giving you your first lesson. Axe helped me build it."

"Fab, you're the best." I didn't want to, but I started to cry.

She gave me a hug. "No crying." She put the door on the tray table, pulled out one of the tools, and went to work showing me how to use each tool.

We laughed while I enjoyed the show-and-tell.

"Are you two having a good visit?" Mother asked, walking in the door. "What is that?" She pointed to the doorknob stand.

"Fab brought me a get-well gift. She's teaching me to pick locks."

My mother clearly struggled for something to say, looking from me to Fab and back again. "That sounds practical," she said, pulling up a chair.

Fab picked up the case and showed us both how to pick locks.

* * *

The hospital was finally kicking me out, but not before I proved I could walk down the hall and back by myself. The going was slow, but I got it done.

Mother had brought me a cotton beach dress to wear, since all I had was that disgusting brown dress and a hospital gown. Trying not to jolt my aching arms, I slid the beach dress over my head and slipped on a pair of sandals. All I wanted was to go home and curl up with Jazz.

"Thought you might need this," Zach said as he walked in the door. He handed over the cane he'd used after being shot in the leg, then put his arms around me and peeked inside the neckline of my dress. "This is one of those dresses I like," he whispered in my ear.

"You have no hospital manners."

"I came to take you home." He kissed me gently.

"What about Mother?"

"She's totally good with me picking you up. She's on her way to your house now. We're just waiting for the wheelchair escort to take you to the car."

"I'm impressed you got her to agree. She must like you."

"Wait till Brad gets back and finds out Madeline and I are bonded. Tight," he said, crossing his fingers.

A nurse arrived with the wheelchair. At last, it was time to go home.

# Chapter Thirty-Six

Zach helped me into his Escalade. I was excited to be leaving the hospital. "Ready?"

"I miss my hairy bedmate, Jazz."

He reached out and took my hand in his. I rolled down the window and let the fresh air blow in my face. I never thought I'd leave the Everglades alive. I figured Will would kill me and toss what was left of me to the alligators to eat.

The sight of my house brought tears to my eyes. "Home at last," Zach said, helping me out of the massive SUV.

"It's good to be here." I smiled. Jazz met me at the door and stood howling at my feet.

"Welcome," Mother, Fab, and Axe called out in unison from the kitchen.

I walked into the kitchen, and they all stood around the island. In the middle of the counter sat a large vase of deep-red hibiscus.

"Hi, everyone." I smiled. "The flowers are incredible. A work of art, Florida-style."

"Plus, there's pizza and beer," Axe pointed out.

"Beer? My favorite," I said, making a face. "What kind of pizza?"

"Shrimp scampi," Mother said, coming across the room to kiss me.

"You guys are the best."

I sat quietly, eating and listening to the talk and laughter. I enjoyed being home and, best of all, sitting with friends and Mother—the fastest way to get well.

Eventually, I slid off the stool and tapped my spoon against my glass. "Your attention please," I said, looking serious. They all looked a little surprised. "Thank you for this special homecoming, and most of all for saving me from a madman. I didn't give up hope. I knew you'd find me, and you did. Anything I can ever do for any of you, I'm your woman."

We moved from the kitchen to the living room, and I curled up in an oversized chair with Jazz on my lap, listening to small talk about new clients they'd acquired. I tried hard not to yawn, but I was losing the fight.

I felt someone touch my arm and jumped. When I opened my eyes and saw Fab standing next to me, I realized I'd fallen asleep in the chair. "You fell asleep," she said. "We have to go."

"It's rude of me to go to sleep," I apologized.

"You just got out of the hospital. I'll come by tomorrow and check on you. I'll bring you a caramel latte, double whip. Call me if anything creepy happens. I'll bring my big guns, and we'll play shootout," she said.

"You do realize that your saving my life makes us good friends?"

Though she was clearly caught off guard, from the look on her face, she wasn't opposed to the idea. I wanted to laugh but was afraid I'd hurt her feelings.

"See you tomorrow." She waved good-bye and left, taking Axe with her.

Zach came over and whispered, "I'll be back in the morning."

When everyone had left, I put my arms around Mother and hugged her. "You're the best. Thanks for always being calm under pressure. Hearing your voice in the midst of the chaos gave me a few moments of sanity. I've been waiting ever since I woke up in the hospital to have a private moment with you."

"I'm focusing on the fact that you're home and healthy. Good thing the little bastard is in jail," she said.

"My thoughts exactly."

"I realize you're just out of the hospital, but I'm not leaving without you telling me how you met these people. I want the *entire* story, Madison," she said. "I'm staying until you're back on your feet and ready to be by yourself."

"Now that you've met everyone, do you like them?" I asked. I wanted the answer to be yes.

"I do. Fabiana's my favorite. You wouldn't

know it to look at her, but she's one fierce chick. She won me over completely when she taught me how to pick a lock." Mother laughed.

"I need more practice. No fair you caught on like you picked locks in another life."

"When you're feeling better, you should throw a pool party. Make it a barbecue and invite all your new friends. A good time to introduce Brad to everyone," she suggested.

"About Brad..." I started.

"I'll tell him what happened. Well, maybe not every detail." She sighed, and hugged me. "He'll just be happy you're alive. Now go to bed before you fall asleep on my shoulder."

"I'm happy you're staying. Come on, Jazz. Time for bed." He raced ahead of me and beat me up the stairs.

* * *

It was late morning when I woke up, and had to remind myself that the nightmare was behind me and I was safe. I appreciated having clean sheets, something I'd always taken for granted in the past. They smelled fresh, not like dirt, and no cockroaches were running across my legs. The best part was Jazz on the pillow next to me, sound asleep.

The phone rang. I thought about letting it go to voicemail but answered.

"Madison, this is Howard Sherman. How are you?"

"Relieved to be home," I told him, getting one of my stomach aches.

"I have good news for you. Tucker Davis couriered over his resignation as executor. He included all the records for The Cottages and the estate filings he'd completed."

I exhaled with relief. "That's great. Did you ask him to resign?" It was hard to believe Tucker would go away of his own volition.

"No, he sent it by messenger and offered no explanation." I could hear the curiosity in his voice.

"What happens from here?" I asked, surprised by the turn of events.

"You, or someone of your choosing, will step in as executor. The actual duties are limited, with the exception of running the property, and there's no reason you can't handle everything. I'll prepare all the documentation the court requires. Ernest Whitman has finished the financial statements, so you may operate The Cottages as you wish with no interference from anyone."

"Who's been looking after the property? Tucker?"

"He's kept a low profile since all this became public. A Fabiana Merceau came to my office and told me she'd take charge until you were able. I assumed she had your permission?" he asked, sounding worried.

"Oh yes, sorry, I forgot." Fab was the perfect choice. No one would put anything over on her. Had I told her Joseph had health problems? I wouldn't want him roughed up too badly.

Mr. Sherman sounded relieved that I was pleased with Fab stepping in. "Since no one's contesting, I'll have the estate wrapped up in a few months."

"I'm happy everything will soon be official."

"I'll send you a copy of the court filings, and Ernest Whitman will also be sending you a final estate accounting."

"I really appreciate all of this."

"Call me if you need anything or have any questions."

I lay against the pillows, scratching Jazz's ears, relieved Tucker was out of my life. I never wanted to lay eyes on him again, the man who'd planned to ruin and then kill me. Zach had said he wouldn't be prosecuted. There was certainly no fairness in that, but I'd bet my meager piggy bank that Zach had something to do with Tucker deciding not to make any more problems.

Against the white shower walls, my body was a gigantic black-and-blue mark, with tinges of healing yellow starting to show. I stepped under the warm water and let it spray all over me until my skin was wrinkly, obsessed with being clean after the grime of the trailer. Never before had bugs walked all over me like their personal doormat. When I finally shut the water off, I was pleased my body smelled like the freesia fragrance of my favorite shower gel. The thought of anything snug panicked me a little, so I slipped on a long hot-pink tee-shirt dress with deep slits up the side. I planned to sit outside by the pool and enjoy the fresh air and sun, then go for a swim to stay cool. Maybe talk my mother into playing some poker for pocket change and clean her out. She was quite the card shark with her "take no prisoners" attitude.

Downstairs, Zach sat at the kitchen island with Mother, drinking coffee and eating a cinnamon roll. They'd certainly formed a bond. *Wait until Brad sees this.* I almost laughed out loud. He had no choice now. He'd have to come around.

"What's for breakfast?" I asked from the stairs.

"I went to that wonderful Bakery Café this morning," Mother said, "for egg soufflés and Danishes, and even picked up a couple of chicken Caesar salads for lunch."

Zach helped me onto a stool, and Mother handed me my coffee and a pecan braid. "You two will have to stop spoiling me," I said.

"No way," he said, kissing me.

"Thank you."

"For what?" He stared at me, trying to anticipate my next words.

"For getting Tucker out of my life. The only thing better would be telling me he's going to jail."

"Not unless Will agrees to testify against him.

Seriously, I doubt that'll happen. He's lawyered up and not talking. Also, as of right now, Will won't be charged with the murder of Oscar Wyatt. All they have is your testimony, and it's not enough. The biggest problem is there's no independent evidence linking him directly to the crime."

"Does this mean he'll be getting out of jail sometime soon?" A feeling of panic swept over me. If Will got a second chance, he wouldn't waste any time in killing me. Would I have to live my life with one eye over my shoulder?

"He's looking at a minimum of twenty-five years here in Florida and, after that, another long sentence in Georgia. He'll be an old man before he gets out, if ever."

"How did you get Tucker to resign?" I looked at Zach.

"Don't ask me. Fab informed me that she'd handle everything. The next thing I knew, she went flying out the door with Slice behind her, and then Tucker resigned as executor." Zach laughed.

"Did she hurt him?" I asked, a big smile on my face.

"When I ran into him yesterday, he had two black eyes." He smirked. "Looked like Slice's handiwork. Those two already had a past."

"Soon as I'm back to normal, I'm throwing a big thank-you pool party for everyone. You guys took care of everything for me and continue to be on call."

"You've done plenty for me too, babe, most of which I haven't been able to show my thanks for in the way I want." Our eyes locked in a sizzle of chemistry.

"Care to enlighten me?" Mother asked, breaking the sexual tension. She'd obviously been listening to our conversation as she worked around the kitchen.

"I planned on telling you today," I reassured her. I hoped she wouldn't regret asking to hear details and, once she got over the shock, that she wouldn't be angry.

"Are you two a couple?" She clearly wanted the answer to be yes.

"We have each other's backs." I smiled at Zach.

"Maybe we should go on another date." He winked at me.

"I'd like that."

"How's your therapy going?" Zach asked.

"I didn't like my therapist. I realize it's arrogant when you think you're smarter than the person helping you, but that's how I felt. She had zero sense of humor, so I found a new one. I called him this morning, and we had a long talk."

"Him?" Zach questioned suspiciously. "What kind of therapy happens over the phone?"

"The same kind that happens face to face. He has a flexible schedule and makes house calls." I wasn't going to confess that my new therapist was Doc Rivers. Zach would find out sooner or later.

"Did talking help?" he asked.

"Yes, and he made me laugh a couple of times. The conversation wasn't all tense and serious. When he told me I'd eventually be able to put this whole drama behind me and move on, I believed him."

Zach's cell phone rang. We looked at each other, knowing he had to leave. I was surprised when he sent the call to voicemail.

"You know—"

I tried not to sulk. "Later."

"Very soon." He kissed me.

* * *

Finally, the day came to return my mother to her friends and busy life. She looked bored, and I felt guilty.

Together by the pool, I told her everything. Starting with how I first met Zach, when he showed up on my patio with a gunshot wound, and every odd adventure in between. She wasn't angry when I told her about my new life and all the things that had happened since arriving in The Cove. She was more hurt that I didn't trust her.

I took her to The Cottages and introduced her to Joseph and Miss January and made sure she met Kitty. She wasn't happy with me because I didn't tell her ahead of time that the cat was dead.

I was no match for Mother when it came to playing cards. I now owed her a box of hand-rolled cigars, my IOU. I'd surprise her with the same kind Zach had given her. When we hugged good-bye, I started to cry. This experience had made us closer than ever—we weren't just mother and daughter, but friends.

"I'll come this weekend and stay overnight. We can go to South Beach for dinner."

"No crying. If you need anything, call me first. And no more hearing about things after the fact," she said, tears in her eyes.

"Love you." I waved as she drove away.

# Chapter Thirty-Seven

Time to return to my daily routine. It was comforting to know my mother was only a short drive away. Brad would be home soon, and I expected he'd come and stay for a few days. He might stay even longer if I could find him a girlfriend. It would serve him right if I started meddling in his personal life.

It didn't take me long to get tired of sitting around the house. I walked and swam everyday as part of my therapy. I could now walk without moaning and groaning, and the bruises were nearly gone, fading from blue to yellow to nothing.

I knew just where I wanted to go on my first solo outing. Fab had called earlier and told me that Zach had decided to go home early to catch up on paperwork. Except for quick kisses, we hadn't had a single private moment since I'd gotten out of the hospital. We were always surrounded by people.

I called Jake's, placed an order, and then ran upstairs to throw on a short tropical print skirt and a coral tee top. All the walking on the beach with Mother had left me tanned, so makeup wasn't necessary. I added a touch of lipstick and shoved my hair into a clip.

Sandals in my hand, I looked forward to getting behind the wheel of my SUV. Mother had insisted on doing all the driving while she stayed with me.

Mother told me that Spoon had had my SUV towed to his shop to repair the beating and banging it took. What she hadn't said was that he'd returned it in mint condition. I inspected every inch, and you couldn't tell it had endured an evening of bumper cars. And it ran like a dream on the way over to Jake's.

I made a pit stop on the way to Jake's. My first act as owner-manager of The Cottages had been to knock on Miss January's and Joseph's doors and inform them about the changes. I hoped Kevin would let Julie and Liam move back soon. I'd put out the word that I was looking for a local girl to work in the office. In addition, I planned to refurnish and update each unit with fresh paint and fixtures. Next stop: Jake's.

"How's it going?" Jake waved.

"I get stronger every day," I told him, sitting at the bar. I didn't need to tell Jake anything. He already knew the details, and probably better than I did. "How about half a margarita?"

He raised his eyebrows. "Half?"

"I'm thinking a little tipsy, not drunk."

"You're crazy."

"You think that's the first time I've heard that?"

"Your order's ready," he said, handing over a large shopping bag. "Who's all the food for?"

"Nobody." I smirked at him.

"Whatever." He snorted. "'Nobody' hasn't been here in a while. Tell him to stop by. How come your card shark mother let you out of her sight?"

"Cleaned you out, did she?"

He made some sort of noise and shook his head.

"This food smells heavenly." I picked up the bag and left.

\* \* \*

I pulled into the driveway of Zach's warehouse, grabbed the shopping bag of food and Zach's cane from the car, and made the slow climb up the stairs. I set my stuff down on the doorstep, took out my leather case of tools, and picked his lock. Sticking my head in the now-open door, I called to him.

"Over here!" Zach yelled from his desk. "Did you just pick my lock?"

"Yes, I did," I said smugly, pleased that my first try was a success. "Fab got me a set of lock-picking tools as a get-well gift." I showed him my case. "She also gave Mother and me lessons. Mother was better at it than me."

"You two," he said, shaking his head. Dressed in black sweat shorts and a Miami Dolphin workout shirt, he came closer. With every step, he looked better and better. "What's this?" He picked up the bag.

"Lunch from Jake's. You hungry?"

He helped me up on a bar stool, took the containers out, and put them on the bar. "Starved." He ran his hand up my bare leg. "In the past, I never gave a single thought to women's clothing, except for how fast I could get them off and throw them on the floor. Then I met you. I like the way you dress," he said, his hand disappearing under my skirt.

I wrapped my legs around his waist, pulling him close to me. "I came here to say thank you for saving my life."

"So, no more IOUs?" he asked, kissing me.

"Are you delusional? I have more than you anyway," I gloated. "But we're pretty even on the life-saving thing."

"How about you show me your thank you and I'll show you mine?" He buried his hands in my hair, and I inhaled the warm, male scent of him. He drove his mouth down on mine in a hungry kiss that left me senseless.

~*~

## About the Author

Deborah Brown is an Amazon bestselling author of the Paradise series. She lives on the Gulf of Mexico, with her ungrateful animals, where Mother Nature takes out her bad attitude in the form of hurricanes.

For a free short story, sign up for my newsletter. It will also keep you up-to-date with new releases and special promotions:
www.deborahbrownbooks.com

Follow on FaceBook:
facebook.com/DeborahBrownAuthor

Join private Facebook group:
Deborah Brown's Paradise Fan Club:
facebook.com/groups/1580456012034195

You can contact her at Wildcurls@hotmail.com

Deborah's books are available on Amazon

amazon.com/Deborah-Brown/e/B0059MAIKQ

## PARADISE SERIES

Crazy in Paradise
Deception in Paradise
Trouble in Paradise
Murder in Paradise
Greed in Paradise
Revenge in Paradise
Kidnapped in Paradise
Swindled in Paradise
Executed in Paradise
Hurricane in Paradise
Lottery in Paradise
Ambushed in Paradise
Christmas in Paradise
Blownup in Paradise
Psycho in Paradise
Overdose in Paradise
Initiation in Paradise
Jealous in Paradise
Wronged in Paradise
Vanished in Paradise
Fraud in Paradise
Naïve in Paradise
Bodies in Paradise
Accused in Paradise
Deceit in Paradise
Escaped in Paradise
Fear in Paradise
Theft in Paradise

Available on Amazon
amazon.com/dp/B074CDKKKZ

## BISCAYNE BAY SERIES

Hired Killer
Not guilty
Jilted

amazon.com/dp/B09BRFYYYN

## LAUDERDALE SERIES

In Over Her Head

amzn.to/3Y4w7AL

Made in United States
North Haven, CT
19 June 2025

69974564R00186